Princess Callie

and the

Totally Amazing Talking Tiara

Book 1

of the Callie Chronicles

Princess Callie

and the

Totally Amazing Talking Tiara

by Daisy Piper

Chapter One

The Message

Callie Richards was an ordinary girl, at least as ordinary as a motherless girl could be.

She lived with her father in a big-sized house in a small-sized town. Callie loved her father, and she knew that he loved her. He took good care of her. He always hugged her and called her Sport, which always perplexed her as she was no good at sports, but she appreciated the sentiment. He tried very hard.

Callie knew that compared to a lot of other children--children who lived in far-away lands without televisions and cereal and beds--she was lucky. She had all those things and more, and she knew the children in those other lands who didn't have those things would think Callie Richards was very lucky indeed.

But Callie was not lucky. In fact, Callie thought she was probably the unluckiest kid to have ever lived. Because even though she had a big television, her choice of a variety of delicious cereals, and a big, soft double bed, complete with a homemade quilt, Callie did not have the one thing in the world that most other children took for granted.

A mother.

Callie had had a mother once—of course she had. It was difficult to be born into the world without one. Callie's mother had been the best mother in the whole entire world—the whole entire galaxy, even.

And her mom had always told the best bed-time stories when Callie was little--fantastic stories about her mom really being a princess from a magical land, where fire-breathing dragons flew through the air and unicorns pranced through the streets of the Royal City. In some of the stories, *Callie* was the magical princess-- the white-blond streak in her red, wavy hair proved it. In some of her mom's stories, Princess Callie had to fight an evil queen.

They had shared many special times together, laughing and giggling, wrapped up in a warm quilt, while Callie's mom told the next installment of the magical story.

But those days were gone now.

Since her mom had died two years ago, Callie had felt out of sorts inside, like a huge part of her was missing. And that kind of thing was hard to explain when you were eleven, going on twelve. Dr. Sam, her counselor, said that what Callie felt was completely normal.

Callie thought that if this was normal, she didn't want to know what *abnormal* felt like.

So instead of focusing on the fact that she missed her mother terribly, and sometimes even pretended that her mother was still alive and had just been kidnapped, and would come home as soon as she could escape the evil clutches of whoever was holding her, Callie concentrated on being normal and ordinary, like the other kids at school who *did* have mothers, which at Maplehurst Middle School (it was a small school) was all of them. For the most part, it worked.

But Callie didn't know that on her twelfth birthday the so-called ordinary life that she worked so hard at preserving would never, ever be ordinary again.

Today was her twelfth birthday.

She wanted to say that it had started off ordinarily enough, even for a birthday, but it hadn't. She'd woken up in her bed with the strangest feeling that she hadn't really been asleep. Then she remembered the dream about the necklace and the jeweled key; the huge stone gate guarding the city, and the gargoyles smiling down at her in the torchlight. The evil queen and her army were advancing, and an insurmountable task had been placed before Callie.

A mind-numbing fear gripped her heart and squeezed—she couldn't breathe.

She sat up in bed, gasping. She tried to shake the awful feeling that still swirled sickly in her stomach, but it lingered like the aftermath of a bad meal.

Have you ever had a dream so real, you could feel it still in the bed with you when you woke up? And you dashed out of bed and ran to your parents' bedroom, jumping into their bed and trying to explain that it *wasn't* just a dream. The fire-breathing dragon was *real*, and his rough, bony scales were real, and his big yellow eyes were real, and the stinky smoke coming out of his nostrils was real, and he was right now sitting on your bed, eating the rest of your crackers and refusing to leave?

Well, that was how Callie felt right now. She could still smell the sharpness of the damp forest air, still hear the labored breathing of the horses and the muffled sound of their hooves striking the ground, still hear the discordant clang of heavy swords as two huge armies clashed in battle, and she could still hear the terrible laugh of the queen echoing in the still morning air.

And the ravens, cawing and screeching and darkening the sky like a black cloud hurtling towards them.

The worst part of all was that in her dream, the evil queen looked exactly like her mother.

It was the same dream Callie had been having for weeks now, only this was the first time she'd seen the Raven Queen's face. The shock of seeing her mother's beautiful face, her mouth twisted into an evil grin, still made Callie feel weak and sick.

In the dream, Callie was a princess in a magical land. The Raven Queen and her army were trying to kill her. An important battle had been lost, and Callie had failed her countrymen. Soon she'd have to turn and fight the Raven Queen alone, but she didn't know how she was going to do that all by herself. She wasn't prepared! And yet, something deep inside her knew it wouldn't make any difference. She was going to have to deal with it. She had no choice.

Just like the day she had lost her mom.

She'd have to tell Lewis about her dream today at school. Lewis was her best friend and always gave good advice. But she knew what he'd say, "Tell Dr. Sam. Dream interpretation is very important." Lewis was only twelve, but he was the smartest kid in their school. He read books on things no other twelve-year old had even heard of like, *The Physiology of Amoebae, Secrets of Unstable Gases,* and *A Short History of Rocks.* Lewis wanted to be a scientist when he grew up, which was no shock as both of his parents were scientists.

Callie sighed. She didn't want to have any more weird dreams like that one. She wanted to have *normal* dreams about normal things, like cute boys and shoe shopping and hair accessories. And moms being there when you woke up.

Pushing that thought away, Callie swung her feet to the floor, hopped out of bed, and went to wash up in the bathroom. Still in her pajamas, she headed downstairs for breakfast with her dad.

As she rounded the corner into the kitchen, a kazoo bleated slightly off-key, sounding like something between a sheep with a stuffed up nose and a goose whose voice was changing. Balloons and streamers in vibrant colors decorated the kitchen walls, the ceiling, the table, and even the chairs. A colorful banner read *Happy Birthday, Callie!*

Her dad, Ben, wore a silly-looking party hat. He blew on his kazoo again, and the paper tube attached to it rolled out and poked Callie in the eye.

"Oops! Sorry, Sport." He put his arm around her and gave her a hug. "Happy Birthday, Calandria."

Calandria was her *full* name. Actually, her full, full name was Calandria Arabella Philomena Teresita Anastasia Richards. The only living person who knew that besides her dad was Lewis, who had been sworn to secrecy on the matter. All those funny names had apparently been her mom's idea. Anastasia was her mom's name, but her friends had called her Ana.

9

Her dad winked at Callie, his blue eyes twinkling with pride. "My little girl is all grown up, and looking more and more like her mother every day."

Callie smiled, though her heart knotted painfully. Even though two years had gone by since her mom had died, Callie still missed her each and every day. It made her heart ache, she missed her so much. Though she knew it was impossible, Callie wished more than *anything*, and that included all the money in the world, all the candy you could eat without it killing you, or a super-cute boyfriend, that she could have her mom back.

She didn't tell her dad that. In fact, Callie didn't talk much to her dad about her mom anymore. Because her dad had a new girlfriend, Sharon, who was about as different from her mom as a stick of celery was from a brick of gold.

Sharon was very pretty, had short blonde hair, and always wore stylish clothes and jewelry. She had her nails done at a salon. Callie's mom had never even worn makeup, never did much to her straight dark hair, and her nails had always been broken from digging in the garden. Callie's mom had worn faded jeans and gone barefoot most of the time. Sharon, on the other hand, looked like she had just stepped out of the pages of a glossy magazine. She was a lawyer. She had her own house, her own car, two walk-in closets, and an evil cat named Wallingford.

Callie tried very hard to like Sharon, but the fact remained that she just *didn't*. Because when you're a kid, you have an extra sense that lets you know immediately when an adult doesn't like you. And Callie knew without a doubt that Sharon didn't like *her*.

But for some unknown reason which Callie couldn't understand, her dad really, really, really, *really* liked Sharon Hennessey. In fact, as far as Callie was concerned, the *liking* was reaching dangerously high levels.

But Callie knew her dad had been through a hard time, too. For whatever reason, Sharon made him happy. Callie thought there was no one on this earth who deserved to be happy more than her dad.

Looking at him now, marching around the kitchen with a silly hat on his head, blowing on a kazoo and singing "Happy Birthday," made Callie giggle. She had an idea that maybe he was getting more enjoyment out of her birthday than she was.

"I have an extra special gift for you, Cal," he said, looking very proud of himself. "Something you've never, ever gotten before. Something rare and beyond price."

This peaked Callie's interest. Perhaps it was the trip to France she'd been begging for?

Her dad whispered in her ear, "I'll give it to you later tonight."

"What is it?" Callie asked, knowing he wouldn't tell her, but feeling compelled to ask.

"It's a surprise, silly. But one that I'm excited about, too."

Callie gasped. Maybe it *was* the trip to France! Because her dad would definitely be going on the trip, too--she was only twelve. She couldn't go to France by herself. Of course, they'd probably have to bring *Sharon* with them. But even that thought couldn't diminish Callie's excitement.

"But first you have to go to school," he said. "Now, eat your cereal, Sport. If you're late, your principal, Mrs. Proctor, will be calling me again, and to tell you the truth, Cal, she scares me." He poured Callie a bowl of alphabet cereal--her favorite--and gave it a splash of milk.

Callie took it and went to sit at the table, while their dog, Bo, a golden retriever, wagged his tail hopefully.

She laughed. "This is *my* breakfast. Go eat your own."

Bo ignored her suggestion, probably because his food dish was empty. He continued, with only the determination a dog can show, to stare pointedly at Callie's cereal with a wide doggy grin on his face.

Callie waited for the cereal to get soggy. As she did, thoughts about her strange dream swirled in her memory. Suddenly time seemed to stop. The kitchen drifted away in a fog and she was transported back to the palace in her dream, with all the sights and smells and sounds she remembered....

Callie was sitting on a dazzling throne. She wore a beautiful silver-white gown and a spectacular diamond tiara on her head. A magnificent court stretched out before her. The walls looked as if they were covered in gold. The floor gleamed like mother-of-pearl. People in richly-colored gowns and robes milled about, but they all seemed to be looking to her, waiting in anticipation for some kind of ceremony to begin. A mysterious voice spoke above the din:

When one is two and two are one,
King Eldric's Magic has begun.
The Queen will call the Princess home,
To sit upon the Enchanted Throne.

All of a sudden, Callie felt dizzy, as if she'd been somewhere very high up and had come plummeting down quickly, like on a roller coaster.

"What a weird dream," she said to herself, trying to focus her eyes and shake the tingly feeling that swirled in her stomach.

Bo barked, as if he knew something strange was happening, too.

Callie looked down. There was a message in her bowl. The letters of her alphabet cereal had arranged themselves into a sentence:

It wasn't a dream

Callie gasped. She closed her eyes again, her heart hammering. She whispered, "Yes it was."

She looked down again.

No, it wasn't

It wasn't a dream

Callie gasped louder. This time, her dad looked up from across the kitchen where he was buttering his toast at the counter. "Did you say something, honey?"

Callie grabbed her cereal bowl and gave a half-hearted laugh. "Me? Say something? Nope. Uh, Dad, I'm just going to go into the family room and watch a little TV before school, okay?"

"Sure Honey," he said, beaming. "It's your birthday. Knock yourself out."

Callie scurried into the living room and placed the cereal bowl on the coffee table. She pointed a finger at it and said, "All right, who are you, and what are you doing in my cereal?"

I'm someone who has been watching over you since the day you were born

Callie trembled. Now her cereal was spelling words it didn't even have letters for. Then a glimmer of hope ignited in Callie's heart. "Mom?"

No

Though I was close to her

This was unbelievable, and yet Callie wanted, *needed* to know more. "Are you a ghost?"

I am very much alive

"If you're alive, why can't I see you?" Callie demanded.

You will see me soon

Little One

Callie stared down at the message in the bowl. Her mother had called her "Little One" as far back as she could remember. She gulped.

"Where are you?" she asked.

In the World

In Albion

"Where's that?" Callie wanted to know, thinking that, even for a bowl of cereal, it was being a little evasive.

You will find us

"Huh? Look, whoever you are," Callie said firmly, "I'm not going to any 'Albion.' I want to go to France!"

We need your help

"Help? You want a twelve-year-old to help you? You must be really desperate."

We need you now

Time is running out

Callie felt a shiver creep down her spine like a big, leggy spider. Either the cereal was for real, or this was the best practical joke Lewis had ever dreamed up.

Her army draws near

"Army? *Whose* army?" Callie said, unable to shake a strange feeling that the cereal was deadly serious. Deep down, she knew whose army it was: The Raven Queen's...

Come quickly

Princess Calandria

"What did you call me?" Callie asked. But the cereal wasn't responding. The letters were all mixed up as usual, no longer arranging themselves into cryptic messages.

Callie spoke nearer to the bowl. "Hello?"

"Callie, honey," her dad said from the doorway, "were you just talking to your cereal?"

She jumped back and almost fell off the couch. "No... I, uh, had Lewis on speakerphone, see?" She picked up the cordless from under the coffee table and held it aloft.

"Oh." Her dad didn't look too convinced. "Well, ask him if he wants to come for pizza tonight."

"Pizza?" Callie asked, confused.

"Yes. Pizza. It's a round food item with pepperoni and cheese on it. We usually have it for your birthday."

It took a moment for his words to sink in. "Oh right! My birthday. Of course. How could I have forgotten that?" She gave a weak laugh.

Her father stared at her for a moment, then nodded toward the phone. "Callie, aren't you going to ask Lewis about tonight?"

"Actually, Lewis had to hang up."

"Well, that was a short conversation." He frowned and felt Callie's forehead. "Are you feeling all right? You're not running a fever or anything, are you?"

Callie pasted on a winning smile. She wanted to say, "Hey, if you just had a conversation with a bowl of cereal, you'd be feeling a little strange, too!" But she didn't. Instead, she said, "Never been better, Dad."

She quickly ushered him out of the family room, knowing in her gut that somehow the message in her cereal and the strange dream were related.

"Now let me get ready for school. I want to look nice for my birthday. It's a big day for me." Callie put her cereal bowl on the counter, gave it a double take to make sure it hadn't started spelling things again, and trotted upstairs.

Once in her room, she flung open the door of her closet and yanked out her favorite jeans and a long-sleeved pink T-shirt. Her dad called from downstairs, *"Callie, you didn't eat your cereal!"*

"Of course, I didn't," she muttered to herself as she got her jeans on and pulled her T-shirt over her head. "It wouldn't stop talking long enough for me to get a bite in."

Callie tried to arrange her mass of red curls into something that didn't look like an electrified mop, but gave up and opted for her usual ponytail.

She was just about to turn away from the mirror when she noticed the T-shirt she was wearing. Emblazoned across the front in dark pink, sparkly letters was the word "Princess."

Weird.

Callie grabbed her backpack and headed downstairs. She had to get to school and tell Lewis about her dream and the weird message in her cereal. What would he say when she told him his best friend was a princess of a mysterious land, and they needed her help to fight an evil queen's army?

Though most twelve-year old girls would have jumped at the possibility of being a princess of a magical land, Callie couldn't shake a foreboding feeling that went along with it. Somewhere deep inside, she knew something had begun which she wouldn't be able to stop.

And that scared her more than anything else in the world.

Chapter Two

A Mysterious Gift

When Callie arrived at school, she made a beeline for Lewis, who was sitting alone, as usual, on the brick retaining wall next to the playground. He had his nose buried in a book called *Astrophysics Made Easy*.

Lewis Farnsworth didn't exactly fit in, which was probably why he was best friends with Callie.

"*Lewis*," Callie whispered as loud as she could.

He looked up and brightened, his dark hair falling into his eyes. "Happy Birthday, Cal."

"Lewis, I have to tell--"

"It's hard to believe you're twelve now, Cal." His eyes took on a melodramatic hue. "It seems like just yesterday we were fighting over Lego blocks, then making up and sharing our apple juice in kindergarten. And look at you now. Twelve. Welcome to the other side." He shook her hand and then started digging in his backpack.

"Lewis, I have something to say--"

"Got a present for you. Use it in good health." He handed Callie a badly wrapped gift, which looked like a big book.

Callie unwrapped it, as it would have been rude not to. "*Thompson's Encyclopedia of Medieval Warfare*. I don't know what to say, Lew. Thanks."

"From my own personal collection." He packed up his books and slung his backpack over his shoulder. "I read it cover to cover—twice. Take it from me, it's fascinating stuff. Never know when it'll come in handy."

"Yeah." All of a sudden, Callie felt funny about filling her friend in on the morning's events. In fact, the more time that elapsed, the more Callie thought maybe she'd imagined the whole thing as a result of some twelve-year-old rite-of-passage/preteen hysteria. But every time she imagined that it wasn't real, a little voice inside her told her not to be foolish, that *of course* it had been real.

She was Princess Calandria of Albion, and her presence was needed immediately to thwart the plans of an evil queen and her army.

Now, why did she have a problem saying that out loud to her best friend?

"Uh, Lew?" Callie began.

"You know, being twelve *rocks*," Lewis said, walking ahead of her across the playground. "Just think, soon we'll have driver's licenses, and cool jobs, and we'll be taller, Cal. Taller!"

The buzzer sounded. Callie and Lewis were carried along into the school in a noisy tide of students. They headed toward their classroom.

Callie's heart raced. She had to tell Lewis about the dream and the message in her cereal... and what it might mean.

"Lewis!" Callie whispered as loud as she dared.

He didn't hear her.

"Lewis, I had a weird dream last night, and I think I might be a magical princess and I have to go fight an evil queen!"

He turned his head then. By the confused and amused look in his eyes, Callie knew he thought she was joking.

It was too late to explain any more, the other kids were taking their seats. Lewis sat next to her, occasionally glancing across the aisle, shaking his head and chuckling. *Chuckling!* Someplace called Albion was under threat from an evil queen (whom they needed Callie's help to thwart), and he was chuckling? She looked down at her desk, pondering the best course of action. Though it was completely forbidden—*completely*--Callie decided there was only one thing to do.

She was going to pass a note.

Ms. Randall, their teacher, was young and pretty and well-liked, but she was very strict with her sixth-graders. No chewing gum. No texting. No passing notes.

As far as Callie knew, only one other person had ever attempted it--Rosie Schwartz, back on the second day of school this year. After "The Incident" as it was later referred to, no one had ever seen or heard from Rosie again. Rumor was that she now went by the name of Dorothy Swanson and attended school in the next town.

Ms. Randall swept into the classroom, looking crisp in an apple-green sweater set and black capris, with her blonde hair pulled back into a low ponytail. She was warm to the kids in her class, but she didn't put up with a whole lot of foolishness, either. Basically, the kids loved her.

The thought of Ms. Randall being disappointed in her made Callie feel almost sick, but the thought of holding in all the strange events of the morning, unable to talk to Lewis until recess made Callie feel even sicker.

"All right, class, settle down," Ms. Randall said. "Take out your math textbooks, please."

Several soft groans erupted from the class.

Ms. Randall ignored their objections, as usual. "Page 72. Let's go over problems three to six...."

As the class dutifully turned to the assignment, Callie ripped a piece of paper from her notebook and glanced around cautiously. She hadn't even written anything on it yet, and already she felt like a criminal.

Callie bit her lip, trying not to lose her place in the problems they were covering in case Ms. Randall called on her, and at the same time trying to write a short note that would convey the seriousness of the morning's events to Lewis. She wrote:

> *Lewis--I'm serious. Something strange happened to me this morning.*
>
> *I got a message in my cereal that said I was a princess and I had to help this place called Albion in their fight against an evil queen.*
>
> *You have to help me figure out what to do!*
>
> *C*
>
> *P.S. Dad said you could come for pizza tonight.*

She quickly folded up the note, her heart beating wildly. This was, without a doubt, the most daring thing Callie had ever done at school. The adrenaline rush had been unexpected, and yet not completely unenjoyable. The next thing she knew, she'd be jumping out of airplanes yelling, "Whoo-hoo."

"*Psst.*" She tried to get Lewis' attention quietly, as she didn't want to alert Wanda Morris, the class bully and the class snitch.

Wanda would have been pretty if she wasn't always in a bad mood. As a result of her prickly nature, her friends were few and far between. In fact, rumor had it that her friends (a grand total of two and who had never been seen in person by anyone besides Wanda) lived three states away and only corresponded with her via email.

To compensate for her unpopularity, Wanda took pride in bullying the kids on the playground and tattling on everyone in class. But Wanda was smart, and did her bullying in a sneaky way. To date, she had never been caught by any of the teachers, and even though Ms. Randall went on record as not approving of tattling, it was difficult for the teacher to ignore Wanda when she reported incidents like, "Morton Dengler just set fire to his pants," or "Toby Taneli put spiders in your desk."

Wanda sat directly behind Lewis. She was very thin as she took no enjoyment out of eating--not even candy. She had beady eyes that, due to habitual frowning, almost disappeared into her face, and those dark, glittery eyes saw things no normal kid's did.

Wanda also had a keen sense of smell, and could differentiate between flavors of contraband gum from clear across the room. Wanda often used her super senses in the classroom to blackmail kids at recess. She had a repertoire of meaningful looks, some of which said things like: "I see you chewing gum. Hand over your lunch money or I'll tell Ms. Randall," and the ever-popular, "Passing notes? That'll be five bucks."

Getting a note past Wanda was going to be harder than getting it past Ms. Randall.

Callie stared at Lewis. Her friend was staring straight at the board, completely engrossed in Math Problem Number Four.

"*Lewis,*" she whispered.

Nothing.

"*Lewis,*" she tried again.

This wasn't working. She had to think of something else.

Then a brilliant idea took hold. She put the folded note inside her notebook and wrote *look inside* on the cover lightly in pencil. It was a risky plan, but she thought it might work. She pushed the notebook off her desk so it went *kerflop* into the aisle, right at Lewis' feet.

A couple of kids turned to look. The commotion got Ms. Randall's attention, too.

"Oops, sorry," Callie said innocently. "I dropped my notebook. Lewis, will you get it for me?"

That seemed to do the trick. Ms. Randall went back to the equations on the board.

Lewis picked it up and smiled at Callie.

She gave him a look that said, "Read the hand written message on the scribbler, idiot!"

Lewis nonchalantly slipped the note out, then turned to Callie with his trademark smile and handed the notebook smoothly across the aisle.

Callie breathed a sigh of relief, but couldn't help glancing at Wanda to make sure they'd gotten past her, too.

Wanda's beady eyes peered at Callie through her narrow little glasses. She knew they were up to something, but it was obvious she didn't know *what.*

Callie felt dizzy. Her blood pressure was going through the roof. She stared at Lewis as he read the note, and was completely unprepared for his reaction.

He laughed.

Out loud.

Then he tried to cover it up by coughing, but he'd gotten the class's attention, and in particular, Ms. Randall's.

"Are you all right, Mr. Farnsworth?" she asked flatly.

"Fine," he croaked, taking out his asthma inhaler. "Just a little coughing fit, preceded by the memory of a humorous moment."

"I see," Ms. Randall said, looking like she didn't.

Callie was stunned. Not only had Lewis laughed at her plea for help--laughed!--he'd botched her brilliant note-passing plan by getting everyone's attention. She glanced back at Wanda, who was staring straight at her with a look that said, "Try that again, and I'm going to tell, big time."

Knowing it was risky, Callie unzipped her pencil case and wrote, *It's true* on her eraser. "Sure, you can borrow my eraser, Lewis," she said, handing it to him.

Ms. Randall glanced behind her, watching Lewis take it and immediately use it to erase part of the problem he was working on. Their teacher returned her attention to the board.

Callie gave Lewis the best "dagger eyes" she could muster. Lewis read the note, his light blue gaze meeting hers. Now he understood she was serious. He quickly used his own eraser to get rid of her pencil-written message. He wrote one of his own on it and passed it back to her.

We'll talk at recess.

"Ms. Randall?" Wanda said sweetly, or as sweetly as a calculating bully can, "I forgot my eraser, too. Could I borrow Callie's eraser, since she doesn't seem to mind lending it out?"

Callie's heart sank. She hadn't had time to erase the message, and now it was going to end up in Wanda's hands.

Ms. Randall turned, looking quite cross. "Yes, you may, Wanda, if you've forgotten your eraser, too. And if there are any others in the class who need erasers, I would ask that you all borrow one *now* so that we may get back to work. After this, if there are any more interruptions, the entire class will be staying after school to do a twenty-question math quiz. Is that clear?"

Wanda looked as if the wind had been taken out of her sails. She didn't even bother to say, "Yes, Ms. Randall." Instead, she snatched the eraser out of Callie's hand and looked down at it. Then she sank back into her desk like a snake coiling upon itself and smiled the most evil smile she had probably ever smiled, which for *her* was pretty evil. She gave Callie a look that said, "You're *so* busted."

Callie's heart did flip-flops. She didn't think Wanda would say anything during class because of Ms. Randall's threat. But Callie knew Wanda would somehow work this to her advantage. Callie and Lewis had been passing notes on her eraser; the evidence was still there. No doubt Wanda would try to blackmail her or something worse. She wondered how much money it was going to take to keep Wanda's mouth shut.

The rest of the lesson passed in relative quiet. The class was subdued after Ms. Randall's harsh warning, and the sick feeling in Callie's stomach grew worse. Now she had another problem to deal with: Wanda Morris snitching on her.

This day had gone from weird, to bad, to worse! First the strange dream, then cryptic messages in her cereal, then Wanda catching her passing notes. For a birthday, it wasn't going well. Callie wondered what else could go wrong today.

They still had one more class before recess--history. Thankfully, it was one of Callie's favorites. Maybe it would help keep her mind off everything. Ms. Randall instructed them to take out their history textbooks and turn to chapter five on the kings and queens of England.

Someone rapped on the classroom door--"rapped" because that's exactly what it sounded like, not just an ordinary knock. "Rapping" is much more important-sounding.

Ms. Randall furrowed her brow. No one ever knocked or rapped on their classroom door while school was in session--unless it was something serious, like someone in your family was in the hospital. Callie knew this from experience.

All eyes turned toward the door as the children hoped their name wouldn't be called.

Ms. Randall stepped back into the classroom, looking very serious indeed. "Callie Richards, come to the door, please."

Callie's heart did not only a flip-flop, but a swan dive into cement. *Her Dad--what if her Dad was hurt? What if her Dad was dead? She couldn't lose another parent...*

Callie looked to Lewis for strength, and he whispered, "It'll be okay."

She took a deep breath and forced herself out of her desk, forced her feet to move, walking slowly up to the front of the room. She could feel her classmates' eyes upon her, especially two pairs in particular--Lewis' and Wanda's.

The closer Callie got to the door, the more scared she got. She hated being scared. She'd spent far too much time being scared in the past two years.

Ms. Randall held the door open for Callie, her expression unreadable. "Come out into the hallway, please. There's someone who wishes to see you."

Someone who wishes to see you...

Before she could stop herself, Callie wished it was her mom. That would be the best birthday present ever.

But it wasn't her mom. It was never her mom.

In this case it wasn't her dad, either.

It was a man she had never seen before. He was an older man, and taller than most. He had a strange, pointy-shaped beard which hung down off his chin like a long triangle. His moustache curled up at the ends, and his long gray hair was tied back into a ponytail. A gold brocade jacket came down to just above his knees. He wore funny shoes with big gold buckles on them, and white knee socks. His matching gold brocade pants ended just below the knee. A long, thin sword hung from his belt. A hat with enormous brim sat upon his

28

head. A buckle decorated the front, and a long white feather extended from the side. A white ruffled shirt and a burgundy brocade vest topped off the costume.

The strangest thing about him, besides his choice in attire, was his eyes. They were the most unusual eyes Callie had ever seen. They were not blue, or green, or even brown, or a mixture of any of those. They were gold. Shimmering gold. Like his suit. He almost looked like a special effect from a movie.

"This man has a delivery for you, Callie," Ms. Randall said. She bent down, gave Callie's shoulder a reassuring pat and whispered in her ear, "It's probably for your birthday."

The strange-looking man took off his hat with a flourish, extending his foot out in front of him and making a formal bow. "Sir Reginald Abercrombie," he said, and when he said it, he rolled his R's so much it sounded like, 'Sir R-r-r-r-r-r-reginald Aber-r-rcr-r-r-r-rombie. Rr-r-oyal Cour-r-r-ier." He pointed to a heavily embroidered badge on his jacket that said exactly that: *Royal Courier.*

Ms. Randall smiled down at Callie, obviously impressed. "I'll leave the door open." She stepped back into the classroom and stood where Callie could see her. Ms. Randall always knew exactly what to do.

Sir Reginald pulled a package out from where it was tucked under his arm. It was wrapped in brown paper, but it was a very strange, heavy brown paper that looked like it was made from leaves. It was tied with a beautiful blue velvet ribbon. Sir Reginald smiled, and even *that* was odd. He seemed to have more teeth than the usual person.

29

"Package for Miss Calandria Richards," he said, still rolling his R's. He placed the package into her hands with an absolute grace of movement.

He knew her full name--Calandria?

Callie was too stunned to speak. She looked down at the package, which was long and rectangular, but thin--like a tall hardcover book. It was also heavier than one would have expected.

Callie looked up at Sir Reginald. "Is this a birthday present?"

"Yes, it is."

"Who is it from?" she asked. There were no "To" or "From" addresses written on the brown paper. In fact, Callie wondered how Sir Reginald had known where to deliver it.

Sir Reginald said, "I cannot say, Your Royal High--I mean, *Miss Richards*. If I were to name the Personage who had sent this most Priceless Gift to you, on this, the Twelfth Anniversary of your Magnificent Birth, I would be forced to endure the most grievous torture, and finally *death*, that you could ever imagine."

"Really?"

"Really." He nodded.

Callie couldn't help but ask, "Like what?"

He waved his hand around. "Oh, you know, the usual turn on the rack, a little keel-hauling, and then being hung upside down by my toes until I expire. Nothing out of the ordinary."

"Yikes," Callie said.

"But that shall not happen, Miss Richards. For I, Sir Reginald Abercrombie, decorated for Hard-Headedness at the Battle of Tarif, and for Pig-

Headedness at the Battle of Gamaro, would not give you even a hint of the name of the Royal Personage who has entrusted me with this most resolute and honorious task." Then, as if just realizing what he'd said, he covered his lips with his long fingers. "Oops. I said 'Royal Personage.' She'll feed me to the dragons, now."

"What royal personage?" Callie asked.

Sir Reginald looked up at the ceiling and hummed an off-key tune.

"Hey, I said what *Royal Personage*?"

He covered his ears, chanting "I can't hear you, I can't hear you," for a little while. Then he took his hands away from his ears and said, "Promise you won't ask me who Her Royal Personage is anymore?"

Feeling sorry for the guy, Callie said, "Fine."

Sir Reginald let out a huge breath in relief. "Oh, Miraculous Wonder! The honor of the Abercrombie name is preserved! I am not used to being so torn by my duty, Your Royal--I mean, *Miss Richards*. You see, the Abercrombies have been serving as Royal Couriers for over nine hundred years."

As Callie tried to comprehend what he had just said, she glanced into the classroom. Ms. Randall looked back, tapping her watch.

"Uh, I have to get back to class now."

"Of course, my lady. But first, may I impose upon you to sign this as proof of delivery?" Sir Reginald took a parchment scroll out of his inside jacket pocket, followed by a feathered quill pen.

Callie looked at the scroll. Strange swirling letters covered the old parchment, but the words were so small,

Callie could barely read them. "What does it say? The writing's awfully small."

Sir Reginald rolled the parchment out further, squinting at it himself. "It says 'I, Calandria Richards, do hereby accept the aforementioned package, delivered to me on this, the twelfth anniversary of my birth, et cetera, et cetera....'"

Callie peered at it again. It looked like the scroll said a whole lot more than that. She regarded Sir Reginald. "I'm not signing anything I can't read." That was the one useful thing she'd learned from Sharon, her Dad's lawyer girlfriend. Sharon had told Callie to *always* read the fine print.

Sir Reginald seemed close to scowling down at her, but somehow restrained himself. "Of course, Miss Richards. Very wise of you, indeed." He reached into his jacket pocket again and pulled out a huge magnifying glass. "Perhaps this will help."

Callie didn't bother to think about how the oversized magnifying glass had fit into his pocket. She just took it and tried to read the fine print. Unfortunately, some of it was fine, fine, *fine* print.

"I can't read all of it. The writing's still too small."

Sir Reginald shrugged, sadly. "Alas, that is the only magnifying glass I have. And I am sorry to inform you that according to official 'Royal Courier' procedures, I cannot leave the package in your care unless I have a receipt of delivery. I will just have to take your birthday present back, I'm afraid."

Callie sighed. She really wanted to find out what was in the package, and who had sent it to her. It *had* to be her dad--didn't it?

But with everything else that had happened today....

She took the quill pen and signed her name on the bottom. "Okay, there. I've signed it. Happy now?"

Sir Reginald smiled down at her and said slowly, *"More than you could ever imagine."* He put his hat back on. "My duty is done. Thank you for choosing 'Royal Courier.' Good day."

Sir Reginald walked jauntily down the hallway, humming the same off-key tune, and disappeared around the corner. Callie rejoined the class, taking her seat while curious eyes looked over at her and her mysterious package. She looked out the window to see Sir Reginald climb into a delivery van that, sure enough, had the words "Royal Courier" emblazoned on the side. But when he pulled away, the van shuddered and bucked, careening sharply left and then right. It almost seemed like Sir Reginald didn't know how to drive, which was odd if he had a job as a courier.

Lewis whispered, "What's in the package, Cal?"

"I don't know." Callie shrugged.

Ms. Randall directed her to put the package away in her desk until recess. Callie did as her teacher asked, but as the history class went on and they learned about the kings and queens of England, she couldn't stop thinking about what could possibly be in the package. Callie was so excited about that, she'd almost forgotten about Wanda and the fact that she still had Callie's eraser. Unable to stop herself, she glanced back at Wanda, and was shocked by what she saw.

A look of pure hatred, directed squarely at Callie, burned in Wanda's eyes. Callie shivered. Then she remembered that Wanda's own birthday had been two weeks ago. No one had delivered any special packages to the classroom for *her* birthday. She hadn't worn any new clothes to school the next day, either. Come to think of it, there was a rumor that Wanda's parents didn't even celebrate birthdays.

The buzzer finally sounded. Callie tucked the mysterious package under her arm as the kids began shuffling outside. Lewis walked next to Callie. "I'm sorry, Cal. I didn't mean to laugh at your note. It just took me off guard, you know?"

Callie gave a half-hearted smile. "I know. It wasn't your fault. It *was* a weird message. And now we have Wanda to worry about, too."

"Don't worry about her. Just tell me what happened this morning."

Callie was just about to tell him as they walked onto the playground, but waiting for them outside the door was Wanda Morris. She squinted her beady eyes at them and crooked her finger. "Over here, morons. We have a little business to discuss."

Callie and Lewis exchanged a look. They knew they had no choice but to follow.

"Passing notes, huh?" Wanda said imperiously. "I wonder what Ms. Randall would say if I showed her this *eraser?*" She held it aloft, the words, *We'll talk at recess*, still written across it in pencil.

"What's to say you didn't write it yourself?" Lewis asked.

Wanda made a face, as if the two people she was talking to were obviously the *stupidest* people on earth.

"The fact that your writing looks like Egyptian Hieroglyphs?"

Lewis pondered for a moment. It was true. He was left-handed and had very distinctive handwriting.

"No one else in class writes like *you*, ding-dong," Wanda said. "All I have to do is show this to Ms. Randall--"

"And the whole class stays after school to write a math quiz," Lewis said. "Great idea. You'll be even more popular with the class than you are now. And we both know you don't want to write that test either, so give the eraser back."

Wanda narrowed her eyes. She didn't like being beaten at her own game. "Well, if we did have to stay and write the test, it would be because of your little girlfriend, here. I'd just be doing my duty as a responsible student, reporting people who pass notes. I'm sure Ms. Randall would take my side."

She had a point.

Callie sighed. "How much do you want? I assume you're going to blackmail us."

Wanda held out her hand, looking completely proud of herself. "I prefer to call it a donation to the Wanda Morris College Fund. Just think, Callie, you and all the rest of these jokers will be paying towards my higher education. Today's donation will be ten dollars."

"Ten dollars! That's not fair," Callie protested.

"Newsflash: life isn't fair, numbskull. I would think a girl without a *mother* would have realized that by now," Wanda said nastily.

Callie's heart did a painful flip-flop. She felt her eyes welling up with tears but fought valiantly against them. She took a deep breath to try and steady her emotions.

"Ten bucks or the class writes Ms. Randall's test," Wanda said. "Take your pick."

Callie reluctantly dug in her pocket and pulled out the ten dollar bill her dad had given her that morning. At this point, she would have paid any amount of money to make Wanda go away.

Before Callie could hand over her birthday money, Lewis shoved a balled-up bill into Wanda's hand. "There. Now give us back the eraser, Wanda. And in case you didn't know--which judging by your behavior you obviously don't--it isn't cool to make fun of someone whose mother died. And speaking of mothers, at least Callie's mother loved her, which is more than you can say about *yours*."

This time it was Wanda's turn to be speechless with shock. Her expression darkened like a sky before a thunderstorm, and her eyes narrowed dangerously. She shoved the ten dollar bill into her pocket and hissed, "*Later, Losers*," then stomped away.

Callie let out a deep breath. Lewis put a comforting arm around her shoulder and led her over to their favorite spot on the retaining wall that surrounded the playground. "I'm sorry about that, Cal," he said. "Wanda Morris is getting worse every day. Talk about dysfunctional."

"I know," Callie agreed. "I think what you said might be true. Maybe that's why she's so mean to everyone...her parents don't really love her."

Lewis gave a lop-sided grin. "Forget about her. Open up your package!"

Callie felt a whoosh of excitement course through her stomach. She gently untied the velvet ribbon and put it in her pocket. "I wonder what it could be?" she mused, unfolding the stiff brown paper.

Lewis craned to get a better look. "Do you think it's from your dad?"

"It must be. Who else would have a gift delivered to me at school?" She lifted out a rich-looking rectangular case covered in burgundy leather. The top was embossed with gold. Intricate swirls and designs combined to form the letter A.

"Open it," Lewis said.

Before she could stop herself, she blurted, "I'm afraid." She couldn't explain it, but somewhere deep inside she knew that whatever was in that case would have a huge impact on her life.

Lewis looked puzzled. "What's to be afraid of? It's just a case with a present in it. It can't hurt you."

Callie had the same funny feeling as she'd had after her dream and the message in her cereal. "The dream...." she mumbled, slowly opening the case.

What she saw there made her gasp. It made Lewis gasp, too, and Lewis was not much of a gasper.

On a bed of dark blue velvet was the most spectacular jeweled necklace that Callie had ever seen. It was covered in brilliant stones, which to Callie's untrained eye looked like diamonds, but they had a soft pink hue. They sparkled in the sunlight. Unable to stop herself, Callie lifted the beautiful necklace from the case. The pink stones formed a long chain, and hanging from the bottom of it was a jewel-encrusted key. One large stone on the top of the key had the image of a unicorn cut inside it. It was the most beautiful thing Callie had ever seen.

"Wow," Lewis said. "Your dad sure outdid himself this year."

"I don't think this is from my dad," Callie said. Her dad loved her, but he would never buy his twelve-year old daughter a priceless necklace for her birthday. It looked like it was worth a lot of money.

"If he didn't send it, who did?" Lewis asked.

"Maybe this will tell us." Callie pulled out a thin scroll tied to the inside of the case. It seemed to be made of the same strange parchment as the proof of delivery she had signed. She unrolled it, and gasped again. "It's a map! And there's another poem. Just like the one in my dream. It went like this:

When one is two and two are one
King Eldric's magic has begun
The Queen will call the princess home
To sit upon the Enchanted Throne."

"What does this one say?" Lewis asked.

Callie took a deep breath. "At the top it says *Royal Summons*." Then she read:

"The key will open the magic door
Found beneath the forest floor
The unicorn will lead the way
And protect you both night and day

Make your way through the Grimstead Gate
Come and claim your royal fate
Proceed to the Palace of Arraband
Our country's fate lies in your hands."

"A unicorn? A door in the floor? What the heck does that mean?" Lewis asked.

Callie felt a chill shimmy down her spine, but it was a strange chill--one of excitement and trepidation combined. It couldn't be a coincidence. Now there was a mysterious key, a map and a royal decree to contend with.

She touched her friend's arm. "Lewis, there's an old statue of a unicorn in our back garden. It's covered now by weeds and ivy."

The house was set on a huge property and bordered a shady forest of maples. Her dad had never been much of a gardener, and since Callie's mom had died, everything had been allowed to grow over.

"What does the map say?" Lewis asked, reaching over to look at it.

Callie held it across her lap so they could see it better. The swirling letters said, "Royal City of Arraband" across the top, and showed what looked to be a fairly large city surrounded by a wall with several gates of entry.

"Look here," Callie exclaimed. "It's the Grimstead Gate! Lewis, that was in my dream, too. And here's the palace in the middle of the city." She pointed at it.

"Hold on a minute," Lewis warned. "We don't even know who sent you this. Cal, come on. You can't seriously believe all this."

"You think I'm making it up?"

"No, I don't think that. I just think, maybe you should talk to Dr. Sam about it."

Callie put the necklace back in its case and slammed it shut. "I don't need to talk to Dr. Sam. What I need to do is look for that door tonight. Something strange is going on, and I want to find out what it is. If you don't want to help me, I'll do it alone."

"Callie--" Lewis began.

"And by the way, Dad's having the pizza delivered tonight at seven. Be there." She packed up her things and stood, then stopped.

Staring at them from the nearby trees was Wanda Morris with a very strange expression on her face. Then Wanda slunk back towards the school like a snake.

Chapter Three

The Door in The Floor

That evening, after the pepperoni pizza had been eaten, the birthday candles had been lit, and the cake and ice cream had been gobbled up, Callie received the worst news she had gotten since learning of her mother's death.

Her dad and Sharon calmly announced that they were getting married.

The funny thing was, *this* had been the extra special surprise her dad had told her about that morning. The "something rare and beyond price." Callie had been hoping the mystery gift was a trip to France.

It wasn't a trip to France.

It was a new stepmom named Sharon Hennessey.

Somehow, the news had formed itself into a knife that was right now sinking into Callie's heart and causing her unbelievable pain. Before she could stop herself, Callie looked at her dad and blurted, "How could you do this? Don't you love Mom anymore?"

Her dad looked a little shocked at his daughter's outburst. "Of course I do, Callie. Nothing can change that."

Callie stood up, completely oblivious to the fact that Lewis was sitting quietly in the armchair and was witnessing the whole terrible scene. "Well, if that's true, how can you want another wife? You and Mom didn't get a divorce, you know. You can't marry someone else. You can't do this to her, Dad!"

Her dad looked hurt, more hurt than she'd seen him look since the horrible day of her mom's car accident. Callie immediately felt bad. Worse than bad. Horrible. She didn't want to hurt her dad, but she didn't want him to forget about her mother, either.

Because if he could forget about her mother, then maybe someday Callie would, too, and that thought terrified her.

She grabbed a picture off the mantle. It had been taken during their last family vacation. They'd gone sailing and fishing on Chesapeake Bay. There they were, the three of them on the deck of the *Miss Amy*, holding tight to one another, smiling and laughing as her dad held a huge fish up by its tail. Two weeks later, her mother was dead.

Callie showed the picture to her father. "We're a family, Dad. I want our lives back the way they were. I want *Mom* back."

"*Callie...*" His voice was choked with emotion as he stood and went to her.

But Sharon stood, too. "Callie, could I have a word with you, alone?"

Callie was momentarily shocked--she had never really spent any time alone with Sharon before. It seemed like Sharon was already taking her new job as stepmom very seriously.

"Ben," Sharon continued gently but firmly, as she might in the court room, "why don't you take Lewis out onto the veranda for a few minutes so you can talk about baseball?"

Baseball? Ha! Callie wanted to say. *If you knew even an iota about Lewis, you'd know he isn't interested in baseball.* But as she saw her dad obediently steer Lewis onto the front porch, what she really wanted to say was, *Dad, don't leave me alone with her.*

Sharon looked down at Callie with a forced smile. If this was Sharon's attempt at relating to kids, it was falling as flat as a three-ton pancake. "Callie, I realize our news might have come as a shock to you...."

That was an understatement.

"I know you're still dealing with your mother's death, and probably will be for the rest of your life."

Callie's heart began to beat faster. Somewhere deep down, she knew that Sharon was trying to be helpful, but right now her efforts were anything but.

"It's been two years, Callie," Sharon said as gently as she could. "And though you may not be, your dad is ready to move on with his life. And that means having a new wife--*me*. And I know you probably thought your dad would never, ever want a wife other than your mom. But... he does."

Callie couldn't believe this. Though it was obvious Sharon was trying really hard to tone it down, no one had ever spoken to Callie so bluntly before. Especially not about her mother's death.

"Callie, I love your father very, very much. He's been through a hard time, too. And now, he has a chance to be happy again, with me. I want to make him happy, Callie. I want us *both* to make him happy. In order to do that, we're going to have to work together, okay?"

If it was possible, Callie felt worse than she had a few minutes ago.

43

What Sharon had said was true. Though Callie knew it was selfish, she had hoped deep down that her dad would never meet anyone and never date anyone, and never, ever remarry. Because it would have made Callie's life a whole lot simpler.

Sharon continued, "This is going to be a difficult transition for all of us, no doubt about it. And I'm hoping that together, all sides can reach an agreeable resolution to this problem...."

Callie couldn't believe it. Sharon was using legal jargon while attempting to relate to her twelve-year-old, soon-to-be step-daughter.

"I've drawn up a proposal for you to peruse," Sharon continued, handing Callie a thick set of papers. "Since I'm going to be your new stepmom, I think we should set aside one day a week to get to know each other better. Forge a bond--'Girlpower,' and all that. I've put together a list of activities you might find interesting...."

Callie scanned Sharon's list: a tour of the legal library at Sharon's office...reorganizing Sharon's closet...cataloging Sharon's shoes...and about a dozen other things you'd only agree to in order to get out of a Turkish prison. The only thing that was missing was cleaning Sharon's bathroom with a toothbrush.

This woman didn't have a clue. That was what worried Callie.

"And now, I have a favor to ask of you," Sharon said seriously. "As young people, it's very common for us to concentrate on ourselves, while forgetting that there are others around us who need our consideration."

Callie detested the term *young people*. It was usually used by adults who didn't understand kids.

"I'm asking, Callie, that you begin putting your father first."

Callie's heart sank. Was Sharon insinuating that Callie had been putting her dad *last*?

She hadn't been--had she?

Sharon patted Callie's shoulder as if she was trying to tap down a nail. "I just want you to think of him--of his feelings--during this time of transition. Okay? Promise?"

Knowing it was futile to argue with Sharon-The-Super-Lawyer, Callie nodded.

"For a verbal agreement to be binding, both parties have to speak," Sharon pointed out, sweetly.

Callie stared up at the woman who was going to be her stepmom. She wanted to laugh bitterly, but she kept it inside. Thinking of her mother's beautiful face on the last day she'd seen her alive, Callie said, *"From now on, I promise to put Dad first."*

Unable to stand Sharon's presence for one more moment, Callie rushed to the door. She ached to see a friendly face, to have her dad's arms around her, comforting her and telling her everything would be all right, but tonight, everything had been irrevocably changed. If she kept her promise to Sharon, she'd have to learn to start taking care of herself, even if she was only twelve.

Callie stepped out onto the veranda. Her dad immediately got up, his brow furrowed with worry. Before she knew it, his big, lanky frame was beside her and his strong arm was around her shoulder, pulling her close. "Everything okay, Sport?" he whispered into her hair.

To her own surprise, she pulled away. She didn't want to be reminded of what she'd just lost, and she knew without a doubt that after tonight, her relationship with her father would never be the same again.

"I just need to be with Lewis for a while, okay?" Callie managed to say in a somewhat normal voice. Already she was breaking her promise to Sharon. She wasn't putting her dad first right now. But she was doing the best she could without making another scene.

"Okay...." her dad said tentatively.

To Callie's deep satisfaction, Lewis stepped up beside her. "I think Callie needs a little space right now, Mr. Richards. She'll be fine with me."

At that moment Sharon opened the screen door and poked her head out, saying, "Ben, why don't you come in and let Callie and her little friend have their visit?"

Callie saw Lewis glance at Sharon in annoyance.

Little friend?--she could almost hear Lewis thinking--they both hated that term almost as much as *young people*.

It made Callie's heart swell with pride. She may not have her dad anymore, but she had Lewis. And he saw right through Sharon, just like Callie did. He led her off the veranda and steered her onto the gravel path that led to the backyard. "We'll just be in the back garden, having a heart-to-heart. Don't worry, Callie, *I have Kleenex*," he said loudly.

They made their way down the dark path to the backyard, and once they were safely away from the house, Callie stopped trying to hold back her tears. By this point in their friendship, Lewis was bomb-proof. Unlike a lot of other boys, or men for that matter, Lewis wasn't scared of a crying girl. The fact that Lewis had two younger sisters probably helped.

"It's okay, Cal," he said, offering her a Kleenex. "You're allowed to cry. I have to say it--for a birthday, *this takes the cake.*"

Callie wiped her nose, unable to laugh at Lewis' joke. "What am I going to do? Sharon and Dad are getting *married*! She's going to live in our house and bring her horrible cat, Wallingford, and make Dad forget that Mom ever existed." Callie stood up, pacing around like a tiger in a cage. "This can't be happening."

Lewis shrugged. "I know it's unfair, but I think you're just going to have to accept your dad's marriage to Sharon."

Callie had an awful feeling that her best friend was right, though she didn't want him to be.

"If only I could find the Door in the Floor and go to Albion. Then I could forget about Dad and Sharon."

Lewis stood up. "Callie, Albion isn't real. It was just a dream and you know it."

But Callie didn't know it. She didn't know anything right now. She just knew that she wanted to escape. Going into a magical land where she might be a princess sounded pretty good, considering what her future here looked like.

She pulled the pink sparkly necklace out from under her sweater. "I have to at least look," Callie said. "It's my birthday. Indulge me."

She walked over to the garden shed and opened the creaky doors. Her mom had spent a lot of time out here, potting plants, weeding, transplanting. Now the shed seemed like a tomb.

"What are you doing?" Lewis asked.

She rummaged through a drawer. "Looking for...this!" She switched on the flashlight and practically blinded her best friend. He howled in pain and staggered backwards.

"Oops, sorry. Are you okay?"

"Yeah. I have a spare set of eyeballs back home," he said, rubbing his eyes. "Wait here while I go get them."

Callie directed her friend out of the shed. "Quit whining and help me look." This was great. Her mood was lifting already. She and Lewis were going to have a grand adventure, just like in one of her library books.

"Okay, but only because it's your birthday and you just found out you're getting an icky step mother."

Callie led the way, going to a back corner of the garden which was overgrown with ivy and weeds. She shone the flashlight around upon a sea of thick green vegetation. "The unicorn statue is around here somewhere...."

"All I see are plants," Lewis said helpfully.

"Thank you, Mr. Farnsworth. Now get in there and look *under* the plants."

Lewis obeyed dutifully. Somewhere during his twelve short years he had learned that there was absolutely no use arguing with a woman once she'd made up her mind. "I think I found something."

"What?" Callie felt her heart begin to race as she shined the flashlight on Lewis' hands.

He held out something dark and leggy. "A bug."

Callie squealed and jumped backwards as Lewis chuckled to himself. "That's not funny!"

Lewis kept chuckling. Even though he was the smartest, kindest, most sensitive boy Callie had ever met, the fact remained that Lewis was still a boy, and he still enjoyed scaring girls with bugs.

"You're supposed to be helping," Callie reminded him.

"I am helping. I'm clearing the bugs out of the way," he said with a smile. He wrestled with the greenery, his arm practically disappearing from sight as he pulled apart the dense vines. "Shine the flashlight over here, Cal. I think...I might...have found it!" He fell backwards and landed in a sitting position on the ground.

Callie rushed to help him, but Lewis quickly stood up. "Look, Callie. There it is!"

Callie turned her gaze in the direction he was pointing. "The unicorn...." She shone the flashlight on the face of the stone statue. It almost seemed to hum with life, its smooth carved eyes staring eerily into the night, its spiraled horn pointing up towards the starry night sky.

Suddenly unconcerned with bugs, Callie waded into the greenery, pulling the vines away herself to reveal more of the majestic statue. "This was one of Mom's favorite places in the garden. There's a stone bench around here too. She used to sit out here for hours and read."

"Well, we found the unicorn," Lewis said. "What else does the poem say?"

Callie took the scroll out of her pocket and shone the light on it, reading aloud:

"The key will open the magic door
Found beneath the forest floor
The unicorn will lead the way
And protect you both night and day."

Lewis waded around the back of the statue, looking down. Callie joined him, passing the flashlight over thick twigs, weeds, and vines.

Lewis crouched down, feeling around in the underbrush. "Do you remember there being a door out here, Cal?"

"Well...no. But that doesn't mean it's not here. Keep looking."

They searched and searched, but didn't manage to find anything more than a bunch of tangled vines.

"I hate to say it, Cal, but I think that poem is a hoax," Lewis said, standing.

Callie felt her heart sink. She realized how badly she'd wanted there to be a door in the floor, and a magical land called Albion that needed her.

"All right, Lew. Let's go in." Callie took a few steps toward the house. "It's just been a crazy day. I don't know what I was thinking. You're right, there's no door in the fl—"

The next minute, the ground flew up to meet her. She dropped with a hard thud, landing on her stomach.

Lewis was beside her in an instant. "Callie! Are you okay?" He tried to help her up, but her foot was caught in something.

He crouched down to where it was twisted in some vines. "Whoa, you're really tangled up here, Cal. Just a second...I'm getting it...wait, what's this?" He pulled away some of the thick vines that had ensnared her, and both he and Callie found themselves staring at an old iron ring.

It was attached to something--a wooden door that looked ancient, like it belonged on a castle.

"It's a door," Lewis said, dumbfounded. "It's the Door in the Floor, Cal!"

Callie got her breath back, and felt her heart swell with hope. "It *is* a door--just like the poem said! Help me up, Lewis."

Lewis quickly got Callie's foot free and helped her stand. Her ankle throbbed a bit, and she'd hurt her knee, too, but her injuries weren't foremost in her mind at the moment. "Help me clear this away," she said, kneeling down to pull at the vines and debris.

Soon they had it completely uncovered. It was made from rough-hewn wood and had thick iron fastenings and bolts. It was only big enough for only one person to fit through at a time.

"It might be the door to an old cellar," Lewis said.

"My parents never mentioned a cellar. Mom used to come out here all the time to do her gardening. You'd think she would have said something if she'd found it."

Lewis jiggled the handle a few times, but the door wouldn't open. "It's locked."

Callie shone the flashlight on the door. Sure enough, under the ring, there was an iron keyhole. *"The key will open the magic door..."* she said, quoting the poem. Callie sat back on her heels and slipped the diamond necklace over her head, hoping the jewel-encrusted key on the end of it would fit the lock. She took a deep breath and slid it in.

"Lewis--*it fits*," she whispered. Her heart began to race with excitement and wonder.

Her friend stepped closer. "Wait a minute. We don't know what might be down there."

"But don't you want to find out?"

Used to being the responsible older brother at home, Lewis folded his arms and frowned. "It might be dangerous, Cal."

Callie smiled mischievously. "Let's just take a look."

For a long moment he stared at her, then he smiled, too. "Okay." Though usually the voice of reason, Lewis was still, after all, a kid.

A thrill coursed through Callie's veins. She turned the jeweled key in the lock, and the mechanism clicked. She removed the key and put the necklace back over her head. Then she and Lewis both pulled on the thick iron ring. Callie gasped as the door lifted slightly. A whoosh of stale air came out, smelling of old decaying leaves and other scents of the forest.

Together they managed to wrestle with the heavy door, and soon the hinges creaked. It groaned as it fell open onto the ground with a thud.

Callie's heart beat wildly.

"It's pitch black down there," Lewis said. "Where's the flashlight?"

Hands trembling, Callie fumbled for the light and held it up. What could be down there? What if it was a pit of snakes, or rats, or spiders? Or worse? She took a deep breath and shone the flashlight down.

An old wrought-iron staircase spiraled into the dark depths of the unknown. Callie crouched, trying to shine the light deeper into the chamber.

"Where does it go?" Lewis asked, craning to get a look.

"I can't tell. It's too deep. I can't see much of anything." Callie's skin tingled as a strange feeling echoed in her heart. It was the same feeling she'd had after the dream.

Though she couldn't see anything, she knew this was the doorway to *Albion*. And she had to go through it.

She stepped down onto the wrought iron platform that led to the spiral staircase below.

"Cal--what are you doing? We don't even know if these stairs are safe, let alone where they go!" Lewis protested, following behind her. "There could be something really, really horrible down here."

"I *know* what's down here," she said firmly, shining the flashlight on the filigreed staircase as they made their way down, their feet tapping quickly. "This is what my dream was about, Lewis. And the message in my cereal, and the necklace, and everything! This is the way into Albion, and it's where I have to go."

The air was thick with the pungent smell of damp earth and wet rocks. Down, down, down they went, until they finally reached a large circular chamber at the bottom. An arched doorway was carved into the far wall.

"Look, there's a tunnel." Callie shone her flashlight into a long, stone passageway.

"Do you feel that?" Lewis asked.

"Feel what?"

Lewis held his hand out in front of him. "Air. There's a breeze coming through here."

Callie lifted her hand and felt it brush over her skin. She didn't need Lewis to explain what it meant; she remembered it from science class. If there was air coming through the tunnel, it meant there was something generating it at the other end.

"Wow," Lewis said, stepping toward the mouth of the tunnel. "Look at these carvings, Callie. This is incredible!"

As they stepped into the tunnel, torches on the walls lit themselves, the orange flames softly illuminating the ancient structure before them.

Callie and Lewis walked slowly through the tunnel, taking their time, marveling at the intricate carvings which decorated the walls.

Several scenes showed magical beasts--winged horses and lions, huge herds of unicorns prancing through thick forests, fire-breathing dragons, frightening serpents, and even stranger creatures which Callie and Lewis had never seen before. There were scenes of clashing armies, royal hunts and processions, kings and queens adorned in all their finery, with jeweled crowns upon their heads and scepters in their hands, sitting upon magnificent thrones.

They were deep in the tunnel now, so deep they couldn't see either end. It was a bit creepy. But what was even more creepy was the next panel of carvings. Callie saw a woman, her face obscured by a veil but wearing a crown. Obviously a queen.

But instead of subjects before her, there were birds. Ravens. Hundreds of them. One in particular was perched upon the queen's shoulder, and looked like it was whispering in her ear. One of her arms was extended, and her hand was stretched out over the ravens before her, who all seemed to be waiting for her command. In the other hand, the queen triumphantly held aloft a small round globe. The letter 'T' adorned the top of it.

Lewis stepped closer. "What a weird globe. Whoever they got to carve it certainly didn't know geography very well. I don't recognize any of these continents. Hey Callie, isn't that the lady from your dream? The Raven Queen or whoever?" Lewis asked, pointing.

A cold shiver passed through Callie's heart. "Yes, I think it is. But how could I have dreamt about this? I've never seen *any* of it before."

"That's a good point," Lewis agreed. He stopped for a moment, getting that special look he always got when he had a particularly brilliant thought. "Maybe you didn't dream it after all. Maybe it's precognition."

Callie frowned. "What's that?"

"In layman's terms, precognition means knowing something is going to happen before it actually *does* happen."

"If that's true..." Callie didn't want to think about what that might mean. She had dreamt she was a princess, but she had also dreamt she'd lost an important battle, people had died, and the Raven Queen and her army were trying to kill her.

"I think I like the dream scenario better," she said, turning her attention back to the carvings. Then she saw something that made her heart and stomach do a flip flop at the same time. "Lewis, look at this."

They both peered at the next panel in wonder. It was a detailed carving of a young woman who looked like a princess. She wore a long, flowing gown and an extravagantly jeweled tiara. In one hand she held a sword. The other hand rested on the back of an enormous throne covered in strange writing. Around her neck she wore the pink diamond necklace and key that was now around Callie's neck.

"Callie," Lewis said slowly. "She looks like—"

"*Me.*" Callie stepped forward and touched the carving. Something traveled through her fingertips, like a series of tingly, electric shocks.

"Me, me, *me.*" A voice said from a few feet behind them. "Is that all you ever think about?"

Callie and Lewis turned in horror to see what terrible creature had snuck up behind them in the depths of the secret tunnel. But they already knew who owned that voice.

It belonged to Wanda Morris.

Chapter Four

An Uninvited Guest

Callie and Lewis both stood motionless, mouths agape in horror. It was like they were in a bad dream, only it was worse than a bad dream because it was real. The good news was that if Wanda was down in the secret tunnel with them, at least they weren't hallucinating the whole thing.

"Happy to see me?" Wanda asked in a snarky voice.

"*No*," Callie and Lewis barked in unison.

Lewis shook his head. "Wanda, you can't be down here. How did you even know about this place?"

"She was spying on us today at recess," Callie said. "She must have overheard me talking about the map and the Door in the Floor."

"I wasn't *spying*." Wanda seemed unconcerned. "It's not my fault if you two were talking so loud."

Callie took a step forward. "This is *our* tunnel, Wanda, and you're not pushing your way in on our discovery."

Wanda tossed her head importantly. "Newsflash: it's a free country, morons. I didn't see a 'No Trespassing' sign on the way in, so I have just as much right to be down here as you do." She jabbed a finger at Callie. "You don't get to hog all the good stuff, you know. Just because you got a stupid necklace for your birthday doesn't make you *special*."

Callie's heart pounded with anger. First her dad's marriage to Sharon--and now this?

"Wanda, I think you should go," Lewis said flatly.

She ignored him, and proceeded to examine the depictions on the wall. "Right. Like I'm going to let you two take all the credit for discovering this place."

"We *did* discover it," Callie pointed out.

Wanda gave a sinister smile. "Your word against mine. I'm sure the news crews will see it my way when I explain how my two friends, Callie and Lewis *assisted* me in my discovery of whatever's at the end of this tunnel."

Callie was stunned. "You wouldn't..."

"She would," Lewis said, staring at Wanda's self-satisfied smile. "Wanda, let me recommend a personal development course to you: it's called *How to Win Friends and Influence People* by Dale Carnegie. Just as an aside, what you're doing right now is a good example of how *not* to win friends."

Wanda narrowed her eyes. "Like I'd want either of you to be my friends. You guys are *losers*."

Callie folded her arms. "Yeah? Well, if we're losers, how come you follow us around everywhere? And eavesdrop on us?"

"Yeah," Lewis agreed. "If we're such losers, what are you doing in this tunnel with us? You'd better go home."

Wanda glared at them. "Nice try, idiots. I'm not going back, and you can't make me."

"Wanda," Lewis said, shaking his head, "since you seem to be missing the obvious point of why you're not welcome here, I'm going to make it simple: You torment the kids in our class--including us. You blackmail people, and you turn up where you're not invited. You're mean, and you're nasty. We're sick of you. I can't say it any plainer than that."

Wanda's eyes blazed with anger. "Yeah? Well, I'm sick of you, too!" She pointed a finger at Callie. "I'm sick of you having everything you want: clothes, shoes, diamond necklaces for your birthday, and now *this*!"

Callie was stunned. Wanda was so wrong. Callie *didn't* have everything she wanted.

Wanda continued her tirade. "Callie Richards-- Daddy's little princess! And you're the teacher's pet at school, too. Just because your mother died, everyone treats you like you're special. You have everything handed to you on a platter, and I'm sick of it." She took a step toward Callie, her eyes dark and glittery. "This time, Wanda Morris is going to take a little bit for herself. And you can't stop me..."

Callie stood silently in shock, her head swimming. She had always known Wanda disliked her, out of jealousy or whatever it was that got under Wanda's skin. But now Callie understood that Wanda didn't just dislike her. Wanda *hated* her.

Wanda pushed past them, shining her flashlight down the long, dark passageway. "I'm going to find out what's at the end of this tunnel. For once, Wanda Morris is going to be the special one, got it? And don't even think about getting in my way." She gave them both a seething stare. "Later, losers..." With that, she disappeared.

Lewis came to stand next to Callie. He put his arm around her as they watched the glow of Wanda's flashlight grow fainter until they couldn't see it anymore. "Are you okay, Cal?"

"Lewis, I'm scared. Wanda really *hates* me."

"I know. What can I say, she's whacked in the head."

Callie nodded. "Maybe we should go back."

"No. We're not going to let Wanda Morris ruin our exploration of your birthday tunnel. We're not going to let a bully intimidate us out of our own discovery!"

Lewis grinned as a thought occurred to him. "Hey, maybe there's a man-eating monster at the end of this tunnel, and he'll eat Wanda! Then when we walk by, he'll be full and he won't touch us."

"Yeah," Callie said, trying not to think about Wanda and her threats as they continued on. Was Wanda truly dangerous? Had her jealousy made her so unhinged that she might actually cause harm to Callie or Lewis? She hoped not.

"Hey, Lewis, look at this," Callie said. They had gotten so wrapped up in the scene with Wanda that they hadn't noticed something strange about the carvings on the walls.

There weren't any.

"What happened to the carvings?" Lewis asked, touching the smooth wall beside them. The opposite wall was bare as well.

"I don't know. Let's go back and find out," Callie said, retracing their steps the short distance back to where they'd been.

She touched the carving of the princess--the one that looked like her. But the next panel, and all the panels after that, were bare. "The carvings end here, with this one."

"What do you think it means?" Lewis asked.

Callie shrugged at Lewis, but kept what she thought to herself--that this was a hall of records, and the carvings ended because the events they depicted hadn't happened yet.

"I think I see something up ahead," Lewis said, pointing to a faint light.

Callie felt a whoosh of excitement. "I see it, too. Come on!" They walked quickly, heading toward an orange glow. They were running, now, not knowing what they were even running to, or if there would be danger. Yet they were unable to stop themselves.

"I can see it," Callie panted. "It's a road or something."

"I see it, too!"

Up ahead, through the mouth of the tunnel, they could make out the edge of a winding road. There was a high stone wall on the left side, a thick forest off to the right, and not a soul in sight.

Callie and Lewis came to a stop at the tunnel exit, and quietly surveyed the mysterious road before them. The stone wall stretched as far as they could see in either direction.

The far-off sound of horses, carts, the jingling of harnesses and the clip-clop of hooves echoed in the night. They heard gruff voices, a door slamming, a bottle smashing on the cobblestones.

"It must be a theme park, or something." Lewis said.

"There aren't any theme parks in our part of the state."

"Oh, yeah."

"Which way do you think we should go?" Callie asked.

They both looked at a road sign nearby. In swirling letters, it proclaimed:

Royal City of Arraband - 2 parthons,
Grimstead Gate - 1/2 parthon.

It pointed right. Below that it said:

Forest of Dead Souls - 5 parthons.

This pointed left. At the bottom it said:

This Sign Made Possible By A Grant From The Department Of Improvements To Road Signage, Kingdom of Albion, Hon. Horatius P. Montague, Minister of Transportation. Working Together To Give Albians Better Roads

"Better roads?" Lewis remarked, pointing at the dusty, bumpy road before them. "Haven't they heard of paving?" He turned his attention back to the places listed on the sign.

"Forest of Dead Souls," Callie said. "Let's skip that for now. Royal City of Arraband--that's the city on my map!"

She pulled it out and shone the flashlight on it. "It's the capital city of Albion."

"Cool, and the gate's pretty close. Only 1/2 a parthon away--whatever that means-- but I'll bet it's not far off."

"The poem said we should proceed to the palace which is in the center of the city," Callie said. "We can use the map to navigate the streets. It looks like there's a lot of them. Come on."

Without warning, Lewis reached over and poked her.

"Hey, what did you do that for?" Callie asked.

"Just checking to see if I was dreaming. I'm not. You were right about this place, Callie. I'm sorry I didn't believe you."

Callie's heart warmed. "It's okay, Lew. Even I had a few doubts. But I'm glad you're here with me. I couldn't have gotten this far without you."

He gave her his trademark grin, and Callie smiled, too.

They used Callie's flashlight to guide their way down the bumpy road. Soon they came upon a big double wooden gate. It stood in the middle of the wall, flanked by two torches that burned orange in the black night. Above the gate, two hideous looking gargoyles stood guard. A weathered iron plaque proclaimed *Grimstead Gate* to passersby.

Callie's breath caught in her throat and her heart pounded painfully in her chest. "Lewis, this place was in my dream. It's exactly the same--the gate, the torches, everything! But I've never been here before. How do I remember a place I've never been?"

"Beats me, Cal. Maybe we've discovered another dimension. You know, this would make a great science project. Something like this would garner a lot of attention in the scientific community. We'd have our pick of universities lining up to give us scholarships."

"*Scholarships*? Lewis, we're only in the sixth grade," Callie pointed out.

"It's never too early to start planning for your higher education." He grinned.

Then something happened that made Callie's breath catch in her throat. A voice came out of the night. Then another one. They weren't just any voices. They were gruff and scary, and seemed to be talking about her.

"I tell ye, it's her."

"Her, who?"

"Princess Calandria—of the Royal House of Arraband."

"'Ow d'ye know?"

"I've seen pictures, so I 'ave."

"Where? Where 'ave ye seen pictures?"

"In the Albion Times, if ye must know. I'm a regular subscriber--the Arraband Chronicle and Gargoyles Weekly, too. I like ta keep up on current events, which is more than I can say about you."

Callie shone her flashlight around. Even with the glow from the two torches it was still quite dark. "Uh... Hello?"

"Uh-oh. I think she heard us."

Callie looked at Lewis. He seemed as uncertain as she did, but he said, "We did hear you. Where are you?"

Callie shone the flashlight around the gate, but they still couldn't see anyone who might be attached to those strange voices.

"Up here."

Callie slowly shone her flashlight up the wall above the gate. A hideous face looked down at her and grinned brightly. *"Hi."*

Callie screamed in fright and fell back onto the dirt road. Lewis shouted in fright too, but managed to stay on his feet. The gargoyles were talking!

"Now look what ye done. Ye've killed her, ye great dolt. The Only Hope of Albion. The queen will 'ave yer head for this."

"The queen'll 'ave my 'ead? I'd like to see 'er try to get this 'ead off. It's been attached for more than a thousand years. And for your information, I didn't kill 'er. I startled 'er. She's getting up. See for ye'self."

Lewis pulled Callie to her feet.

"Are you all right, Princess?"

Callie shone her flashlight up at the statue. A concerned face stared down at her. It was a hideous, frightening face, but it was definitely full of concern--for her.

"Um... are you talking to me?" Callie asked.

The horrifying face laughed. *"Well, I don't see any other princesses around 'ere, d'you, Kevin?"*

Callie shone the flashlight further to the left of the stone figure. On the opposite end of the gate, another stone gargoyle looked down at them, laughing and holding his tummy. *"No I don't, Terry!"*

She shone the flashlight back and forth between them, just to make sure she was seeing what she thought she was seeing. "Lewis?"

"I see," her friend replied. "Way cool."

"Hey--stop that. Ye're blindin' us with that bloomin' light, Yer Highness."

"Sorry, I--what did you call me?" Callie asked.

"Yer Highness, of course," one of them said.

65

"He means 'Yer Royal Highness,' Yer Royal Highness," the other one said. "But allow me to introduce me'self. I'm Terry." Callie shone the light on the gargoyle closest to her. "And this is my brother, Kevin."

She shone the light on the other one, who said politely, "Hello."

"As ye can see, I'm the better looking one," Terry said proudly.

"But you both look exactly alike," Lewis said.

Terry scowled at them. "No we don't. And oo's this? Yer manservant? A might lippy fer my taste, if ye don't mind me sayin', Yer Royal Highness." The gargoyle pointed a long, skinny finger at Lewis. "When ye get to the Palace, they'll put ye in a pot, make a stew out of ye, and feed ye to the royal dragons. And from the looks o' ye, it'll be a thin supper."

"I'm not her manservant. I'm her *friend*," Lewis said defensively.

"Friend, is it?" Kevin said. "We'll see how long 'e lasts at Court, eh Terry?"

"Yeah... lot's goin' on at Court these days. Everyone preparin' fer your arrival," he said to Callie.

"Preparing?" Callie said. "You mean, they knew I was coming?"

Terry gave a broad grin. "Of course. It's been all over the papers fer weeks. Look—'ere's today's Albion Times." He held up a newspaper. "Headline reads: 'Princess Calandria Arrives Today--Big Party at Palace!'"

"A party--for *me*?" Callie asked, confused.

Terry said, "Sure enough. It's yer birthday, in't it? It's all 'ere on the front page. 'Ave a look."

Terry tossed down the newspaper, which was quite heavy, not like regular newspapers at all. The paper was rough and brownish, like the paper on the birthday gift delivered by Sir Reginald, and it was covered in the same swirling script they'd seen on the road sign and Callie's map.

Callie gasped. There was a picture of *her* on the front page!

Lewis read the article aloud:

"Bureau Chief Tertius Lombardi reporting —

On what is sure to be one of the most important days in our history, Princess Calandria arrives today in the Royal City of Arraband (with her usual full entourage) to begin her royal duties on this, the twelfth anniversary of her birth.

Tonight, Queen Arabella will be hosting a banquet in Princess Calandria's honor, which will include a host of dignitaries and nobility. After a tour of the Royal Treasury, the stables and grounds, the princess and her guests will be treated to royal entertainments before a grand finale of what is being touted as one of the most spectacular fireworks displays in the city's ten-thousand-year history.

Palace spokesman Pontius Hastings released the following statement: 'On behalf of Her Royal Majesty Queen Arabella, I would like to thank all those involved in the careful planning of this glorious event. The long-anticipated arrival of Princess Calandria will prove vital to our nation's future.'

Political pundits have predicted that Princess Calandria (who has been fully briefed on our situation) reportedly possesses a magic far more powerful than any in Albion's history, and will undoubtedly be the answer to our people's prayers.

Albians--rejoice! Our princess has returned!"

Callie stared at the newspaper article, unable to speak. She blinked a couple of times, thinking that might help. It didn't. The *Albion Times* still showed her picture on the front page, and the article still said she was the answer to Albion's prayers, and it still said the queen was throwing a huge party in her honor, and it still said she was a magical princess, besides.

It was more exciting than anything Callie had ever dreamed of: a royal banquet, magical powers.... Yet, she somehow felt that the article wasn't telling the full story.

"I hate to tell you this, but there are errors in this article," she said to one of the gargoyles.

"Oh yeah? Like what?" Terry asked.

"Well, like here, it says I have a 'full entourage.' That isn't true. I only have Lewis." She gestured toward her best friend.

"Ye mean your manservant?" Kevin shrugged. *"So it's a small entourage."*

Callie pointed at the article. "And see here, where it says I've been fully briefed? That's not true, either. I've only been partially briefed."

"Partially?"

Callie nodded. "I had a message in my cereal this morning."

Terry shook his head and gave his brother a meaningful look. *"Well, that's the Department of Information Dissipation for ye. Phorbus Crumbly's been the Director for three-hundred years, and they still 'ave the same problems they did back in King Cadmus's reign. Don't know what they're doing in these* government departments, anymore. And this is 'ow they spend our taxes, on mismanagement...."

The two gargoyles began bickering about government spending, until Callie cleared her throat. "Ah-hem?"

Terry gave a toothy grin. *"Sorry, Princess. Ye'll 'ave ta forgive us. In over a thousand years of sitting on this wall together, my brother and I have never been able to see eye-to-eye on two things: politics and dentistry."* He pointed at his brother. *"See? 'E refuses to visit the dentist for his regular twenty-year check up. And just look at 'is teeth. 'Orrible. What would Mum say, Kev?"*

Kevin stuck his nose in the air, looking hurt.

Callie raised her eyebrows. She hadn't known that gargoyles were so concerned with oral hygiene. It seemed to be a touchy subject, so Callie tried to redirect their attention back to the front page of the *Albion Times*. "And see here, where it says I have magical powers? I don't."

Kevin peered down at her keenly. *"Are ye sure?"*

"Pretty sure," Callie replied.

"Pretty sure isn't totally sure, though, is it?" Kevin said pointedly. *"Maybe ye do 'ave magical powers. Ye just 'aven't discovered 'em yet."*

Terry nodded. *"Often times, there's something right under our nose which we never saw before. Just because we didn't see it doesn't mean it wasn't there the whole time."*

Callie thought about the gargoyle's words. That was true about the Door in the Floor. Just because she hadn't been aware of it didn't mean it hadn't been there the whole time. Could the gargoyles be right? Could

Callie really possess magical powers? It seemed impossible. Yet, up until recently, talking gargoyles had seemed impossible, too, but here she was, having a serious conversation with two of them.

"But enough o' this chit chat," Terry said. "You and yer 'entourage' better get to the Palace quick, or ye'll be late fer yer own party!"

"Bye, Princess," Kevin said, amiably. "Good luck!"

"Yeah, Good Luck, Princess. And one more thing..." Terry leaned down and gave an evil-looking smile. "Trust no one."

Callie was shocked. "What did you say?"

Terry leaned down again, dramatically, "I said, 'Trust no one...'"

"I know what you said!" Callie huffed.

Terry sat back. "Well, if ye know what I said, why'd ye say, 'What did ye say?'"

"Because it's a contradiction in terms," Lewis offered.

"That's right!" Callie agreed. "If I trusted no one, that would include you two."

Terry smiled. "Exactly...!"

"She's going ta make us proud, Terry," Kevin said, wiping a tear from his eye. "So very proud!!"

Terry blew his nose loudly, wiping his tears, too. "That's right, Princess--remember those words, for they'll serve ye well. Things aren't always as they seem. Trust no one. Especially that other girl 'oo came through 'ere just before ye. I really didn't like the looks of 'er."

"You mean, Wanda?" Callie asked, anxiously.

Terry shrugged. "Afraid I didn't get 'er name."

"Did she have long dark hair, tied back in a ponytail?" Lewis asked, stepping forward. "And was she wearing glasses?"

The gargoyles commiserated for a moment, then nodded. *"That sounds like 'er, yeah. She was also wearing a nasty grin,"* Kevin said, demonstrating. He actually looked a lot like Wanda when he did.

"Which way did she go?" Callie asked, her heart pounding with concern. Even though Wanda had declared herself Callie's enemy, she was still one of their classmates, and Callie was worried about her safety.

Terry pointed in the direction of the tunnel. *"Back that way, I reckon."* According to the road sign, it was also the direction of the Forest of Dead Souls.

A huge wave of trepidation swept over Callie. Her dream about the Raven Queen chasing after her in the woods...the horrible scene in the tunnel with Wanda.... Somehow, it was all connected. But how? Why?

And why did Callie seem to be at the center of it all?

She had to find the answers to these questions and others that plagued her as well. She suspected the answers would be found at the Royal Palace of Arraband.

Just then a strange sound, like thunder, rumbled through the night. Only it wasn't thunder--there wasn't a cloud in the sky.

"Lewis?" Callie looked to her friend.

He stepped toward her and took her hand as the rumbling grew closer. It sounded like a hundred horses galloping toward them, but there was nothing coming down the road. The sound was coming from behind the gate.

"What is it?" Callie shouted up at the gargoyles, who were looking back at something behind the huge stone wall. They didn't seem to have heard her over all the noise.

"Here they come!" Terry shouted.

"Here *who* come?" Lewis yelled, but his question was ignored.

The massive wooden doors creaked open, and what Callie and Lewis saw inside made their jaws drop.

A mounted regiment of military guards--dressed in old-fashioned uniforms--stood in formation. One man rode forward on a magnificent dappled gray stallion.

His hair was pulled back into a queue and tied with a ribbon. He wore a dark blue jacket, decorated with silver embroidery and silver buttons down the front. His trousers were black like his boots, which flared out over his knee. He looked like something out of one of their history books in school. He was handsome, with sandy blond hair and piercing blue eyes.

But what happened next shocked Callie even more.

The man looked down at her and spoke curtly, "I'm afraid there is no time for pleasantries, Your Highness. You are in grave danger, here. If you value your life, you will come with me *now*."

Chapter Five

The Raven Queen

Wanda Morris was an ordinary girl, at least as ordinary as a girl whose parents didn't love her could be.

She would have liked to say she lived with them in a big house in a small town, but that wasn't totally true. Their house was big, and it was in a small town, but Wanda's parents didn't live there. Not really. Wanda and her housekeeper, Mrs. Crossley did. Wanda's parents, Ron and Marlene, both traveled a lot for their jobs. In fact, they traveled so much that they were sometimes gone for months at a time. It was Wanda's greatest fear that her parents had actually forgotten about her and were living in another country without her.

Because Wanda's parents were never home, they had hired a housekeeper to look after the house and to look after Wanda. Mrs. Crossley was an older lady with gray hair, whose two passions in life were watching television and warming up left-overs. She didn't love Wanda. In fact, she barely took any notice of her at all.

Wanda's life had been like this for so long, she couldn't remember it being any other way, ever. She knew the other kids at school had parents who spent time with them, helped them with their homework, took them to the park for picnics, took them to movies, and gave them hugs before bedtime. She knew that these other kids had parents who thought they were special, and who really loved them.

This knowledge drove her crazy.

And one person in particular drove her especially crazy--Callie Richards, the girl whose mother had died in a car accident two years before. From that day forward, Callie had been the *special girl* in class. The teachers always took time to give Callie an extra smile--they didn't do this for Wanda.

Callie's father always picked her up after school, waiting by the car with open arms to give his girl a big hug. Wanda's father didn't do this. He couldn't--because it was hard to pick up your daughter at school when you were on a business trip in another country.

Callie's best friend Lewis always looked out for her, took her side, and made her feel better when she was sad. Wanda didn't even have a best friend. She only had two kids she corresponded with via email whom she'd met briefly through a state-wide school function. And they didn't bother to correspond with her very much.

Each day at school was torture for Wanda, because it was a constant reminder of what she didn't have, and what others did. When Callie Richards' mother died, it had left Callie with only one parent. Wanda had two parents, but together they didn't even add up to *one*. In Wanda's opinion, Callie was the lucky one.

That fact that Callie took every opportunity to throw this in Wanda's face made her want to scream. Callie always had the best clothes; her dad showered her with gifts even when it wasn't her birthday.

For Wanda, it was just one more injustice she was forced to endure. Somehow, Callie Richards had become the symbol of everything wrong in the world. In Wanda's world, at any rate.

Now, because of Callie and the way she'd *flaunted* her sparkly necklace on the playground, and *bragged* about the secret map, and *selfishly* had everything handed to her on a silver platter, Wanda was in a strange place, walking down a dirt road next to a dark forest, and getting a little scared. And Wanda hated being scared. Only weaklings got scared. So she did the only thing she could do. She told herself that whatever happened, she would be okay. She had learned a long time ago to rely on herself, and so far, she'd never been disappointed.

She didn't want to go back through the tunnel just yet, because she didn't want Callie and Lewis to beat her at this little game. They thought they were *so* clever.... Well, they weren't. And it was up to Wanda Morris to teach them that. She was going to discover something amazing in this place, wherever it was, and she was going to take all the credit.

Wanda turned her head when she heard the sound of jingling harnesses down the road behind her. She shone her flashlight through the trees and caught a glimpse of a carriage ambling down the road toward her. Her heart gave a little skip at the sight of it, though she didn't know why.

The carriage came closer. It was drawn by four magnificent black horses. Except, as they got closer, Wanda saw that they weren't horses at all.

They were...*unicorns.*

They were as big as draft horses--with a spiral black horn in the middle of their foreheads. A glowing lantern hung suspended from each corner of the carriage, swinging back and forth eerily as the vehicle rolled toward Wanda. There was a gold emblem on the door, with two intertwined ravens, wings extended, and a crown in the middle.

The carriage drew near, and Wanda gulped. The driver on top wore a long, black oilskin coat and a tricorn hat; the collar of his coat was so tall that only his eyes were visible. He pulled on the reins and yelled "Ho!" to his team. The unicorns slowed their pace immediately; the carriage itself was now right beside Wanda as she walked, ever faster, down the road.

She didn't dare look at it, as it creaked and groaned beside her like a beast. She just put her chin down and kept walking faster.

A sound made her look sideways. She saw the blind go up in the carriage. For a few moments, no one appeared. The sight of the empty window was almost unbearable. Then a figure came into view.

"What a pretty little girl you are," a melodious voice said. "Are you lost?"

Wanda glanced up at the carriage window. The veiled face of an extraordinarily beautiful woman looked out at her. Wanda didn't say anything for a moment. Instead she watched the mysterious woman's dark eyes as they studied her through the sheer black veil.

"No," Wanda replied. "I'm not lost."

"Oh. I see. Where are you going?"

Wanda pointed her flashlight in front of her. "*This* way."

"How fortuitous." The woman angled her head a little. "May I offer you a ride in my carriage, as we are both going the same way?"

Wanda rolled her eyes. "Newsflash: Kids aren't supposed to accept rides from *strangers*." For an adult, this lady was sure behind the times.

"Oh." The lady nodded. "Very prudent of you. I see now that you aren't a little girl at all. You are a young woman, and an intelligent one, at that. I must say, it is quite refreshing." She rapped on the roof of the carriage. *"Driver, keep to a walking pace. We shall escort our new friend to wherever she is going on this splendid evening."* She said to Wanda, "This forest is full of dangerous creatures, as you know."

Wanda *didn't* know--and she didn't know what to say either. Instead, she continued to walk briskly along the lonely road, the carriage creaking slowly beside her. All the while she felt the woman's eyes upon her. It was a little unsettling.

The silence was almost unbearable. Before she could stop herself, Wanda asked, "Where are you going?"

"Home. To my castle," the woman replied.

"You live in a castle?"

"Oh, yes. I am a very important lady. A queen, you see."

"A queen?" Wanda couldn't believe her ears. A queen was talking to *her*?

"Yes," the woman replied. "My lands border these of Albion. We are neighbors."

"Oh." Wanda scoured her brain for other topics that might be suitable to discuss with a queen... "So, what's your castle like?" She winced. It was a lame question.

"It is quite magnificent," the queen said. "It has spiral towers, spacious banquet halls, and stables for a thousand horses. It is a shame you can't visit. Since my husband the king died, it has become a very lonely place for me."

A castle? That was better than a palace if Wanda had anything to say about it.

"My friends Callie and Lewis are going to visit some palace around here," she lied. Callie and Lewis weren't her friends, but she decided to skip over that part. "Have you been to the palace?"

"I have been inside it many times," the queen said.

"Is your castle *bigger* than the palace?"

"Oh yes," the queen said, waving a hand. "It is almost twice the size. I should so like to show you its halls and galleries, and all my royal treasure rooms. But I would not want to keep you from your pressing personal business."

Wanda bit her lip. She didn't really have pressing personal business. And she really wanted to see the queen's castle. "Well..."

"Yes?" the queen asked, politely.

"Maybe I could come, just for a little while. But then I'll have to go home." Though why she had to go home, Wanda didn't know. Mrs. Crossley wouldn't even notice she wasn't there. She'd be too busy watching TV to care.

"How delightful!" the queen said. "Yes, yes, you *must* come. It is settled. And I shall host a royal banquet in your honor."

A banquet...in Wanda Morris' honor? No one had ever hosted a banquet in Wanda's honor before, royal or otherwise. Not even a birthday party.

"We shall have jugglers and fire-eaters, magicians and minstrels, and courtly dances. Come, come—" the carriage door opened. "We shall plan it all as we ride."

Wanda stepped toward the door of the carriage, no longer worried about accepting rides from strangers. This lady wasn't a stranger, she was a queen. And she wanted to show Wanda her castle, and throw a party for her.

For the first time in ages, Wanda's heart warmed with hope.

And for the first time in even longer than that, she smiled.

oOo

"*Who are you?*" Callie demanded. "*And why am I in danger?*"

The officer stared down at her, his horse prancing restlessly. "I am Hugh FitzWarren, Lord Graydon, Captain of the Queen's Royal Guard. I am under orders from Queen Arabella herself to escort you to the Palace of Arraband. We have horses for you and your manservant." He indicated two saddled mares which stood patiently nearby.

"I'm *not* her manservant," Lewis said flatly. "I'm her *friend*. And we're not going anywhere with you until we see some I.D."

The man frowned down at them. "What is this *I.D.*?"

"Identification," Lewis explained. "You know--a drivers license, credit card, passport. The usual."

"I do not have any of these things you describe," he said impatiently.

"How about a library card?" Callie suggested.

"No," he said rifling through his jacket pocket. "But if you insist on confirmation of my identity, perhaps this will do." He tossed down an extendible spyglass. Engraved on the side were the words, *Presented to Lord Graydon, Captain of the Queen's Royal Guard for Loyalty of Service by Her Royal Majesty, Queen Arabella.*

"We were hoping for something with a picture," Callie said.

"Yeah," Lewis echoed, examining the engraving on the spyglass. "This doesn't tell us anything."

Lord Graydon looked like he was going to blow a gasket.

Just then two men on horseback came galloping around a bend in the road. Pulling their horses up to a short stop, one of them said quickly, "My Lord, we found fresh carriage tracks in the road. The carriage is being pulled by a team of four. Judging by the hoofprints, it's a team of unicorns. They stopped about two parthons down the road, then continued on. We rode to the edge of the Rianca Pass, but there was no sign of anyone." The soldier patted the neck of his tired mount, then looked down at Callie and removed his hat. "Your Highness." The other one followed suit.

The captain nodded. "It was undoubtedly her, then. No other team could have escaped through the Pass so quickly." He shook his head, slamming his fist against his thigh. "That the Raven Queen would be so brazen as to approach this close to Arraband's walls.... Her powers must be growing stronger."

A chill passed over Callie's heart. "Excuse me. *Who* did you say?"

His green eyes met hers. "Queen Miranda of Tor-Enrith. Pretender to the Enchanted Throne of Albion. Queen of the Ravens. Dark Witch of the North. And the woman who would see you, and the rest of us, dead."

"Well, she doesn't sound very nice," Lewis said, glancing at Callie. "I'll bet she'd benefit from a Dale Carnegie course."

Lord Graydon ignored Lewis' remarks and directed his gaze at Callie. "Your Highness, we must make haste. You are in danger, here. For the last time, I ask you to come with me. The next time," he said, placing his hand on the grip of his sword, "it will be an *order*."

Callie gulped. Lord Graydon was one of the most intimidating people she had ever met. She couldn't really imagine arguing with him and winning. She handed his spyglass back to him. "Okay, don't have a freak-out, already. We'll come with you." She glanced at Lewis, who didn't try to hide the fact that he objected and was still waiting to see the proper I.D. But Callie had a feeling about Lord Graydon. She felt compelled to trust him. Even though her friends, the gargoyles, had warned her about just that very thing.

As the guards helped her and Lewis onto their horses, Callie knew that to most people, what she was doing would seem a little crazy. Maybe a *lot* crazy. She was proceeding into a strange land that was under threat from a neighboring queen. But that was part of the reason she had to continue on this strange journey. Because of the Raven Queen. Because in Callie's dreams, the Raven's Queen's face had looked like exactly like her mother's.

Though she had never admitted it to herself before this moment, Callie had a horrible, horrible realization. She knew that in a secret corner of her heart, part of her hoped--part of her prayed--that by some strange turn of events, the Raven Queen *was* her mother. Because that would mean her mother wasn't really dead. Callie would be able to have her mom back, just as she'd always hoped. And if her mom had somehow become this evil queen, Callie could try to help her become good again....

Callie's heart throbbed in her chest as she contemplated exactly how she would feel about that. Would she be willing to have her mother back, on *any* terms?

As the horses proceeded down the cobblestone street, Callie struggled to figure out what it all meant. Somehow, Callie and her mother were connected to this place. Her mom's favorite reading spot in the garden had been near the secret Door in the Floor. Had her mother somehow known about this place, too? Had her mom been here before?

Callie didn't know the answers to those questions yet. But now, she was more determined than ever to find out the truth. And the first person she was going to ask was Queen Arabella.

Chapter Six

The Royal Palace of Arraband

Callie couldn't believe her eyes as they rode through the heart of the city. "Lewis, are you seeing what I'm seeing?"

"I sure am, Cal." He pulled his horse up beside hers. Callie and Lewis had taken riding lessons last summer together, and it was sure coming in handy now. "It's pretty amazing."

Callie thought that was actually an understatement. The palace wasn't just amazing. It was the most unbelievably spectacular, super-duper colossal thing she had ever seen before. Blazing torches stood along the roadway like streetlights, and they lit the city sky to an orange glow.

The palace stretched across three or four city blocks. The center structure was a massive rectangular building at least ten stories high. It had four huge, domed turrets on each corner, with another domed lookout post on top of each of those. A flag in the royal colors of red and gold flew proudly atop each dome. Two flanking wings with tall, yellow stone arches ran along each side, and there were hundreds of windows reflecting the torchlight and making the palace sparkle like gold.

The kicker was that the palace looked just like the one in her mom's stories.

In front of the palace, the grounds boasted beautiful gardens with walkways decorated by marble statuary and urns. People milled about, horses and grand carriages passed by, and all of the people seemed to be staring at Callie. A few of them pointed. A few of them even bowed.

Lord Graydon shouted, "Make way! Make way for the Princess!"

And people did.

Soon Callie, Lewis, Lord Graydon and his men had passed through the palace gates to the grand entrance. Two huge golden doors marked the entrance to the palace; they were decorated in ornate carvings, strange writing, and a coat of arms with two dragons intertwined under a crown.

Lord Graydon hopped off his horse and helped Callie off hers, leaving Lewis to dismount on his own. He gave his men their instructions, and said to Callie, "Your Highness, if you will follow me."

Callie and Lewis exchanged a look, then practically had to run to keep up with the Captain of the Guard as he proceeded past the sentries at the door, who didn't blink an eye at them.

They entered the palace. Callie's first impression was that she'd never seen so much marble--there were marble floors, marble pillars, and marble statues of important-looking people.

Her second impression was that she had never seen so much gold. There were gilded engravings around the doorways and on the ceilings, and gilded scrolls at the top of the marble columns, and gilded statues of yet more important-looking people on top of the columns themselves.

Callie's third impression was that the people here sure dressed funny.

They passed by women dressed in luxurious eighteenth-century gowns with long, billowing skirts of heavy brocade. They looked like they came straight out of a history book. The men wore heavy brocade jackets with short pants and white stockings, and shoes with big buckles.

In short, Callie guessed that these people were almost four-hundred years behind the times in fashion sense, but she didn't mind. In fact, Callie *loved* all these clothes!

She and Lewis scurried to keep up with Lord Graydon, whose long legs made his stride almost twice as long as theirs. The long marble hallway seemed to go on forever, and they passed through archway after archway after archway.

"I wonder where we're going?" Callie said.

"Probably to the dungeon," Lewis replied calmly. "After all, didn't Terry and Kevin say that once we got here, the queen would have me chopped up and made into a stew?"

They kept walking, and Callie was shocked to see a familiar face.

"Sir Reginald!" she exclaimed, smiling at the sight of him.

"Your Royal Highness," he said, beaming. He bowed to her with a flourish, and kissed the back of her hand. "Oh, my dear, you have arrived safely! How it warms my heart to see you. Undoubtedly you have put the gift I delivered to good use."

Callie took the necklace out from under her sweater. "Reggie, you'll never believe this. It opened the Door in the Floor!"

Sir Reginald grinned. "I know."

Callie wanted to laugh. "Well, if you knew, why didn't you tell me that in the first place?"

He held up his hands. "Oftentimes it is best to figure things out for one's self, instead of being told what to do. Besides, I had my orders from the queen, and I told you what would happen to me if I displeased her." He drew his finger across his throat.

"I was told they might make a stew out of me," Lewis added.

Sir Reginald regarded him seriously. "Oh yes. Indeed, I see why they might. Many an opinionated manservant such as yourself has ended up in a stew, dinner for the royal dragons."

Lewis' lips compressed into a thin line. "I'm *not* her manservant. I'm her *friend*."

"Indeed?" Sir Reginald raised his eyebrows. "It is lucky, then, that you are under the princess's protection, young man. For the queen is very traditional. Is she not, Lord Graydon?"

"Her Majesty is, indeed," Lord Graydon replied. "And if I do not deliver the princess to her Majesty immediately, it is *I* who will be made into a stew."

"Of course." Sir Reginald stepped back and made for them to leave, but Callie stopped.

"I'm nervous about meeting the queen," Callie said. "Is she nice?"

Sir Reginald exchanged a look with Lord Graydon. "She is the queen, my dear. Just be yourself, and you'll be fine. Now, run along. I shall see you later this evening at the banquet."

Callie gulped as Lord Graydon led them onward down the endless marble hall. What if the queen didn't like her? What if she was mean? What if she *did* make a stew out of Lewis?

Yet, Callie had come too far to give up now. She wasn't going to let fear get the best of her. She had to talk to this "Queen Arabella," whoever she was, because Callie was convinced that the queen had information about why the Raven Queen looked exactly like her mom.

They came to a doorway with two serious-looking guards outside it, and stopped. Lord Graydon said a few words to the guards in hushed tones, and then, as if by magic, the doors opened inward into the most exquisite room of all.

Because it contained the queen.

If you have ever been in the presence of someone who seemed to fill up an entire room just by being there, and who seemed to have an indescribable quality of complete confidence and absolute elegance, and who seemed to speak without saying a word, then you will know what Callie felt when she beheld Arabella, Queen of Albion.

For a moment or two, they stared at each other. The queen stood beside the fireplace, dressed in a jewel-encrusted gown of heavy golden satin, with a stiff, standing collar. The sleeves were bunched and tied with fancy ribbon. Diamonds, topaz, and pearls decorated the gown in intricate patterns of flowers and filigrees.

Around her neck, the queen wore a sparkling diamond choker along with several ropes of diamonds and pearls. Atop her head was a magnificent tiara of white diamonds, which quite took Callie's breath away.

Yet, in all of this, it was the queen's face that was the most glorious of all. She was beautiful, with cool blue eyes and graying blonde hair which she wore pinned up in the back. When she spoke, her voice was one of quiet command. "Lord Graydon."

The Captain bowed to his queen. "Your Majesty, may I present to you, the Princess Calandria."

Callie gulped. Not knowing what else to do, she curtsied.

The queen studied her for a moment, and Callie thought she saw a wave of emotion pass across her face. But the queen controlled herself easily. She said, "You are your mother's daughter."

Callie's heart did a flip. She took a step toward the queen, a strange premonition coming over her. "You knew my mother?"

"I knew her very well," the queen confirmed. "She was my eldest daughter. I am your grandmother, my dear."

Callie was stunned. Yet, there was a recognition in her heart. "You're my *grandmother*?" Callie had only known one set of grandparents--her dad's. Her mom's parents had both died long before Callie was born. At least, that was what she'd been told.

The queen said simply, "Yes."

"I need to sit down," Callie said shakily. It was still a lot to take in all at once.

Queen Arabella waved a hand at Lewis.

Lewis waved back at the queen.

The queen frowned. "Whatever is wrong with your manservant? Is he hard of hearing?"

Now it was Lewis' turn to frown. "I'm not her manservant, Your Majesty, and I'm not hard of hearing, either. I'm her *friend*, Lewis Farnsworth, Esquire, of the Paxton Lane Farnsworths--winner of the Maplehurst Middle School's Science Award three years in a row, graduated first in my class at the Turner Institute's Summer Science Program for Pre-Teens, and the son of the famous scientists Drs. Frederick and Maria Farnsworth."

The queen raised an eyebrow. "Is that a fact?"

Lewis folded his arms across his chest. "That's a fact."

"Your accomplishments sound most impressive, young man. I apologize for the misunderstanding." Queen Arabella waved a hand at one of the footmen standing along the side of the room. He quickly brought a gilded chair for Callie to sit on. This hand-waving thing was certainly effective in getting people to do things.

Callie sat on the chair while Lewis stood beside her, his hand resting on her shoulder while she tried to process what the queen had said, and what it meant for her future.

Queen Arabella swept majestically around the room as she explained the story to Callie. "I know it must come as quite a shock--"

That was an understatement.

"And I apologize for the way in which you were told of your birthright. But I am afraid we had no choice." She exchanged a look with Lord Graydon, then regarded Callie. "We intended to ease you into your role here, but circumstances would not allow us to wait any longer. You see, our nation is in grave danger, and according to the Scrolls of the Ancient Kings, *you* are the only one who can save us."

Callie felt dizzy. She had fantasized about this moment, about finding out she was really a princess-- what girl didn't?--but somehow, even with all that had happened, she hadn't been prepared for the reality of this majestic queen telling her in all seriousness that the entire fate of their country depended on a twelve-year-old girl named Callie Richards.

"Are you sure I'm the one you're looking for?" Callie asked. "Maybe it's a mistake. Maybe I only look like the girl you want."

The queen smiled sadly, as if she knew exactly what Callie was feeling. "No, my dear. You are the princess we seek. You wear the mark which the Ancient Kings predicted, a mark which shows you to be the One."

"I do?" Callie asked, wondering what it could be.

The queen nodded. *"Your hair."*

"My *hair*?" Callie said in disbelief, tugging at it. "You mean this hair, which I've spent the better part of my life fighting with and wishing it was anything but red and wild and so curly I can't even get a brush through it? This hair, which always made me feel like a freak?"

The queen's expression turned a little stern, then. "Yes, young lady. *That* hair--the color of which no one

90

else in our land possesses. The snow-white streak within it sets you apart from all others, and proves that you are the Royal Princess whom the Ancients foretold. You are Calandria Arabella Philomena Teresa Anastasia Richards. Daughter of the Princess Anastasia and her Royal Consort, Benjamin Richards. Grandaughter of Irene and Walter Richards, and of Tarquin and Arabella, King and Queen of Albion. There is no mistake. Apart from your hair, you are the image of your mother--my daughter, Ana. *And you are the rightful heir to this kingdom.*"

Callie's head swam. Could this woman be right? Could this all be real? And if it was, how was Callie going to save an entire kingdom, when she couldn't even remember to bring back her library books on time?

Callie's heart pounded as she tried to process all this new information. She--a royal princess? And her mom had been a princess, too? For real?

Though she had been dying to ask the queen, now that she had the opportunity, it was difficult to actually form the words. Still, she managed to say, "Tell me about my mother."

A bittersweet expression clouded the queen's eyes. "She was my joy. A laughing, intelligent child, always getting into mischief, always trying to do things herself." Queen Arabella shook her head. "Once she got something into her head, there was no way to change her mind about doing it. The spirited, intelligent child grew into a spirited, intelligent young woman. And then...we lost her forever."

Callie stared at the queen, willing her to continue as questions swirled in her mind.

"She fell in love," the queen said, then added coldly, "With an entirely unsuitable young man. Your father, Benjamin Richards."

Callie felt her temper rise at the queen's words. "My father is a wonderful man, and Mom loved him!"

"There is no doubt that Ana loved him," the queen shot back. "More than she loved her own country, more than her own family, more than her duty as a princess of Albion. Because of that love, she abandoned her birthright, her people, and broke her father's heart. And mine, too."

"But why?" Callie wanted to know. "Couldn't she and Dad come back here to live?"

The queen sighed. The recollections of time seemed to make her tired. "It was forbidden by the king himself. Ana knew that when she went through the tunnel into your world. That was what hurt us so badly. And being Ana, nothing would dissuade her from getting what she wanted. She wanted to marry your father."

"But how did they meet?" Callie asked, confused.

"Your mother had received a gift for her eighteenth birthday. It was an enchanted looking glass, said to reveal your true love."

Callie listened intently as the queen told the story.

"On the fateful day when Ana peered into the looking glass, she saw your father, Benjamin Richards. One look at him told us that he was not from Albion. He was not from Tor-Enrith, either, our neighbor to the North, nor from any other land we knew of. It was a great mystery, and one that Anastasia would not let go of, for every time she looked into the glass, your father's image was there. The glass had never been known to lie, for it had been used successfully for many centuries. Ana would not give up. She enlisted fortune tellers, wizards, priestesses, goblins, and anyone else known for possessing powers of second sight. No one knew who the mystery man was. Ana was grief-stricken. She vowed to find her true love, no matter what the cost. Little did any of us know how grave that cost would be."

A cold shiver ran over Callie's skin as she thought of her mother's car accident. Was that what the queen was talking about?

Queen Arabella continued. "Years passed. The man's identity was still unknown. Then one day, an old priestess came to the palace. She requested a private audience with Princess Anastasia, and revealed the truth about the man in the glass--that he could not be found in our world at all, for he lived in the Land of Ur. That is the name by which we call your world."

"Ur?" Lewis asked, intrigued. "We call it *Earth*...I guess."

The queen nodded and continued. "Ana was overjoyed. After years of searching, she had finally found her true love and was determined to be united with him in marriage, as the looking glass had foretold. To do that, she would have to travel into the land of Ur, but such a thing is forbidden in our world, except by Royal Decree. Of course, over the years, a few of our creatures have defied our laws and found their way into Ur and become part of your legends."

Lewis said excitedly, "You mean, like dragons and unicorns and stuff?"

Queen Arabella nodded. "Fifteen-hundred years ago, it was quite a problem. Hundreds of dragons found their way into the Land of Ur, creating havoc among your people, who were completely ill-equipped to fight such beasts. Finally, we found how they were getting through--a cave near Mount Arratus--and we blocked the entrance. Eventually the dragons in your world died out, as did the unicorns, and other creatures too numerous to mention."

Callie and Lewis shared a glance. They had just completed a unit at school about mythical beasts and legends--St. George and the Dragon. Now they knew it hadn't been a fable at all.

Callie spoke up. "But why was it forbidden to go into our world? What was the big deal?"

"It is too dangerous for us," Queen Arabella explained. "Time passes differently here than in your world, and though we look alike, the physiology of our bodies is different as well--our life spans, the way we breathe. No one knows what long-term exposure to your world would do to us. And of course, in your world, there is no magic."

"Magic?" Callie asked, though she had heard the queen quite plainly.

Queen Arabella continued, "Not as we define it, at any rate. Of course, there are people who claim to be magicians in your world, but they merely perform parlor tricks. They have no real powers."

"Powers?" Lewis asked. "What kind of powers are we talking about?"

Callie and Lewis stared in shock as the queen reached out and pointed toward a vase of cream-colored roses. One of the roses lifted, as if by an invisible hand. Then it floated gently across the room to hover in front of Callie. She reached out and plucked it from the air, lifting it to her nose. Sure enough, it was a real rose.

"Can anyone in your world do that?" The queen asked.

Callie shook her head, still trying to take in what she'd just seen.

"Of course not," The queen said. "Magic is a very rare hereditary trait, even here. To our knowledge, it is possessed only by the Royal Family of Albion."

Callie gasped. If that was true, then... "You mean, my mom had magic powers?"

"Yes, my dear, in our world. As do you."

"Me?" Callie stammered, thinking back to the article the gargoyles had shown her in the *Albion Times*. It had said something about Callie having a power greater than anything Albion had ever seen. She hadn't thought it was for real.

The queen continued, "Ana knew when she went through the tunnel into your world that she would never be allowed to return to Albion. It was against our laws. But it didn't change her mind. The love she felt for your father, even then, was too strong for her to deny. She chose him over her royal duty to her family and her country."

Callie tried to process all that the queen had said. It seemed impossible, and yet, somehow, Callie *could* believe that her mother had been a princess from a magical land. Her mother had always seemed to possess an inner radiance. And it was true that Callie's parents had loved each other deeply. They had always held hands when they walked, always looked at each other with pure love in their eyes, and they had never argued about anything.

"But there is more to this story than I have told you," Queen Arabella said.

"More?" Callie said, dumbfounded. *How much more could there be?* "You've already told me that dragons and unicorns are real, that my mom was a magical princess, and that I'm supposed to be one, too. Yeah, right, there must be something you missed."

The queen looked directly at Callie, her expression dark. "There is. The Raven Queen is your mother's twin sister."

"What?" Callie asked in disbelief. Fear swam in her stomach. "The Raven Queen--I saw her in my dream. She had my mother's face."

The queen nodded soberly. "Miranda--the second born twin. Now the Queen of Tor-Enrith, our sworn enemy for countless generations."

"She's the one who wants to destroy Albion?"

"Yes." Queen Arabella walked about the room as she explained. "She's always had her sights set on Albion's throne."

"The message in my cereal said that her army was approaching," Callie said. "Was the message from you?"

The queen nodded. "It was, though I had no idea it would appear in your cereal. I'm afraid my powers are not what they once were. At any rate, Miranda's husband King Gregor died under mysterious circumstances a few months ago. Since then, Miranda's reign has become even more terrible than that of King Gregor himself. She is obsessed with invading Albion and taking the Enchanted Throne for herself. She believes *she* is the true heir--which is utter nonsense, of course. In Albion, the power of rule is passed down through the first-born heir--be they male or female--of the reigning monarch. Your mother, Princess Anastasia was our firstborn, and you are hers. Upon Ana's death, you became next in line to the Enchanted Throne. Upon my death, *you* will be Queen of Albion."

Lord Graydon added, "Unless the Raven Queen is victorious, conquers our nation, and destroys Albian life as we know it."

Queen Arabella nodded gravely. "That is why we need your help, Calandria. The Scrolls of the Ancient Kings prophesied these happenings: '*When one is two and two are one, King Eldric's magic has begun.*'"

Callie continued, "'*The Queen will call the princess home, to sit upon the Enchanted Throne.*' What does that mean—'*when one is two and two are one?*'"

The queen explained, "The Priestesses of Arundel say this: '*When one is two*' refers to the twins, your mother and her sister; they were once one being who became two. '*And two are one*' refers to your parents, Ana and your father. The purity of their love for each other transformed two beings into one, and you are the living legacy of that love. The rest of the riddle is self-explanatory. I have called you home to take your rightful place as Princess of the Royal House of Arraband. The time has come, Calandria. You must do your duty to the people of Albion."

Callie took a deep breath, and stood up for the first time since the queen had begun her speech. Her head was still spinning from all that she'd heard, and though part of her still had trouble believing it, and part of her didn't want to--she knew that Albion was real. And she was in over her head, big time.

She said slowly, "First of all, my name is Callie. Second of all, I appreciate the thought, and it's great that you want me to be your princess and next in line for the throne and save you from the Raven Queen and everything, and third, I'd like help you out...but I just can't."

Queen Arabella stared at Callie with an expression of such quietly controlled shock that it was almost worse than if she'd yelled. *"What did you say?"*

Callie tried to keep her knees from knocking together, because her legs had now started to tremble at the queen's obvious displeasure. "I said, I'm real sorry, but I can't help you. I have to go home, now."

The queen's eyes narrowed. "I heard you, young lady, and I am sorely disappointed in you." Then to Lord Graydon, "Call in Sir Reginald."

Callie's heart thudded with fear. Was the queen going to do something horrible to Sir Reginald because Callie had dared to disagree with her? He had mentioned something about being hung upside down by his toes until he expired. Callie's stomach turned at the thought. She looked at Lewis for help, but even he seemed unsure of what to do.

The great doors opened on their own, and soon Sir Reginald was beside them, holding a long parchment scroll that looked all too familiar.

Sir Reginald made his customary bow to the queen, saying, "Your Majesty." Then he made one to Callie. "Your Royal Highness."

Queen Arabella held out her hand. A pair of gold spectacles floated across the room, then hovered in front of her. She placed them on her nose and gestured to Sir Reginald, who unfurled the parchment scroll with great flourish. It rolled along the floor until it finally bounced against a chair leg across the room.

"Sir Reginald," the queen began, "is this the contract which you presented to my granddaughter Calandria Richards in the Land of Ur?"

He nodded. "Indeed, Your Majesty, it is."

"Hey," Callie protested, "that's the proof of delivery from my birthday present!"

The queen continued, "Sir Reginald, would you please read aloud the relevant passages for the benefit of those in the room?"

"Of course, Your Majesty. A-hem..." He pulled out a magnifying glass. "I draw your attention to section XXVII-B, which states, and I quote, '*I, Calandria Arabella Philomena Teresa Anastasia Richards, of Fourteen Shamrock Drive in the Land of Ur, do hereby solemnly agree, on this the twelfth anniversary of my birth, to assume all of my royal duties as Princess and Heir Apparent to the throne of the kingdom of Albion, including, but not limited to:*

i) shall endeavor with all of my strength to completely and utterly defeat any threat to

the kingdom of Albion, especially from that of our sworn enemy, the nation of Tor-Enrith, and any of her agents, representatives, leaders, and/or monarchs

ii) shall swear allegiance to the sovereign nation of Albion, vowing to uphold its laws and traditions as laid out by the Scrolls of the Ancient Kings of Albion, the Royal Constitution of Albion, and the rules and regulations set out by the Municipality of the Royal City of Arraband

iii) shall agree to partake in any instruction, course, or tutorial that might better enable me to execute my royal duties as deemed necessary by her Royal Majesty, Arabella, the Queen of Albion.

Furthermore, if I, Calandria Richards, fail to comply with any of the above covenants, warrants or agreements set forth herein, the queen may take action against me, including, but not limited to: imprisonment of my friends, family or known associates for as long Her Majesty deems fit, until the aforementioned covenants of this contract are satisfactorily executed, as decided by Her Majesty, Queen Arabella of Albion. Signed this day, blah blah blah, blah blah blah...'" He pointed to her signature.

Callie was speechless. She shot a scathing glare at Sir Reginald. "You tricked me into signing that! You told me it was a proof of delivery."

Sir Reginald regarded her with a pained expression. "I had no choice, Your Highness. I was under orders from the queen."

The queen snatched the contract out of his hands. "Indeed, Sir Reginald, you did your duty most admirably, and are to be commended." She regarded Callie. "You signed the contract, my dear, and you are bound by it."

"But I didn't know what I was signing!" Callie protested. "It's not fair."

The queen's eyes blazed. "Not fair? What a sorry excuse. If life were fair our country would not be under threat from Tor-Enrith. If life were fair, I would have my daughters back. Both of them!" She tapped the contract with her finger. "This agreement is binding, Calandria, and you will be held to it. If you do not abide by this contract, I will be forced to pursue drastic measures." She eyed Lewis. "You don't want your little friend here to end up in the dungeon, do you?"

"You wouldn't..." Callie whispered.

"She would," Sir Reginald said uncomfortably.

Callie couldn't believe this. This wasn't how it was supposed to be! Finding out you were a princess was supposed to be *fun*. Traveling to a magical land was supposed to be a grand adventure, but it wasn't fun anymore. Somehow Callie and Lewis' secret adventure had turned into a labyrinth of deception, lies, legal wrangling and blackmail.

"How can you be so *mean*?" Callie demanded, close to tears.

The queen looked down at her regally. "I am a queen, my dear. I am interested in results, and I will do whatever it takes to get those results--especially when the very future of my country and the lives of my subjects are at stake."

"But what about my dad?" Callie asked, fighting a lump in her throat. She missed her dad so much right now, it hurt. She wanted him to come and fix everything, wipe her tears away and take her home. "He'll be worried about me."

"Time passes much slower here. A month in Albion is but a few minutes in your world. In the Land of Ur, you have not even been absent for a full second. Your father will not even know you are gone." Queen Arabella studied Callie for a moment. Then she took off her spectacles and said, "And now, I would like a few moments with my granddaughter. Alone."

Chapter Seven

Arabella

The queen walked slowly around the drawing room, her satin gown swishing along the polished marble floor. Callie was alone with her now. Lord Graydon and Sir Reginald had led away her only friend. Not that Lewis had wanted to go with them, but he knew as well as Callie did that it was no use arguing with the Queen of Albion.

Queen Arabella turned to regard Callie. The woman's cool blue eyes seemed to look straight through her. It was very unnerving.

"I know what you're thinking," she said.

Callie wanted to laugh. Sharon had said the same thing to her only a little while ago, and Callie had thought the same thing then. *You couldn't possibly know what I'm thinking.*

The queen shot Callie a look as if she had heard her very thoughts. For all Callie knew, she had. Nothing would surprise her, now. The queen said, "You're thinking that I am a cold, unfeeling woman. Calculating, ruthless, even. I cannot deny it. I must be those things, in order to rule this land. But what I do, I do for the good of the people." A softer tone crept into the Queen's voice. "I know it has not been easy for you since the loss of your mother."

At the mention of the most horribly important event in her life, Callie looked up. "How did you find out about

Mom's death? Did you know when it happened?" She remembered all too well the exact moment *she* had known.

The queen said quietly, "We have ways of monitoring your world from here. When Ana left us, her father and I always watched over her, though our magic could not protect her in your world. We were as powerless as you and your father on the day of the accident. We could only stand by and watch our princess die."

Callie felt tears prick her eyes. She had gotten very good at pretending that day had never happened. She didn't need Queen Arabella stirring up such painful memories. Yet, they seemed to have a life all their own. It was as if the memories themselves were hungry for life, and refused to be forgotten.

"I don't want to talk about it," Callie said, abruptly.

"There are many things we do not want to do," the queen explained, "and yet we must."

"Why?" Callie demanded angrily.

"It is the nature of life itself," the queen said, looking pensive. "It is a struggle, my dear, for all of us. It is the grand challenge that we must rise to, no matter how difficult it is to do so. Otherwise, we might as well give up, throw down our swords, and surrender. I, for one, am not prepared to do that. Whoever said life was easy? It isn't. Not even for a queen. Or a princess. Like you."

So many thoughts swirled in Callie's head, she felt dizzy. "This is all happening too fast...I'm not ready for this."

"Most things in life, we are not ready for, my dear."

Callie looked up at her, unconvinced.

"Take me for example," Queen Arabella said.

"You?"

"Yes, *me*. I wasn't ready to become a queen. I wasn't ready to become a mother." Queen Arabella walked with such grace around the room that she practically floated. "I wasn't ready to lose a daughter. I wasn't ready to defend my country against the threat of the Raven Queen--*my own child*. I'm still not ready. Life happens to us, my dear, whether we are ready for it or not. Most often, we are not ready for what befalls us, but somehow, we struggle through. That is how we are victorious. We strive to do our best, even when it is difficult, even when it is impossible. Now, that is what I am asking of you, Calandria. I am asking you to rise to the challenge, and accept your duty as a royal princess and protector of this land, even though it is going to be difficult for you."

"But I'm only twelve," Callie said, shaking her head.

The queen raised her eyebrows. "And you're going to let that stop you?"

Callie paused. "Normally, I would. Yes."

"Well, look around you!" the queen said in exasperation. "This, my dear, is not 'normally.'"

At last Queen Arabella was talking sense.

Callie felt a pain in her chest, like a knife plunging deep. It was the same feeling she'd had on the day of her mother's death, and at times of stress afterword. And this day ranked pretty high up there on the old stress-o-meter.

"I can't help you. Please don't ask me to. I'm not qualified. I'm just a kid in sixth grade who doesn't have a mother, and who has to go see a therapist because she's so screwed up about it!" She cursed the tears that filled her eyes, and wiped at them quickly.

Then the queen did something for which Callie was completely unprepared. Queen Arabella of Albion, in her grand jewel-encrusted satin gown, dazzling jewelry and magnificent diamond tiara, sank down onto the floor before Callie. Arabella knelt before her, and took her granddaughter's hand in hers. "My dear, I know your heart is wounded, dreadfully wounded by the loss of your mother...."

Callie gulped because the queen had once again hit it right on the mark.

"But we need you *now*. You are the one whose coming the Ancient Kings foretold. You are the only one who possesses the power to defeat the Raven Queen and ensure our country's safety."

"But I don't have magic powers!" Callie argued. "Yes you do. There is a magic within you, which you have yet to understand," the queen answered. "And it is more powerful than any our world has ever seen. You must only learn to use it, though that in itself will not be without its challenges."

Callie shook her head. This couldn't be true. It just couldn't. "I just want to go home," she said quietly.

In fact, Callie had never wanted to go home more than she did right now. She wanted the comfort of her father's arms protecting her, his quiet voice soothing her, his strength and solid nature guiding her like it had since the moment her mom had died. But her father wasn't here to help her right now, and what was worse, even if she did go home, she wasn't sure he'd be there to help her, either, not now that he was starting a new life with Sharon....

Somehow, Callie had to handle this problem alone. And it was a pretty big problem.

"Calandria," the queen said, seriously, "if you do not help us, people will die. Thousands and thousands of people, whom you alone have the power to save."

The queen's words sent a numbing chill through Callie's heart, for though she didn't want to admit it, something inside her knew that the queen was telling the truth. She looked into her grandmother's eyes; they were so blue, so open and honest.

"Please help us," Queen Arabella said quietly. "*Please.*"

Callie's stomach tied into a painful knot. She felt horrible. Scared. In between that, she felt something powerful stirring within her. Callie had no idea what it was, but it felt like a glimmer of hope...of strength...of possibility. *"I don't know how,"* she whispered.

The queen clasped Callie's hand. "You will. When the time is right."

Callie was uncertain. How could she, Callie Richards, possibly take on all of this responsibility? How could she not? She didn't know what to do. She wished Lewis was here to advise her....

The queen rose to her feet then, and Callie did, too.

"Make me one promise." Queen Arabella rested her hand on Callie's shoulder. "Do not give me your decision now, in the heat of the moment. Rather, think it over, and give me your answer in the morning. Tonight, stay as my guest here at the palace. Enjoy your position as Princess Royal at the grand banquet and ball, which I am hosting in your honor. Get to know the people of Albion, as I do. One night is all I ask. In the morning, I will accept your decision as final."

"And you won't put Lewis in your dungeon if I say no?" Callie asked, worriedly.

The queen huffed. "I suppose I could refrain. The dungeons are quite full, anyway."

The dungeons were full?

Callie soberly followed her grandmother across the room.

"There is so much to do, yet! You must be fitted for your gown and your hair must be arranged," Queen Arabella made an opening motion with her outstretched hands, and the great gold filigreed doors opened by magic. She glanced back at Callie and motioned for her to walk more quickly. "Come, come--we have not much time! Your presentation at court is little over an hour away, and I want you to look your best."

Callie trotted after her, down the glittering marble and gilded halls. "What about Lewis?"

"You needn't worry about him. Your friend will be in attendance. Lord Graydon and Sir Reginald will assist him with his wardrobe. I will make sure he is seated next to you at the Royal Table."

Callie struggled to keep up with the queen, who walked at a clipping pace as they passed through the royal hallways of the palace. Soon they reached another room decorated in pale blue, white marble, and gold. A canopied four-poster bed stood at one end. The bedroom even had a sofa and a huge fireplace!

"This is your room, Calandria," the queen said, showing her inside. "It was your mother's room when she was a girl."

Callie's heart skipped a beat. *Her mom had slept here?* Somehow, Callie could sense it. She felt her mother's energy here, just as she did in parts of her own house, or in the back garden. It was a wonderful feeling.

"And now, we must get you dressed." Queen Arabella rang a long, red velvet bell-pull. A gong sounded somewhere. A group of six ladies, all dressed exquisitely, entered the room from another door. They regarded Callie with expressions of admiration and awe.

"These are your ladies in waiting," the queen explained. "They will assist you in whatever you need, they will watch over you when I cannot, and they will guide you in matters of dress and etiquette." She introduced them one by one. "Lady Florian, Lady Arden, The Countess of Harvill, Baroness Northrop, Lady Lynford, and the Duchess of Kenryk."

The first lady curtsied to Callie. "Your Highness."

Callie started to curtsy back, but the queen gently touched her arm and whispered, "You don't curtsy to them, my dear. They curtsy to *you*. The only person you curtsy to is me, and that is only in public, you'll see."

The rest of the ladies in waiting greeted Callie the same way. They seemed to be in awe of Callie, in particular, of her hair. They marveled over the unusual color and, of course, the white-blond streak which marked her as Princess and Protector of Albion.

Of all the women, the Duchess of Kenryk was the most beautiful. She had thick, chestnut hair and wore a gown of sapphire blue. She curtsied and smiled up at

Callie, but something in her eyes lacked warmth. "I am pleased to finally meet you, Your Highness. Roarke has spoken of nothing but your arrival for days, now."

"Roarke?" Callie asked.

"Your cousin, the Duke of Kenryk. My husband."

"Oh..." Callie looked toward the queen, who answered, "Your second cousin once removed, dear. Roarke is the son of my late brother, Anders."

The duchess smiled and laughed gently. "Oh, but Your Majesty, Roarke does not make such distinctions, nor let them get in the way of his duty. Already he vows to love the princess as if she were his own sister."

The queen eyed the duchess and said, "Yes. Your husband generally does what he wants."

The duchess bowed her head. "Only to please Your Majesty, of course."

"Of course," the queen said, looking completely unconvinced. She turned her attention back to Callie. "And now there is no more time for talk. We must get the princess ready. Lady Florian and Lady Arden, bring in the selection of gowns, if you please. Baroness, would you supervise the hair arrangements, since I know you are so gifted at it? Lady Lynford, would you and the countess please have my personal jewelry chest brought in? The duchess and I will assist the princess in her choices."

As the women quickly and efficiently followed the queen's orders, Callie felt a wave of excitement wash over her. A royal banquet and ball were being thrown in her honor. It was unbelievable and yet, it was all absolutely real.

Callie's breath caught as the ladies brought out several stunning gowns for her to choose from. There was one of pale, rose-pink silk, another of soft green, another of lavender, and yet another of sky blue. Like Queen Arabella's, the blue gown was decorated with jewels on the front bodice and skirt. Diamonds and pearls twinkled in the candlelight.

"This one?" Callie asked timidly, pointing to the dazzling blue gown.

The queen smiled. "Oh, yes. That will do marvelously. Do you not agree, Edwina?" she asked the duchess.

"A wonderful choice, Your Majesty. Your Highness has exquisite taste." The duchess took the gown in her arms and directed the other ladies to assemble the assorted petticoats and other things a princess wore underneath such a garment. Soon, behind a gilded screen, the ladies were helping Callie into her gown.

"It's heavy," Callie remarked.

The duchess explained, "It is the jewels, Your Highness. You are wearing over fifty carats of diamonds alone."

"Please, call me Callie," she replied, tugging at the sleeves.

The young duchess gave a smile. "I would be honored, *Callie*. And let me also say that it is a great honor indeed to be attending the heir to the throne of Albion. The news must have come as quite a shock to you, and now you are a stranger in a strange land, with so very much responsibility thrust upon you. It must be difficult. Frightening, even."

Callie gulped.

The duchess continued, fussing with Callie's gown, "But you must not let the nobles at court intimidate you. Certainly, you are a new face to them, and you are only still a girl, but as the queen says--you are the Princess Royal. You must command their respect."

All of a sudden Callie felt very unsure of herself. "So, there are going to be a lot of people there tonight?"

"Oh, yes. Over two thousand people will be there to see you."

"Two thousand people...to see *me*?" Callie felt slightly sick to her stomach.

"Of course. It's all the City of Arraband has been talking about for weeks. The people are anxious to meet the princess who shall save us from the Raven Queen. Why wouldn't they be?"

Now, besides feeling slightly sick, Callie felt slightly faint. She wasn't sure if she could pull this off, let alone all the other stuff she was expected to do as a princess and protector of Albion.

"Hurry up, ladies!" the queen shouted across the room. "We have no time to dawdle."

The duchess adjusted Callie's sleeve, then they quickly emerged from behind the screen.

"Come, come, we must choose your jewelry," the queen said. "Baroness, you may start arranging the princess's hair."

Queen Arabella waved Callie over to a chair and plunked her down in front of a gilded chest. The top opened to reveal several expanding velvet trays that sparkled with jewelry: strands of diamonds, rubies, sapphires, pearls, emeralds, and many others that Callie didn't even know the names for.

The queen fished through them. "I know, I know, I should have had the entire royal collection brought out--these are only the favorites from my personal collection, but they will have to do."

"You mean there's *more*?" Callie asked in disbelief.

To her surprise, the queen laughed. So did the other ladies. Queen Arabella patted Callie's hand and said, "Your innocence is so endearing--of course it is not your fault, dear. How could you possibly know? Yes, there is more. Much, much more in the royal treasure rooms here at the palace. I shall arrange a tour, of course, if you wish it."

Callie nodded enthusiastically. She'd jump at the chance to see more of the entire royal collection of jewels. "Could I try some of it on?"

The queen smiled. "It is your privilege as a princess." Then she whispered, "Sometimes I like to go through all of the treasure rooms and try on the pieces, one by one. In truth, it takes about a week to do it; one of my few guilty pleasures. That, and Fragorian fudge."

This time it was Callie's turn to laugh.

The queen placed several long strings of diamonds and pearls about her neck and rings on her fingers.

Callie looked down. "I'm so shiny, I think I need sun-glasses."

"What are sun-glasses?" the queen asked, quizzically. "A glass in which you see the sun?"

"They're glasses that protect your eyes from the sun's brightness. They're dark, but you can see through them. We call them *shades*."

The queen looked intrigued. "I must have my craftsmen fashion me a pair of these shades."

113

Callie grinned, trying to picture her grandmother, Queen Arabella of Albion, in shades. Now *that* would be cool.

"There," the queen said quietly. "I think you are ready." She motioned Callie to step over to the mirror.

Callie gazed at her reflection and saw a princess--a beautiful princess in a glittering gown and jewels, with her hair piled up into a curled and braided arrangement.

"*Wow...*" was all she could say.

The queen stopped short. "But wait. How could I have forgotten the most important thing?" She disappeared behind the jewelry chest for a moment, then returned and stood behind Callie. "Every princess needs a tiara." She placed a spiked diamond-fringe tiara upon Callie's head.

"Double wow..." Callie said, almost breathless. "I get to wear a crown?"

"*We're not a crown,*" a chorus of voices said.

"*We're a tiara.*"

"*Yes, we're a tiara... Aren't we, Stan?*"

Callie looked up because the voices were coming from the top of her head. "Did someone say something?"

"*We did!*" the group of voices answered.

Callie looked toward her grandmother, who seemed completely unfazed by the whole thing. "Princess Teresa's Talking Tiara," she said simply.

"A talking tiara?" Callie asked, unbelieving.

"*Of course,*" one of the voices answered. "*Where have you been living--under a rock?*"

"*She's been living in the Land of Ur, Donald,*" another answered. "*It's not her fault.*"

"I say, Beryl," another commented, "She does have a most comfortable head, does she not?"

"Very comfortable, indeed," a little old voice replied. "Reminds me of her mother's--the Princess Anastasia."

"Now there was a comfortable head!" another said.

"Oh yes, very comfortable," another answered.

Callie stepped closer to the mirror and peered at the sparkling diamond tiara atop her head.

"Hello, Princess!"

"I say--she's looking at us. Hello! Hello!" a jolly voice sang out.

The jolly voice belonged to a jolly face inside one of the tiara's multitude of diamonds. Callie peered closer. She blinked a couple of times. The little faces were still there, each one inside one of the many glittering diamonds adorning the tiara's spiked fringe.

"Oh, she is pretty, isn't she?" another commented.

"Yes. Very. And dashed smart, too, I hear. I read it in the Albion Times. "

"Over my shoulder, I expect," the queen commented. She turned to Callie. "But there's more to this tiara than the fact that it talks."

"Much more!" the voices said in unison.

Callie was a little afraid. "Like what?"

The queen removed the Talking Tiara from Callie's head and placed it in her hands. "This tiara was passed down from my mother and her mother before her, and on and on back to Princess Teresa. I suppose by this time it knows far too much about the Royal Family of Arraband."

"We do!" the tiara said.

Queen Arabella continued, "Along with being able to talk—quite opinionatedly, I might add--the tiara also protects the wearer from harm."

"Exactly!" the tiara said, all the voices in unison.

"How does it do that?" Callie asked, looking at all the animated little faces as the tiara rested in her hands.

"We'll show you, but you have to promise not to drop us," the tiara said.

The queen said, "Try holding it out in front of you, at arm's length."

"Why?"

"You'll see." Then she spoke to the tiara: "Alright. Show her."

Callie stared transfixed as the tiara began to growl, quivering and shaking in her hand. The spikes that formed the diamond fringe grew taller and resembled teeth. Suddenly, the tiara had turned into a mouth, like that of a monstrous beast. The teeth gnashed and snapped ferociously, and it roared like a lion.

Callie screamed, and though she'd promised not to, she dropped the tiara, faces down, onto the floor.

All of a sudden, the growling beast was gone. There were muffled exclamations:

"Ow!"

"My nose... I think I hurt my nose!"

"Are you alright, Effie?"

Callie quickly bent down to pick it up, hoping it wasn't going to snarl and gnash its teeth at her again.

"You promised not to drop us!" the voices admonished.

Callie said sheepishly, "I'm sorry, but you frightened me."

"We were supposed to frighten you! It was our 'frightening' demonstration!" Stan said. *"That's it--no more demonstrations. Each time we do one, someone has to go to hospital. Donald might have a sprained nose. Do you know how long they take to heal?"*

Callie felt terrible. "I'm sorry about your nose... Donald?" She peered at the little faces, trying to decipher which one had a sprained nose.

A stuffed-up voice replied, *"It's okay, Princess. I'll get used to a flat nose."* He moaned.

Queen Arabella said imperiously to the tiara, "If you are quite done feeling sorry for yourselves, I should like to take the Princess down to the Banquet Hall. Don't forget, you have been a servant to the Royal Family for centuries. It is your job to protect the Royal Personage whose head you adorn. Some of you may be injured whilst doing your duty, it is true, but you must bear it as the Royal Tiara that you are."

"We will, Your Majesty," it said soberly, though Donald's voice was a little more nasal than the rest. *"We'll do our duty to you, Princess. Even if some of us lose a nose while trying."*

While Callie digested that thought, the queen placed the tiara on her head. She and her footmen ushered Callie out of the room and down to the Banquet Hall.

"We are here, my dear. And remember--you curtsy to no one inside that room. They curtsy and bow to *you*. Deep breath!"

The doors opened. Callie didn't have to be told to take a deep breath, for when she saw what was beyond, she gasped.

Chapter Eight

A Royal Banquet

Callie tried to steady her nerves as she looked into the huge banquet room. Over two thousand people were seated at large, round tables inside. Red and gold banners hung from the arched ceiling in swags down the marble walls. Hundreds of candelabras glowed with light. Ladies and noblemen all craned their heads to catch a glimpse of Albion's newest princess.

"I go first," Queen Arabella whispered. "Then you will be announced. You will walk in and proceed to the Royal Table and sit next to me. Nothing to it."

"I think there might be *something* to it," Callie stammered.

A trumpet sounded. Then the majordomo proclaimed, *"Her Majesty, Queen Arabella of Albion."*

"That's me," the queen said, then proceeded with all the pomp and circumstance one could imagine as she was escorted to the Royal Table at the far end of the room.

Callie's heart raced. She didn't think she could do this, but she was going to find out.

"Her Royal Highness, Princess Calandria of Albion," the voice announced.

A hush descended over the room. It was as if no one dared to breathe, and that included Callie. She felt butterflies whiz crazily through her stomach to crash in a mangled heap.

A gentleman appeared beside her--the Captain of the Queen's Royal Guard, Lord Graydon, the man who had threatened to arrest Callie and Lewis earlier. "Your Highness," he said.

For some reason, Callie felt a very strong urge to faint, but she forced herself not to because she didn't want to miss anything. Instead, she took Lord Graydon's arm.

Soon, she stood at the grand table beside the queen.

"Lewis Farnsworth, Esquire, of the Land of Ur," the voice said. *"Noted Scientist and Royal Advisor to Her Highness, Princess Calandria."*

Lewis walked in. Instead of his usual worn jeans, wrinkled t-shirt and scuffed-up sneakers, he was dressed in a dark green velvet jacket with gold embroidery and buttons down the front. A ruffled white shirt and black pants and boots completed the outfit. He looked kinda... handsome.

Lewis came to stand beside Callie. "You look beautiful, Cal," he said with a smile.

"She does! Doesn't she?" the Talking Tiara said.

"Huh?" Lewis asked, dumbfounded. "Is that tiara *talking* to me?"

Before Callie could reply, it said, *"We certainly are."*

"Ignore them. They'll talk your ear off." Callie smiled. "But don't make any sudden movements, either. It should really be called the Attack Tiara."

Lewis seemed intrigued by this but said nothing as more dignitaries joined them at the Royal Table. The queen sat down, then the rest of the table followed suit.

"We have some wonderful delicacies prepared for this most special occasion, Calandria," the queen said. "I'm sure you and your friend will find our Albian cuisine most delicious. Ah--they are bringing in the first course."

Hundreds of footmen appeared, carrying huge silver trays on their shoulders. Soon they were placing steaming bowls of soup in front of the noble guests.

"Smells delicious," Callie remarked. She looked down. The steaming golden broth tickled her nostrils and made her stomach growl with its mouth-watering scent. Then she noticed something odd about the soup...something in it was moving.

Callie dropped her spoon, hoping her eyes had been playing tricks on her. She looked closer. There were little fish-like creatures swimming in the soup!

The queen dipped her spoon into the bowl before her. The creatures wriggled and swam about in the broth as she raised it to her mouth. "Fresh Cadamorg in Thistle Butter Broth," Queen Arabella said. Then she took a mouthful of the strange soup and everyone else followed suit.

Callie and Lewis looked at each other in alarm. *What are we going to do?* Callie whispered.

"Pretend to sip the broth," Lewis answered quickly. "We don't want to appear rude. They might put us in the dungeon!"

Callie forced herself to scoop some broth into her spoon. She'd managed to avoid the feisty little cadamorgs, but the mere thought of them swimming around in the broth made her want to hurl.

While everyone chowed down around them, Callie and Lewis managed to dump a few spoonfuls of the soup behind them into a nearby plant. Soon, their bowls were half-empty. The footmen began clearing them away.

"I hope the next course is better," Callie whispered.

"Me, too," Lewis agreed. "I'm getting hungry."

Another team of attendants brought in steaming trays and set them down. At first glance, the cooked creature on the silver platter looked like a lobster. It had legs--lots of them. It had beady little eyes, antennae sticking out of its head, and looked like a giant spider. Some julienne vegetables had been placed around it as a garnish.

"Oh, how delightful!" the queen said. "Boiled Husanik...one of my favorites." She reached over and grabbed a leg, then ripped it off of the hard shell and began to suck the meat out of it as if through a straw. The others at the table followed suit.

Callie and Lewis each took a leg. They exchanged a glance, then pretended to suck on it as the queen had done. Sir Reginald did the honors of cracking the hard shell of the body, revealing steaming, pink meat within. The rest of the creature was heartily enjoyed by those at the table. When they were finished, all that was left were the antennae.

"This is going from bad to worse," Callie whispered to her friend. "They bring out more and more food, and still there's nothing for us to eat."

Lewis looked pensive. "That's what you call a 'cruel irony.'"

After that course was cleared, the footmen re-appeared again with deep silver bowls. "I hope this is something we'll like," Callie whispered. A footman placed her bowl in front of her. It was full of little round morsels of something that smelled pretty delicious. Except one of the morsels opened its eyes and blinked up at Callie. Then it cooed.

"Mmm! Fresh Baby Pachu'aa," the queen said. "Very difficult to find this time of year." She picked one up in her spoon, then swallowed the cute little creature whole.

Callie looked at Lewis in desperation. "I am not eating one of those things!" she whispered.

Lewis gave a pained smile. "I'm with you on this one, Cal. We'll just have to hope no one notices."

But someone did notice. Queen Arabella leaned toward Callie and said, "You aren't eating, dear. Are you not feeling well?"

Callie gulped. "I'm feeling fine. It's just that...well...some of this food is a little strange to us. Like this, for example. We can't eat this. It would be gross."

"I see. I had no idea our food was so different from yours."

Callie made a face. "It is."

"I can have the kitchen prepare you a special meal, perhaps more like your own cuisine in the Land of Ur," the queen offered. "What would you like to eat?"

Callie gave a sigh of relief at the thought of eating something other than swimming fish soup, boiled spider, and live pachu'aa. "I'd really like a hamburger!"

At that, the queen went perfectly still. So did most of the people at the table. A hush had fallen over the room. "You want to eat...a *hamburger?*" the queen asked, seemingly a little shocked.

"Do I ever!" Callie said, enthusiastically.

"That goes for me, too," Lewis added, peeking around.

The queen sat back, regally. "The princess has spoken. She would like to eat a hamburger. Bring in-- the hamburgers."

The people in the room all began whispering and looking about curiously.

"You must not eat hamburgers very much here," Lewis said to Sir Reginald, who was sitting beside him.

Sir Reginald said slowly, "No...we don't."

When the hamburgers were brought in, it was easy to see what Sir Reginald had been talking about. A footman approached the Royal Table. "Your Majesty, may I present the Hamburgers. Please let me know how you would like them cooked, and what garnish and sauces you will require."

Callie stared in disbelief. A family of five stood in front of the table, all crying and wiping their eyes. The mother clutched her husband's arm and said, "Oh, Kenneth--I'm going to miss ye!"

The father held his wife tighter and choked back a few tears of his own. "Be brave, Matilda...fer the children's sake."

He took a step forward. "Princess...I mean, Yer Royal Highness--we are the Hamburgers: myself, Kenneth; my wife, Matilda; our boy, George; daughter, Susie; and finally, little Blossom." He hugged a little baby with a pink bow on her head. "If our 'umble family has been chosen ta be yer dinner, we consider it an honor. We know ye'll make us proud, and defeat the Raven Queen utterly." He turned to his wife and said, "Goodbye, Mattie...."

The family hugged and cried quietly as they waited to be taken away to the kitchen.

"Well, my dear," the queen said to Callie. "How would you like your Hamburgers cooked?"

Callie rolled her eyes. She couldn't believe this. "I don't want them cooked at all."

"You would prefer them served raw. I see," the queen said.

"No, you don't understand," Callie protested. "We can't eat these Hamburgers. They're *people*. We don't eat people!"

Now it was Queen Arabella's turn to sigh in relief. "Oh, good. For a moment, I was worried. And you think *our* food is disgusting. At least we draw the line at eating a family of five."

The Hamburgers stopped crying. Kenneth asked, "Ye mean, yer not going to eat us for dinner?"

"No," Callie replied, smiling when she saw the expression of relief on his face. "And neither is anyone else. Where I come from, a hamburger is a very different thing."

After Callie and Lewis explained how to make a hamburger like they do in the land of Ur, the Hamburgers were taken back to their table and allowed to finish their own meal. Soon the footmen had returned with more silver platters, but this time, they were covered in hamburgers! There wasn't any ketchup or mustard--the sauce on it was a lovely shade of royal blue, though Callie didn't want to know what it was made from. *"You're not going to eat that, are you?"* the Talking Tiara demanded from atop her head.

Callie assured it that she was, and took a bite.

"Perfectly disgusting, isn't it, Alfie?" said one of the diamonds to another.

"Oh, be quiet," Callie said, looking up.

The final course was some kind of weird purple ice cream with dark speckles in it. Callie had been just about to eat a spoonful, when Queen Arabella mentioned that the dark speckles were Porfirian Sweetbugs.

Needless to say, she and Lewis regretfully passed on dessert.

Chapter Nine

In The Castle of the Raven Queen

"Here we are, my dear," Queen Miranda said, smiling as she stepped out of the carriage. "Welcome to my home."

Wanda looked up at the castle's dark spiraled towers stretching into the night sky like long fingers. Square windows in the towers glowed with light high above them.

"What's that noise?" Wanda asked uneasily, hearing a thick fluttering.

Queen Miranda smiled. "Those are my ravens." As if reading Wanda's mind, she continued, "Do not be afraid--they shall not harm you."

"I'm not afraid," Wanda said, bristling. "I've never been afraid of anything. Especially not a bunch of dumb birds."

The queen ascended the grand, stone staircase to the castle doors and said over her shoulder, "These birds are not 'dumb.' They are intelligent. I have trained them to serve me--you will see." Then she stopped and turned abruptly, gently touching the underside of Wanda's chin. "And I know you are not afraid of anything. That is why you and I are going to be such good friends."

What was that supposed to mean? Wanda followed the queen up the grand steps. Queen Miranda raised her arms and made a sweeping motion. The huge wooden doors--which had to be twenty feet tall and probably six feet thick--opened as if by magic.

Wanda knew that at this point, most other kids would decide it was time to go home, but Wanda Morris was not like most other kids. She did not want to go home. She wanted to see more. The whole thing intrigued her. She sensed something powerful and she wanted it--whatever it was--for herself. Besides, she hated it at home.

Queen Miranda motioned for Wanda to follow, and swept through the doors into a large entrance hall, where the fluttering of wings echoed off the walls. The whole place gleamed in the torchlight: black marble floors, pillars, solid gold statues, paintings of important-looking people. "This is pretty cool."

The queen didn't comment, but the expression in her eyes said that she knew what Wanda meant.

Wanda looked up at a black raven flying toward them. Strangely, she didn't feel afraid.

The queen held out her arm and the bird landed gracefully upon it. "Argus--one of my sentinels," she said. The raven ruffled his glossy black wings and eyed Wanda coolly, while Queen Miranda stroked his chest. Then he walked up the queen's arm to perch on her shoulder.

In the back of her mind, Wanda thought it was a little strange that no one else had come out to meet the queen--only a raven. Wasn't she supposed to have courtiers and things like that?

"I am so happy that you will be my guest here at the castle," Queen Miranda said. "Since the king died, this has been a lonely place for me. I have always longed for a daughter, but the gods were not kind to me and my beloved Gregor. He died before I could give him an heir. But let us not think about that." She clasped Wanda's hand. Her dark eyes shone with an unnatural gleam which strangely didn't detract from her beauty, but seemed to make her more beautiful. Her voice was melodious, like bells. "*You* are here now, and your youthful presence will be just what the castle needs. In fact, you may stay as long as you like. It is my hope that you *will* stay...."

Wanda didn't know what to say, though already she was tempted. No one had ever invited Wanda to stay as long as she liked anywhere before. Usually, they were always trying to get rid of her--the kids at school, even her mom and dad.

"Let me take you on a tour." Queen Miranda gestured toward an arched doorway. They walked up a staircase and into a gallery, high above a magnificent throne room. "Behold the Throne of Tor-Enrith, sacred seat of the chosen rulers of our land from time immemorial."

The throne itself was gleaming black, and covered in strange carvings. Red rubies were the only jeweled ornamentation--they adorned the carved crown that sat at the top of the throne.

Queen Miranda led them down the stairway to a silver door at the end of the gallery. She motioned with her hands again and the heavy door opened. "One of my personal treasure rooms...."

Wanda felt her eyes almost bug out of her head as she tried to process the sight before her. It was like something out of a fairytale--fat chests with gold coins spilling out of them littered the floor. Velvet sacks of precious jewels full of sapphires, rubies, emeralds, and diamonds, as well as others which Wanda knew were valuable but didn't recognize, lined one wall.

Gold goblets lay scattered about, as if hastily thrown there. Strings of pearls and other precious stones fell out of heavy silver cases. Tiaras and brooches were stacked upon velvet trays. Other jeweled trinkets too numerous to mention were scattered upon tables and shelves, along with dazzling necklaces, adorned with sparkling precious stones the size of quarters.

Queen Miranda said easily, "You may take whatever you like."

"*Huh?*" Wanda said in shock.

"Oh, yes. Take what you like. I have more." The queen chuckled softly as if Wanda had made a joke. "This is only a small portion of my personal treasure. I have many more rooms like this one, filled to bursting."

Wanda's jaw dropped. And Wanda was not much of a jaw-dropper.

"Come," Queen Miranda said, gently pulling Wanda deeper into the room. "Try something on." She reached for a necklace adorned with rubies the size of grapes, separated by diamond collets. Wanda felt a thrill go through her as she touched the priceless necklace that she—*she*--was wearing! Even Callie Richards' birthday necklace hadn't been this beautiful. Even Wanda's *mother* didn't have anything remotely this cool!

The queen gently turned Wanda toward a mirror. "They look lovely on you," she said, touching the exquisite necklace. "The rubies complement your complexion, as well as the color of your eyes. I daresay it was made for you."

"Do you think so?" Wanda asked, breathlessly. She looked in the mirror and had to agree. The ruby necklace *did* make her look sort of pretty.

"I do," Queen Miranda said, smiling warmly. "It is yours."

"Really?" Wanda asked, still not able to believe the queen would give her any of the treasures in this room, though she had said she would.

"Of course, my sweet. Now try this." The queen placed a ruby and diamond tiara on Wanda's head as if it were the most natural thing in the world.

Wanda stared at her reflection in the mirror and almost wanted to cry. No one had ever thought Wanda Morris was pretty, or special, or deserved to wear a tiara on her head. No one except Queen Miranda. Though she had only known the woman for a short time, she felt like Queen Miranda was the best friend she'd ever had.

Then the queen wiped away a tear and touched Wanda's shoulder. "Forgive me, my dear. It is just...."

"What?" Wanda whispered.

"To see you looking so splendid in my jewels...It is what I had dreamed I would do one day with my own daughter." Her dark eyes filled with emotion. "King Gregor and I longed for a child--a daughter! She would have looked, I think, like you."

"Really?" Wanda said. She looked in the mirror again, at her own face and then at the queen's. There was some resemblance. They both had dark hair and eyes. Wanda's heart screamed out, *If only she could have been my mother!*

131

"Yes." Queen Miranda stroked Wanda's hair. Wanda couldn't remember the last time anyone had stroked her hair, not even her own mom. In fact, she couldn't remember the last time she had actually *seen* her mother in person. Had it been weeks, or months now? Suddenly, that didn't seem to matter.

"Tell me," the queen asked in her melodious voice, "do you have any parents?"

Wanda stared at herself in the mirror, at the jewels that she wore on her neck and the tiara that crowned her head, and as if in a dream she slowly said, *"No...."*

The queen touched Wanda's shoulder. "Perhaps, then, you could be *my* daughter, as I have no child and you have no parents."

Wanda blinked. She knew what Queen Miranda was asking. It seemed somehow horrific and wonderful all at once.

The queen gestured toward the priceless treasures that glittered in the room before them. "If you choose to stay, I will give you this entire room of my personal treasures for your own."

Wanda looked at the priceless jewels, gold coins and other valuables that filled the treasure room. *All this could be hers?* She tried to estimate the value. Ten million? Twenty million? And that was a conservative guess. It seemed impossible, and yet she knew she was wide awake. She wasn't dreaming.

The queen smiled gently. "No, my dear, you are not dreaming. All this--and much more--will be yours if you choose to stay. We could have such fun together, you and I. We are two of a kind. Say you will stay."

Wanda looked at the queen in the mirror. She tried to remember what her own mother looked like, but couldn't. Somehow, that didn't bother her. Maybe she was under some kind of spell, or maybe she knew deep down that her mother probably didn't remember what Wanda looked like either....

"I'll stay," she said simply.

oOo

Even though the Hamburger family had almost been cooked up and served to Callie for dinner, they didn't hold it against her. Later that evening during the ball, they even let Callie hold their baby, little Blossom, who was certainly the cutest baby she had ever seen. Their daughter, Susie, tugged on Callie's sleeve and asked, "Are you going to save us from the Raven Queen? She wants to feed me and George to her ravens. And Blossom, too."

Callie felt a wave of emotion pierce her heart as she saw the fear in the little girl's face. "Don't worry. She won't feed you to her ravens."

"Do you promise?" Susie whispered.

Her parents looked on with concerned expressions, waiting for Callie's answer.

"I promise," she said, wishing she hadn't made the promise, but unable to stop herself from trying to comfort little Susie Hamburger and her family. The thought of anyone trying to harm this little girl or her brother and baby sister made Callie feel sick. She was suddenly sobered by the situation.

What if it was true? Could the Raven Queen really be that evil? Lord Graydon had assured her that it *was*

133

true, along with more that he refused to tell her. Suddenly the thought of abandoning the people of Albion--people like the Hamburgers and their children-- to the clutches of the Raven Queen seemed unthinkable.

After the ball, Queen Arabella, along with Sir Reginald and Lord Graydon, took Callie and Lewis on a tour of the palace.

"This may be of interest to you, Calandria," the queen said, as she led them into a long gallery with high ceilings. Priceless paintings of stern-looking people from centuries past hung on the walls. "This is the Royal Gallery. These are all members of the Royal House of Arraband, my dear. They are your ancestors."

Callie was impressed.

Queen Arabella gestured toward the first painting. "Sir Reginald, would you do the honors? I know of no other who knows more about our history than you."

"Of course, Your Majesty." Sir Reginald stepped forward, looking quite proud. "This painting shows King Enoc, who ruled about a thousand years ago, and is credited with defeating the Mulbar forces."

Callie and Lewis peered closer. There was something strange about King Enoc's face. He didn't seem to have a nose, and he had a big bump on his chin. "What's that?" Callie asked, pointing toward the bump.

Sir Reginald gave a pained smile. "That is King Enoc's nose. It...fell off...at the Battle of Everard. It was later re-attached."

"*To his chin!*" Lewis whispered, giggling in Callie's ear. Then he said aloud and very importantly, "You could say he had a 'nose for battle,' then."

This got a muffled laugh from Lord Graydon and an expression of quiet mirth from Sir Reginald.

Queen Arabella was not impressed, however, and gave them a stern look.

They passed by a large clock on the wall. The clock face looked like a real person's, with eyes that followed them as they walked by.

It called out, "Nine of the Clock, and all is magnificently well, Your Majesty."

Callie and Lewis were amazed.

Queen Arabella, however, merely nodded and said, "Thank you, Sir Ambrose."

The clock blinked in acknowledgement. But when Callie looked back at the curious timepiece, she felt a shiver go through her. The eyes in the clock face had changed. Callie could have sworn the eyes had been brown, and now they were blue.

Unable to take her gaze away, she pulled on Lewis' sleeve; all the while, the strange blue eyes watched her.

"Lewis," Callie whispered. "Look at the eyes in the clock. They were brown and now they're blue. And they're watching us!"

Lewis turned to look, but as soon as he did, they had changed back.

"What are you talking about, Cal?" Lewis asked. "They look brown to me."

Callie's heart skipped a beat. Had she been seeing things? She could have sworn the eyes had been blue. Probably just a trick of the light. And yet, as the group moved through the room, Callie's gaze kept returning to the clock. All that stared back, however, were the somber brown eyes of Sir Ambrose. *Weird.*

Trying to shake off the strange feeling of being stared at by a painted clock face, Callie turned her attention back to Sir Reginald and his history lesson.

"Next, we have King Ethelred the Great," Sir Reginald continued. "As you can see in the background, his Royal Dragon, Llyr, swoops down in victory against Tor-Enrith in the Battle of Wulffsig."

"Cool," Lewis said. "Do you get to have a dragon, Cal?"

Queen Arabella looked down her nose at Lewis, seeming to disapprove of his informality with the princess. "Yes, she does, young man. Dragons are royal beasts, kept only by royalty, as is our law. It is a tradition that has existed for thousands of years."

"What happens if a regular person keeps a dragon?" Lewis wanted to know.

"Tell them, Sir Reginald," the queen said imperiously.

Sir Reginald explained bluntly, "The offending personage is chopped up, sauteed with a little garlic, perhaps a little butter, and made into a stew for the dragons."

Callie and Lewis looked at each other and started to giggle. Adults could be so silly sometimes when they were trying to fool kids. "Has that ever *really* happened, though?"

Sir Reginald and the queen shared a look and chuckled a bit as well. "Oh, *yes.*"

Callie's smile faded. "What am I going to do with a dragon? I mean, is it really necessary? Goldfish are more my speed."

The queen waved a hand. "Of course they are necessary, Calandria. Every princess needs a dragon to protect her. Tomorrow, if you choose to stay, you will go to the Royal Stables and meet with Ignatius P. Entwhistle—the Royal Dragon Master and author of the runaway bestsellers, *Dragons--Complete Care and Rearing, and Talking with Dragons--Confessions of a Royal Dragon Master*. Both are excellent, by the way. Ignatius advised me that he has a new hatchling ready to come out any day now, and it is important to have the hatchling imprint on the royal personage it is going to serve as soon as it breaks out of the shell." She touched Callie's arm. "This would be your dragon for life. It will protect you and fight to the death for you."

Callie gulped. It was a lot of responsibility to think about. "Do you have a dragon?"

Queen Arabella smiled. "I do. Soren. He has been with me since I was four years old. You will meet him tomorrow."

"Did my mother...?"

"Yes, of course." The queen looked a little sad. "Both Ana and Miranda had their Royal Dragons from an early age: Ana had Loxar and Miranda, Kyros. After Ana went into the Land of Ur, Loxar wasn't himself. Like us, he had lost his princess. When Ana died, Loxar died shortly after. It happens often. When a dragon's master dies, it loses the will to live."

"How did he know?" Callie asked.

"He just knew. Dragons do, you know."

"What about Kyros?" Lewis asked.

"He went with Miranda when she ran away to Tor-Enrith. As far as we know he is still living."

A chill went up Callie's spine.

They came to more modern paintings, and Callie's breath caught when she found herself staring up at the beautiful, familiar face of her mother. Her mom was young in the painting; she looked to be in her late teens, and there was another girl with her, standing slightly behind her, who looked exactly the same--her twin, *Miranda*.

All at once, it became real to Callie. Not that she'd thought she was dreaming. She knew she wasn't dreaming because Lewis was here, too, and he said they were both wide awake. But to see real physical evidence of her mother's presence in this strange land, this magical Kingdom of Albion, was almost too much for Callie to handle. Her throat felt like it had a grapefruit in it, her eyes started to water, and her knees felt weak. She stumbled a bit, trying to keep anyone from noticing, but someone did notice, and he was beside her in an instant.

"Are you alright, Princess?" Lord Graydon asked.

Everyone took notice now, including Lewis who had wandered off with Sir Reginald to examine a statue of King Cadmus.

"You okay, Cal?" Lewis asked, looking a little put out at how Lord Graydon was attending to his best friend.

"Are you ill, my dear?" the queen asked, her brow furrowed with concern.

"No...I'm fine. Really." She pointed to the painting of her mother. "It's just...a bit of a shock, that's all. To see this--it's like she's still here, somehow."

Queen Arabella clasped Callie's hand and said, "She *is*, my dear. In you."

That made Callie want to cry all over again, but instead she gave a brave smile and asked Sir Reginald to continue with the tour of the gallery.

When he led them to the next item, Callie overcame her tears. This was not a painting, but an old slab of stone with broken edges. The stone itself was huge, and depicted four men who, from the tall crowns upon their heads, looked to be kings. The carvings of their faces had been worn down a bit, presumably by wind and rain. It looked like it had once been part of an outdoor structure that had crumbled.

"Who are they?" Callie asked, intrigued.

Queen Arabella explained, "These are the Ancient Kings of Albion. At least, that's who we think they are...."

"You mean, you don't know for sure?"

The queen shook her head. "It is a great mystery that has plagued our historians for centuries. Sir Reginald, perhaps you can shed more light?"

He nodded and began walking around the stone. "Albian historians can trace the history of our nation back at least fifty-thousand years. The first King that we have record of--Eldric the Wise--ruled about forty-eight-thousand years ago. Yet we have found artifacts that date our nation earlier than that, which go back at least sixty-thousand years. But there is a gap in our records. There are at least ten-thousand years missing from our history."

"Missing?" Lewis asked. "How can they just be missing?"

Sir Reginald continued, "We know that our civilization existed at that time, from records that came after, which refer to the 'Time of the Four.' They refer to the Ancient Kings--four of them--who ruled together over a vast empire. But we do not know their names. There is nothing from that time left to tell us what happened--no carvings, no tablets, no writings--save the scrolls, and this stone ruin. It is as if something, or someone, destroyed all the records of this time; or hid them away."

"But why would someone do that?" Callie asked.

"We don't know." Sir Reginald continued, "But we do know that the scrolls talk of an ancient city, a lost city--Antheon. Some historians believe that is where the missing records and treasures of the Ancient Kings can be found. We have been searching for centuries, and we have yet to discover its whereabouts."

Callie looked to the queen. "You said the scrolls of the Ancient Kings foretold my coming to Albion, and they said I was the one who could defeat the Raven Queen."

Queen Arabella nodded. "Yes. It is so. The Priestesses of Arundel guard the scrolls at their temple in Cascia. They are a sacred relic, the only link we have to the four kings who may have founded our land."

Callie recited the words she'd heard in her dream:

"When one is two and two are one,
King Eldric's magic has begun
The Queen will call the princess home
To sit upon the Enchanted Throne.

"Tell me about King Eldric," Callie said. "And the Enchanted Throne."

The queen ran her hand along the edge of the great stone carving. "Eldric the Wise was one of our most famous kings. He defeated the first invaders from Tor-Enrith. He possessed a magic of great powers. It is he who reportedly cast the spell of enchantment upon our throne which holds to this very day."

"How is it enchanted?" Callie asked.

"It holds a spell of protection for the land," the queen began, "as well as dramatically increasing the power of the Royal Personage who sits upon it."

"That is why we are so worried about the Raven Queen, Your Highness," Lord Graydon said. "If she were to sit upon the Enchanted Throne of Albion, we fear her powers would be too great for *anyone* to defeat her. It may be the entire reason she wants to possess our throne--as a tool to amplify her power."

"It is a possibility," Sir Reginald said quietly.

Queen Arabella looked away uncomfortably.

Sensing her grandmother's pain, Callie stepped forward and reached for her hand. "Perhaps you might show us the Enchanted Throne now?"

The queen took a deep breath. "Of course." Then with more official oomph: "We shall proceed to the Throne Room."

They followed Queen Arabella down the white marble hall and soon they were on the threshold of the Throne Room.

The Queen made a sweeping motion. "The Enchanted Throne of Albion."

Callie's gaze fell upon a glittering golden throne upon a pedestal, under a purple velvet canopy. It shimmered in the light from the chandeliers, like sunlight dancing on water. Embedded in the arms and back were sparkling jewels of every color in the rainbow--rubies, diamonds, sapphires, emeralds, yellow topaz....

"Your birthright, Calandria," the queen said.

Callie's body quivered with exhilaration.

"The Scrolls of the Ancient Kings speak of an enchantment that has not yet come to pass," Queen Arabella continued. "The throne holds a power within it which, legend says, will protect our land from harm. According to our records, the Enchanted Throne still waits for the One for whom it was crafted, as foretold by the Ancient Kings:

"Behold the Golden Throne
The seat of kings and queens
But the Royal Throne of Albion
Is much more than it seems

It holds a hidden power
Within its glittering stones
To be unlocked by a princess
The key is hers alone

This ancient key is legend
But does not yet exist
It will be forged upon the day
When fear fades into mist

It will be won in battle
And at tremendous cost
In order to be found
Something must be lost

Then King Eldric's magic
Will sing its ancient song
To weave the old Enchantment
And protect our Albion."

A shiver danced up Callie's spine.

In order to be found, something must be lost...

She had already lost so much. She wasn't sure she could handle much more. Yet, she knew it was useless to deny it. The wheels were in motion even now. She could feel them all around her. Something was happening that neither she, nor anyone else, would be able to stop.

Chapter Ten

The Hatchling

The queen showed Callie and Lewis to their rooms for the night, and left them to prepare for bed. Callie was astonished when the queen introduced her to a little purple creature named Rodney, the Royal Tooth-Brusher. He was bald, had a long nose and spectacles, and sat patiently on a chair until Callie was ready to have her teeth brushed.

"Honestly," she tried, "I can do it myself."

But Rodney would have none of it. "I've been brushing royal teeth for twelve-hundred years, Your Highness. Believe me--it is something best left to professionals. Open wide, please."

Callie obeyed. She didn't want to ask what the toothpaste was made from--it was pink and tasted pretty good, but going by Albian cuisine, it could have been anything from mashed bug eyeballs to troll snot.

As Rodney gently brushed her teeth, Callie asked if there was a Royal Face-Washer, too. Maybe a Royal Armpit-Washer? Rodney assured her that there was.

She supposed people needed jobs...

After Rodney finished and the Royal Pillow-Fluffer had come in to fluff the pillows, and the Royal Bed-Turner-Downer had come in and turned down the bed, the Royal Princess-Helper-Upper helped her into the great soft bed which had once been her mother's.

As Callie lay there in the dark, she felt strangely at home. She thought about all that had happened on this unforgettable birthday, and must have fallen asleep because soon, she was waking up to a frantic pounding at the door.

"*Huh?*" she said sleepily, sitting up.

"Calandria?" It was the queen.

Callie jumped out of bed and raced to the door. She struggled with it because it was so heavy, but suddenly it opened as if on a breeze. Queen Arabella walked in, dressed in a white lace-trimmed robe, her hair in a long braid along the side of her neck.

"What is it?" Callie asked breathlessly.

The queen's eyes were lit with excitement. "*The hatchling*...Ignatius sent word, it is going to hatch within moments. If you have made a decision, now is the time. Once the dragon hatches, it will imprint on the first person it sees, and if you want this dragon for your own, that person must be you. Do you understand?"

Callie already knew her decision. She'd known when she'd held beautiful little Blossom Hamburger in her arms, and when she'd promised Blossom's sister, Susie, that she and her siblings would be safe from the Raven Queen. She was going to stay and help these people any way she could. It was how her father and mother had raised her. "I'm staying."

The queen's face beamed with joy.

"Well, don't just stand there," Callie said, pulling her grandmother out of the room. "We have to be there when my dragon hatches!"

They ran to Lewis' door, pounding and yelling in the same fashion, and soon Lewis was beside them as they

146

ran down the hall with a couple of royal guards escorting them to the dragon stables.

The night was crisp and still as they jogged out onto the grounds. The dragon stables were twice the size of a football stadium. The structure was made of stone-- probably a good idea, as wooden stables might not be the best thing to house fire-breathing dragons. A gold-lettered sign above the doors proclaimed:

Royal Albian Dragon Stables

Ignatius P. Entwhistle, Certified Royal Dragon Master

Soon they were through the doors, running down the dirt-covered floor, past the huge stalls, as Callie and Lewis caught glimpses of the strange-looking creatures within.

A big green eye looked out of one stall and blinked at them; a massive creature with reddish-orange scales moved around in another, trying to get comfortable; in another, long black wings flapped, blowing Callie's hair around; in yet another, a bolt of fire shot up into the air, scorching the stone ceiling.

Callie clutched Lewis' sleeve. "Did you see that? Did you see?"

"It's amazing, Cal!" Lewis enthused.

"Quickly, quickly!" the queen said, ushering them toward the last stall. "I hope we're in time."

They rounded the corner and almost fell over each other as they took in the sight before them. A hulking man wearing an iron helmet with the visor up, gazed down at a purple speckled egg the size of a watermelon. The egg quaked and rocked in a nest on the stable floor.

The man glanced up at them, motioning for them to come closer. With large hands and a wide, stubbled face, he looked like the type of man who could handle dragons, or just about anything else, without blinking an eye.

"Ignatius?" The queen said.

"A matter of moments, now, Your Majesty. Come closer...that's it, Princess." He motioned for Callie to crouch beside him, next to the egg which was now shuddering from within. "Not long, now. Oh, we got a good one here. Look at the way he's using his whole body to weaken the shell...magnificent." He smiled up at the queen. "But what could you expect from the son of the Great Soren?"

"How do you know it's a boy?" Callie asked. "It isn't born yet."

"Shape of the egg. Females will be a bit smaller, rounder. Males will be bigger, more oblong, like this one here. Look, there's a foot."

Sure enough, a golden foot with a sharp talon had popped out of the shell, toes wriggling as the baby tried to squeeze out. The foot itself was almost as big as Callie's hand.

The Dragon Master pointed at the cracking shell. "Watch for the head. You want to make sure the hatchling looks directly into your eyes as soon as he opens his. You may have to move the egg to make sure his head is in the right position."

Callie reached out and screamed a little as another foot popped out. Then she laughed, because the baby dragon was still in the shell, but his feet were now standing--however wobbly--on the ground. He stumbled around like that for a few moments, then out popped a purple wing.

148

"Look at the color!" Ignatius whistled. "He's a beauty, all right. Here comes the head.... Grab it!"

Heart pounding, Callie reached for the cracking egg. She could feel the power of the creature within as it tried to force its way out of the shell.

"I see it--*is that it?*" A purple head the size of a cantaloupe pushed through the broken shell.

"That's it. Turn his head. There you go. Oh. Look at him."

The dragon's eyes were closed--he looked a little cranky. Then he opened his mouth and bellowed.

"Watch out!" Ignatius warned, pulling Callie out of the way as a half-hearted flame puffed out of the creature's mouth. The baby dragon coughed and sputtered--only smoke this time--and his eyelids started to flutter open.

"It's okay, sweetie," Callie said, not really knowing how to comfort a newborn dragon. "You're okay... see?"

The dragon opened its eyes--big yellow eyes--and blinked up at Callie.

"I'm Callie," she said.

"Touch him, touch his wings and his feet gently. There, like that," the Dragon Master directed. "Let him hear the sound of your voice. Good. He'll learn to locate you from great distances just by the sound of your voice."

"Really?" Callie asked, impressed. "What else can he do?"

The Dragon Master smiled. "When he's full-grown, he'll be able to fly at speeds of six, seven-hundred parthons an hour."

"That sounds fast," Callie noted, watching the baby dragon wobble on the ground. Already, he was turning his head at the sound of her voice. He looked around a bit, exploring his surroundings, then looked back at her. "What kind of dragon is he?"

Ignatius explained, "This little fellow is a Great-Crested Ceylx--one of the fastest breeds in the world. They also have the unusual ability to change colors to suit their environment, as a form of camouflage, though as you can see, their natural hue is purple. They can breathe fire up to a range of two-hundred phlegans, roughly a quarter of a parthon, and can be trained to hit a target with dead-on accuracy. The Great-Crested are exceptionally fast learners. Loyal and brave. Like his father before him, I daresay. Right, Your Majesty?"

At that, a dragon in a nearby stall brought his head up to the bars and looked out, his big yellow eye staring down at the queen, his purple wings fluttering in greeting.

"Soren!" she said lovingly, and went to see her dragon. Soren purred happily as the queen patted his snout. Warm steam flowed out of his nostrils.

"Cool!" Lewis said. "Can I try?" The queen nodded, and Lewis reached in and bravely patted the dragon's scaly snout, too. "Wow. The scales are neat, Cal. They're warm. They feel kind of like leather. Will Callie's dragon grow this big someday?"

Ignatius nodded. "Most definitely. It will take about two years for the hatchling to reach that size, but he'll be growing before you know it."

Already the baby dragon had grown protective of Callie, for when Lewis got too close to her, the dragon bellowed again and tried to fly. He only managed to flap sideways across the floor, but he obviously remembered how to breathe fire. All of a sudden, a flame shot out, and Lewis had to jump into the air to avoid getting his feet scorched.

Everyone laughed except Lewis.

"Already taking on creatures twice your size, eh?" Ignatius said, scooping up the hatchling and gently holding his snout shut so he couldn't fry anyone else. "Easy, now."

The dragon struggled and squawked at being confined. His big yellow eyes looked at Callie beseechingly. He gave a muffled bellow which just about broke Callie's heart.

"It's all right," the queen said, touching her arm. "Soren did that, too, when he was first hatched. He'll be fine. Ignatius is very skilled with dragons, and very gentle. He'll take good care of him, and you'll be coming here to the Royal Stables to help train the hatchling. But first, you must choose a name for him."

"A name..." Callie pondered for a moment, watching her brave baby dragon squirm valiantly in the Dragon Master's arms. The baby's bellow almost sounded like *ehhrrllll*. She smiled brightly. "Earle! That's what he's saying. That's his name!"

Ignatius smiled. "Well, come on, Earle. Time for your first feeding. Fresh fortified rinlak milk. Doesn't that sound yummy? Here we go, then."

Callie watched as Ignatius took Earle away for his feeding. She hadn't known she was going to fall in love with a squirmy, purple-scaled creature with big yellow eyes, one who breathed fire and would eventually grow to the size of a three-story building. In her heart, Callie felt completely responsible for the baby dragon. It felt both scary and wonderful.

"Well, I daresay the sun will be rising soon," the queen said, taking Callie's and Lewis' hands and giving a little squeeze. She whispered conspiratorially, "What do you say we sneak into the kitchens and make ourselves something to eat for breakfast? Can either of you cook? Oh. Neither can I. We will have to rouse Cook from her slumber, and she always hates when I do that."

oOo

After breakfast, Callie and Lewis were escorted to the Royal Library. They were given a list of required reading for the study of princess-hood, which read as follows:

The Princess's Guide to Acceptable Footwear
by Cato Fluki

Which Fork to Use, A Guide For Princesses
by Lady Malvinia Lactose, Curator of the Royal Albian Flatware Intstitute

Coping
by HRH Princess Raghnild-Ethelfrida of Tarpethia

Taking Care of You: A Princess's Workbook for Self-Realization
by Lady Primrose Salvia of the Wellness Institute

Someday You Might Have To Cook—A Guide for Royals

by Nunzio Romaine

Magic--Don't be Afraid to Use It
by Dr. Pericles Monsoon

An Extremely Short History of Albion--12 Volume Set
by Sir Humperdinck Perkins

The Scrolls of the Ancient Kings--Abridged Version
Ed. The Priestesses of Arundel,

with a new Introduction by Her Majesty, Queen Arabella of Albion

*Dragons--Complete Care and Rearing * #1 Albion Times Bestseller*

by Ignatius P. Entwhistle

How to Win Friends and Influence People
by Dale Carnegie

"Hey, look!" Lewis said. "My man, Dale Carnegie! Cool. I wonder how that book got into Albion?"

Callie shrugged.

"I guess Dale's reach went farther than I thought. Just goes to show you what the power of positive thinking can do." Lewis looked about the impressive library. "I guess we better get started looking for these books.

They split the list in half--five books each--and browsed while they searched. For two library lovers, the

Royal Albion Library was like hitting the jackpot. There were so many books to choose from! Even though Callie had a specific reading list, she didn't think it would hurt to add to it. After all, she was a princess now and she had to start making decisions for herself.

"Wow, look at this!" Lewis exclaimed.

Callie hurried to join him, wondering what cool book he'd found.

"*Quantum-Sorak Physics and Lyaxion Relativity--A Comparative Study*," he said enthusiastically.

"What's Lyaxion Relativity?" Callie asked. "Hey, for that matter, what's Quantum-Sorak Physics?"

Lewis grinned. "I don't know, but I'm gonna find out. I am *so* gonna ace the Science Fair this year!"

"You ace the Science Fair *every* year." She tugged on his sleeve. "Come on, let's find the other books on my list. I have to learn how to be a princess, pronto. And yes, if you're wondering, I was informed there *will* be an exam. Which is why you have to help me study."

"It's *your* princess exam. Why do I have to help you study?" Lewis asked, gazing at the books dreamily.

"Because you're my Royal Advisor, and if you don't, I'll throw you in the dungeon. Maybe even feed you to Earle." Callie smiled sweetly.

"Ha, Ha."

"It's not a joke, Lew. This *princess* thing is really going to my head. So you just better watch this whole 'displeasing me' stuff, or you'll end up as dragon stew."

He studied her for a moment before she broke into a fit of giggles. "Gotcha."

Now it was his turn to roll his eyes. "Look, Your Royal Specialness, just because you're a princess and you may have magical powers, it doesn't give you the right to take me for granted."

Callie grinned. "I could never take you for granted, Lew. You're the only thing that keeps my feet on the ground. Here, and back home."

Callie could have sworn Lewis's chest puffed out a bit.

"Now come on," she said. "Let's find these books. I have to get busy studying. And if you find any other books that might aid me in my quest for princess-hood, grab those, too. Hint: they would not have *anything* to do with Quantum-Sorak Physics or Lyaxion Relativity. Okay?"

Lewis shook his head. "Okay, but as your Royal Advisor, I have to say there's no telling when you might find a use for such information."

Knowing she wasn't going to win this particular argument, Callie sighed and went back to her list. Soon she had found all the books but one, and had also picked up two more which she thought might be of use: *101 Sneaky Tricks For Defeating Enemies on a Large Scale* by General Tedius Fitzwarren, a relative of Lord Graydon; and *The Albion Times Guide: Best Places to Eat in the City of Arraband*, by Snodley Gyro, Food Editor.

She was secretly hoping she and Lewis would be able to find someplace in Arraband that made french fries, maybe even pizza. If they were going to be staying here for awhile, they'd have to figure out other stuff to eat. Breakfast that morning had been scrambled ciarrai eggs, which were blue and tasted weird, and toasted hundred-grain bread with ballinberry jam, which looked like black tar but tasted much better.

They had both skipped the bloodboar juice.

Callie proceeded down a long shelf of books, her arms already loaded up with heavy tomes. She craned her neck to see the last book on her list: *Magic--Don't be Afraid To Use It*, by Dr. Pericles Monsoon. She checked the number on the list again, and looked back at the shelf.

"Darn," she muttered to herself. The book wasn't there. Someone must have checked it out. It must have been a thick book, because there was a wide space left vacant on the shelf. She gazed through the space, and took a step back, gasping.

A pair of eyes stared at her, but they didn't belong to Lewis. They were blue and very much alive, and they were staring out of the face of the Royal Library's clock, Lady Rathmore! But those eyes weren't Lady Rathmore's, though they looked strangely familiar.

Her heart racing, Callie ducked back behind the shelf again. She had to tell Lewis, but she didn't want to alert whoever, or *whatever*, was spying on her from behind the clock. She decided to play it very cool, and began whistling and walking nonchalantly up the aisle to where Lewis was reading a book called *The Truth About Unicorns*.

"Lewis," she whispered. "Ix-nay on the ock-clay."

"What?" Lewis looked at her like she was speaking some strange language. Which she was.

"I said—"

"I heard you, but I don't know what that means." He looked annoyed that she'd disturbed him.

She blinked a couple of times, really obviously, and twitched her head toward the clock.

Suddenly, Lewis looked concerned. "Are you okay, Cal? I think you've developed a slight tic."

Callie made a *grrr* sound. Sometimes Lewis had no concept of subtlety.

"Up there," she hissed.

"What?" Lewis was getting exasperated.

This wasn't working. She glanced at the clock face again to make sure the creepy eyes were still there. They were. She pulled Lewis around the corner, saying loudly, "I think that book you wanted is over here. Yes, here it is." She positioned him so that he stood where she had been, facing the gap in the shelf. He now had a perfect view of the clock face of Lady Rathmore.

"Whoa!" he whispered, taken aback. *"That clock is staring at us."*

"I know," Callie replied. "That's what I've been trying to tell you."

"What do you think it wants with us?"

"I don't know. But I *do* know those eyes aren't Lady Rathmore's. They belong to someone else. Someone else is back there spying on us!"

Lewis looked at her. "You mean, there might be a secret passageway?" When Callie nodded, he said, "Cool!"

"We've got to find the entrance. Come on."

Finally back on the same wave length, they walked slowly across the floor of the library to the opposite wall where the Royal Clock hung. As they came closer, the eyes kept following them. Then all of a sudden, they stopped.

"Look!" Callie said pointing. Lady Rathmore's eyes once again stared back from the clock face. Then they heard movement from behind the wall.

Quickly they searched, looking for any anything that would act as a switch for a secret door. Nothing worked.

"The passageway might not even open up into this room, Cal," Lewis said.

"Or if there is one, the door could be anywhere, even on the opposite side of the room," Callie added.

They looked over their shoulders to see if anyone might catch them, but the guards stationed outside the great doors stayed there. They were under orders from the queen not to disturb the princess as she tried to study. Obviously, they took their jobs very seriously.

Callie looked around, searching for a clue. Then she thought of the Door in the Floor, and her garden back home. The words from the map echoed in her mind:

The unicorn will lead the way

And protect you both night and day...

She looked down at the pink jeweled necklace--King Eldric's key--that hung from her neck.

"Look for something with a unicorn on it," she said to Lewis, scanning the stone walls, the carvings, and the statues nearby. There were all kinds of royal carvings, but no unicorns.

Then something behind a bookshelf caught Callie's eye. Something in the floor. She stepped over to a wrought iron grate in the marble floor along the side of the wall, like a heating grate. In the center was a unicorn, and something else that looked like a key hole. "Let's see if it works again."

She took King Eldric's key from around her neck and tried it in the lock. It clicked into place, just like it had in the Door in the Floor in her back garden. She turned the key and felt the mechanism stiffly turn into place, like it hadn't been opened in a long time. Lewis helped her pull the grate open. It was just big enough for one person to get through.

"Hmm, let's see...more stairs, going down into a dark pit." Lewis did his best Indiana Jones impression, 'Why's it always have to be...*stairs*?'"

Callie elbowed him. "This is serious. We need a flashlight or something. It's really dark down there."

"Your wish is my command, Princess." He went over to a long wooden study table and picked up one of the lamps that someone had left there. The lamp was an old brass contraption with a handle on top. Callie had seen them used quite extensively in the palace. Lewis and Callie each had one in their rooms. The source of light was a couple of Porfirian Sweetbugs, who, along with being an Albian delicacy mostly used in desserts, were also the source of energy in most of the lighting fixtures in the palace, and in the whole city of Arraband. They were like fireflies, but with Porfirian Sweetbugs, you had to talk nicely to them or they just wouldn't give you any light. Their name referred to the way they tasted rather than their "sweet" personalities. They probably should have been called "Porfirian *Stubborn*bugs."

"Excuse me," Lewis said, gently tapping the side of the lamp. "Could we bother you for a moment?"

The two Sweetbugs opened their eyes, and then closed them again, trying to get back to their naps.

Sweetbugs usually slept in the daytime because they were up at night providing light.

"Excuse me," Lewis tried again. He huffed. "*Excuse me?* Hey. Mr. Sweetbug. Rise and shine, buddy. The princess has a little job for you."

At that, one of the Sweetbugs stirred. He blinked his beady, beetle-like eyes a couple of times, then got to his feet, of which he had eight. He used one of them to kick at his neighbor, who was still trying to doze in the bottom corner of the lamp. The sleepy one grumbled and turned over, sticking his beetley rump in the air, obviously trying to get more comfortable. This of course made a great target for his friend, who began to kick at him. The Sweetbug squeaked in protest while his friend chastised him for not doing his duty to the princess.

Soon, the Sweetbugs were flying around inside the lamp, giving off their famous baby blue glow.

"Let there be light," Lewis said as he brought the softly swinging lantern to where Callie patiently waited.

Callie swung her feet toward the opening, but Lewis stopped her. "You went first last time. And besides, you're a princess, now. I have to protect you."

Callie loved it when Lewis did his manly protective thing. "Sure, Lew."

"Pardon me, Princess." He maneuvered around and shone the light into the opening. He put his feet in and lowered himself down with Callie following.

As tunnels went, it was quite unremarkable. No interesting carvings, no mysterious languages, just a functional stone passageway. It dipped down and then went back up, the steps leading to a small room ahead.

"Look!" Callie exclaimed. "This must be right behind the library clock." There was a small wooden platform for a person to stand on, which raised them to the perfect height for staring through the eyes of the clock face. Sure enough, there was a sliding mechanism in the wall, which, when moved, showed two small oval holes--Lady Rathmore's eyes--which looked out into the library.

"So someone was definitely here spying on us," Lewis said, having a look for himself. "But who would want to spy on us?"

An unsettling feeling rippled through Callie's heart. "I don't know, but I don't like it."

"Ditto."

Then a thought hit Callie. "Do you think they might still be in the passageway?"

"I don't know, but if they really wanted to hurt us, they could have gotten to us by now." Lewis stepped off the platform and shone his lantern further up the tunnel. "I wonder where this tunnel ends?"

"Let's find out."

Lewis grinned. "Yeah. If we run into anyone, I'll just whack them with my lantern." They started up the tunnel. "I hope it's not a monster, though."

Callie hoped so, too.

They proceeded up another flight of stairs, passing by the Royal Gallery--where Callie had first seen the eyes looking at her last night--then they went down again, then up, then around, then down, then up a spiral staircase until they reached another platform. Neither of them had any idea where they were in the palace.

"There's only one way to find out where we are," Lewis said, stepping onto the platform. He slid the mechanism and looked out of the two oval holes. "I think...this is *your* room, Cal."

Callie's heart did a flip. *Her room? Had the mysterious person been spying on her last night, too? Had someone spied on her mother when she'd lived here all those years ago?* Callie stepped onto the platform, and Lewis made room for her. "Look."

Sure enough, it was the blue and white marble bedroom where Callie had slept last night, under the big clock face of Lady Elva--exactly where her mom had slept when she was as girl.

But it wasn't just this new discovery that gave Callie a strange feeling. She took the lamp from Lewis and stepped off the platform. Somehow she knew that there was an entrance into her room from this tunnel. She didn't know how she knew, she just knew. She "felt it in her bones" as her mom used to say. And there was more.

"There's something of my mother's hidden in this tunnel," she said slowly.

"*Huh?* How do you know?" Lewis asked.

"I feel it. I feel *her*." Callie said. She heard her mother's voice then, as clear as day. She whispered in Callie's ear, *Look to the wall.*

Callie swung the lamp around, looking at the dark stone walls. Then she saw it. She reached for a loose stone--she'd known it was loose before even touching it. She pushed away the stone and raised the lantern. The eerie blue light illuminated a small compartment in the wall.

"There's something in it," Lewis whispered, though why he was whispering, Callie didn't know. It was just the two of them…. Or was it?

Callie reached into the compartment and pulled out a dust-covered book. She brushed a finger across the cover. It was encrusted with pink jewels, just like the ones in Callie's necklace. She brushed away the dust, revealing something else, a swirling, gold letter 'A.' For Ana, perhaps?

"It looks like a diary," Callie said, jiggling the strong buckle clasp. "It won't open."

"There must be a key somewhere," Lewis said. "Do you think it's…?"

"My mom's diary?" Callie finished. She held the book to her heart, felt the recognition there. "I *know* it is. And I think I know where the key is, too. *Back home.*"

Callie met Lewis' questioning eyes and explained further, "My mom always wore a little gold pendant on a chain around her neck. It was in the shape of a key, and it had the letter 'A' on top. Lew, the letter looks just like the one on the diary!"

Callie had pestered her mom about the key pendant forever. It was one of their private jokes. No matter how much Callie begged, pleaded, or promised to do chores, her mom would never reveal what the key opened. She would only say that, one day, Callie would discover the secret herself. Somehow, she had known Callie would find it here in the tunnel.

"And there's more," Callie explained. "She said she'd hidden a special gift for me, and when I found what the key opened, I would understand…. She said that one day, this gift might *save my life.*"

"Wow," Lewis said, looking seriously floored. "I wonder what she meant?"

Callie wished she had the pendant here! It was sitting in the little china dish on Callie's bureau, which still held her mom's everyday jewelry including the gold pendant.

What secrets would her mom's diary reveal? Callie's fingers itched to open it.

Could this be what the mysterious person in the tunnel had been seeking? If so, for what purpose? Why had her mom hidden it away in this secret passageway? Had her mom used the passageway herself? For what reason?

More and more questions spun in Callie's head. And she knew that the answers to many of them, and more, would be found inside her mother's diary.

Chapter Eleven

The Pool of Arundel

On Wanda's first night in the Castle of Tor-Enrith, Queen Miranda made good on her promise--she gave Wanda the entire contents of the treasure room for her own. They spent most of the evening trying on the collection of priceless jewels and having a wonderful time, just like mother and daughter.

Wanda gazed at her reflection in the mirror, as she dripped in priceless jewels. The queen was right--Wanda *was* pretty. All the stupid kids at school were wrong. Wanda Morris was pretty, and highly intelligent, and greatly superior to other children in almost every way; Queen Miranda told her so.

The queen told her all sorts of other things, too-- how she, Queen Miranda, had once been a princess of Albion, how she had been betrayed by her own twin sister and forced to leave her home, how she had found solace here in the Kingdom of Tor-Enrith, eventually marrying King Gregor. The worst part of all was how poor Queen Miranda had been cheated out of her rightful position as heir to the throne of her homeland.

"My love for Tor-Enrith could not be greater," the queen explained. "It is my home, now. But I feel I must try to reclaim what my sister stole from me, and eventually take my place as the rightful Queen of Albion."

Wanda couldn't agree more. How dare the queen's awful sister *steal* from her like that? From what Queen Miranda said, her sister had always been the favorite, always had everything handed to her on a silver platter while Miranda had been ignored. Well, Wanda certainly knew what *that* felt like!

"It sounds just like Callie Richards!" Wanda complained, trying on another sparkling tiara. "You remember that girl from school I told you about who came through the tunnel, too? I *hate* her. She's got her 'poor little me' routine down to a science. Everyone falls for it. You should see it--it's disgusting."

"I know," the queen nodded.

"How do you know?" Wanda asked absently, snatching up a couple of diamond bracelets and a few more strings of pearls to try on, too.

"There is more that I have not told you," Queen Miranda said quietly, her eyes becoming moist with emotion.

"What?" Wanda asked, concerned. She hated to see Queen Miranda so upset.

"About your friend, Callie."

"She's *not* my friend," Wanda insisted.

The queen gave an understanding nod. "This Calandria you speak of. She is the daughter of my sister--the one who betrayed me all those years ago."

Wanda was momentarily floored. "You mean, Callie is your *niece*? Her mom was from Albion?"

"Yes. And now, Calandria is here in our world to finish what her mother started all those years ago."

Wanda felt her blood begin to boil. *Callie Richards' mother had been a real princess from a magical land?*

166

She felt her heart beating wildly--with anger, jealousy, and ice-cold envy.

"So that means Callie...."

"Is of royal blood, yes," the queen answered, closely studying Wanda's reaction.

Wanda couldn't believe her ears. "Are you *sure*?"

"Quite sure. And being one of our line, she has inherited magical powers, too, I'm afraid. Though my spy in the Albian Court tells me she does not yet know how to use them."

Wanda felt her heart clench like a fist. She didn't want Callie Richards to be the daughter of a royal princess, or have magical powers. It was all more of the same--Callie Richards trying to flaunt her superiority over everyone else, especially Wanda--and it had to stop.

Queen Miranda touched Wanda's hand. "I am so very frightened, my dear, and I don't know who else to turn to. I think your friend is here to destroy me."

"I told you, she's not my friend. And she's not going to destroy you."

"How can you be so certain?"

"Because," Wanda said firmly, "*I'm* not going to let it happen."

oOo

While Lewis was busy discussing the differences between Quantum-Sorak Physics and Lyaxion Relativity with Sir Reginald, Callie was hanging out with Queen Arabella at the Royal Dragon stables.

As they watched Ignatius with the dragons, they indulged in a little girl talk, too. It was nice, one of the things Callie missed with her mom being gone. She'd told the queen about finding her mom's diary in the passageway. Her grandmother had nodded sagely and commented, "So, that's where it went." Queen Arabella informed Callie that her mother had been keeping the diary for years before her departure from Albion. She also informed her that without the key, no power in Albion could open it--the diary was enchanted.

This news made Callie even more determined to find out what was within her mother's secret diary.

Earle was growing by leaps and bounds each day. He was now roughly the size of a pony, and was currently trying to get the hang of his wings. So far, the baby dragon had suffered what Ignatius described as a "slight concussion" when he'd crashed a few times while attempting to fly. Other than that, he was doing fine. Ignatius had even let Callie hand-feed her dragon some of his favorite treats: Sugared Tabari-roots, which dragons loved. After his snack, Earle had made a loud burp, sending a bolt of orange-hot flame into the air along with a puff of black smoke.

Then they had moved into the main training area, which was like a large indoor stadium, where Ignatius put Soren--Queen Arabella's dragon and Earle's father-- through his paces.

Callie kept saying, "Wow..." over and over as the gigantic winged beast flew in loop-the-loops, singed specific targets with his breath on command, and performed all sorts of agility and speed requirements befitting a Royal Dragon. Then Soren and another dragon, Nexu, demonstrated *Chiagaruu* (the dragon version of flyball) in which they flew at top speeds over hurdles, retrieved a target, turned on a dime, then went back over the course.

Earle watched his father's precise movements with all the enthusiasm of a puppy, and all of a sudden, the sight of her baby dragon trying to emulate his father made Callie sad. She and Lewis had been in Albion for days, now--which, as the queen explained, was only about a minute in the Land of Ur. But for Callie, the time felt as real as ever, and she realized then that she missed her dad, even though she'd been angry at him when she'd left the house the night of her birthday.

Queen Arabella gently touched Callie's shoulder. "What is it, my dear? Why are you unhappy?"

Callie bit her lip. Queen Arabella had been so good to both her and Lewis since their arrival, she didn't want to complain.

"It's nothing..."

The queen tipped Callie's chin up. "That tone isn't fooling me one bit. You're upset about something, and you must tell me what it is."

Callie took a deep breath. She didn't want her grandmother to think she was being disloyal. "It's my dad. I miss him."

The queen's eyes became sadly resigned.

Callie explained, "I've never been away from home for this long before. Since Mom died, we both stay pretty close to home and to each other. Do you understand?"

Queen Arabella nodded. "I'm sorry, dear. Sometimes, I am so excited and happy to have you here with me, that I forget you are only a young girl, after all. It is perfectly natural, what you are feeling, and I think I can help."

"You can?" Callie asked.

"Yes. Come with me." The queen thanked Ignatius for his demonstration and continued excellence of service, then made their apologies, as they had pressing business elsewhere.

"Where are we going?" Callie asked.

"To the Pool of Arundel. To see your father."

Callie tried to absorb what her grandmother had said. "My dad...is *here*?"

"Not exactly." The queen glanced down at her. "But you shall see him there."

Callie's heart leapt with joy. She hadn't realized just how much she was looking forward to seeing her dad.

They passed through the Royal Gardens, through a hedgerow maze which Queen Arabella expertly navigated, and down a path with arbors covered in fragrant white roses. They finally came out onto a grassy lawn with a small reflecting pool.

A bench, which looked remarkably like the stone bench that Callie's mom had loved so much in their back garden, stood nearby. Seeing it here gave Callie a funny feeling.

Next to the bench stood a life-sized statue of a woman with flowing hair in a long gown. The statue gazed down dreamily into the pool. The carving was so life-like, the woman almost looked real. Callie almost expected her to greet them. "Who is she?" Callie asked.

"This is Queen Arundel." The queen gestured toward the statue. "She was the wife of King Eldric the Wise—the king whose key opened the door into our world."

Callie absently fingered the jeweled key that hung from her neck. She could have sworn it felt warmer to the touch than it usually did...

"She looks alive," Callie said, still captivated by the statue.

"She may well be."

"Huh?" Callie said, confused.

"There is no record of Arundel's death in any of our histories. An old legend tells of a dark enchantment which turned an ancient queen into a living statue, alive yet turned to stone. We think this statue may be her, forced to watch each season pass for thousands of years. Imagine what she has seen...."

The thought of poor Queen Arundel being alive in there kind of freaked Callie out. She decided to change the subject. "So, why do you call it her pool? Did she used to swim in it?"

Queen Arabella smiled. "No. It is not that kind of pool. Queen Arundel used to gaze into it, and it would show her things."

"Like what? The future?" Callie didn't want to see the future. Ever since her mom's death, when she had learned that the future didn't always hold happy things in store for you, Callie had tried to avoid even thinking about it.

"No," Queen Arabella replied. "This is a 'seeing pool.' They are a natural wonder, and very rare, even in our world. It is how Ana's father and I watched over her in your world. You simply ask it to show you someone, and you will see their image, wherever they are." The queen's expression grew sad. "It was here that we watched our princess die on that horrible day."

Callie chewed her lip as her heart tensed. She remembered standing helplessly beside her dad in the hospital room as he clutched her mother's hand. It seemed horrible to think that her mom's parents had been standing here helplessly, too.

"How do you work it?" Callie asked, pushing the painful memories away.

"Like this." The queen addressed the pool. "Show me Princess Calandria."

The pool made a *whooshing* sound, and the water turned a silvery blue, then--*zip!*--there was Callie's reflection in the pool. Only it wasn't her *reflection*. It was like a view of her from a different angle, like a camera was filming her.

"Wow," Callie said. "Can I try?"

"Of course."

Callie commanded, "Show me Lewis!"

The pool *whooshed* and *zipped* again, and there was an image of Lewis, deep in discussion with Sir Reginald, surrounded by books in the Royal Library.

Callie was amazed. She had to try it again. "Show me Earle!"

In seconds she saw Earle with Ignatius in the Royal Dragon Stables. Ignatius was trying to train Earle to hit a specific target with his fiery breath, but Earle's aim was a little off. He'd singed one of Ignatius' eyebrows instead.

Then Callie said, "Show me my dad." The pond turned silver-blue, and then, shimmering in the water, was the image of her dad sitting on their couch. With his arm around Sharon.

Callie stared into the cold waters of the Pool of Arundel, and watched as her dad smiled and shared a joke with Sharon, then gave her an affectionate kiss on the cheek. Callie closed her eyes. Didn't her dad miss her?

Suddenly, Callie was embarrassed. Her grandmother stood beside her, watching.

"That's my dad's girlfriend—I mean, *fiancée*, Sharon," Callie mumbled. "They just got engaged."

The queen's expression was unreadable. "I see. Tell me, does Sharon make your father happy?"

Callie paused. "I guess so." Since Sharon had been around, her dad's spirits had lifted. He seemed more like his old self, when her mom had been alive.

"Then why are you opposed to the marriage?" the queen asked bluntly, looking like she already knew.

Callie's emotions were spinning. She didn't want to have to answer that question, because she didn't know the answer herself. "Because...if he really loved Mom, he wouldn't want to marry someone else."

Queen Arabella gave her granddaughter a stern look. "Calandria, your mother is gone. It pains me--it pains all of us--that she is gone. But your father is still alive, and it would be a sin more grievous than you could ever imagine to ask a living person to behave as if they, too, were dead. That is what you are asking your father to do."

At that, tears sprung to Callie's eyes.

"I also know that Ana would have wanted your father to be happy after she was gone. She would not want him to be alone for the rest of his days. She loved him too much."

"He's not alone!" Callie insisted. "He has me."

"A mate is different from a child," the queen explained. "Your mother would not want him to go through life without a companion at his side. She would want you to support your father in this. You know it as well as I do. Your mother would be greatly disappointed if you deliberately stood in the way of his happiness."

Callie wiped away tears. "I don't want to talk about it anymore." She didn't want to talk about it, because her grandmother was insinuating that Callie was somehow betraying her mom in all this. *But Callie was on her mom's side.* She was the only one who was! Everyone else seemed determined to forget her, to forget that her mom and dad had ever even been married.

The queen studied Callie for a moment. "I shall withdraw to the palace now, as I must attend to affairs of state. I think you also require some privacy with your thoughts. But do not be late for your Magical Theory and Application lesson with Dr. Pericles Monsoon. He has come all the way from his home in the Marpesian Mountains to be your tutor. Though he is a distant cousin of mine, he demands punctuality from all his royal students, including you. Dinner will be at six sharp in my sitting room. I shall see you and Lewis there."

With that, Queen Arabella took her leave.

Though Callie hated to admit it, she had never really thought about what her *mom* would want for her dad's future. Would her mom really want her dad to marry someone else? If only she could ask her, and hear it straight from her mom. It might make things easier.

She gazed into the pool, at the mysterious silver-blue water, and before she could stop herself she said, "Show me my mom."

She waited, uncertain what such a request might bring. If her mom was alive, as Callie had always secretly hoped, and just kidnapped someplace...

The waters remained still, smooth as glass.

There was nothing to show. The Pool of Arundel could only show you living people, or living creatures. And Ana Richards--former Princess of Albion, wife of Ben Richards and mom to Callie--was gone.

Callie cried quietly, the cold tears sliding down her cheek and dripping onto the leg of her jeans. But as she cried, she felt a presence nearby, watching from behind her, within the trees. How she knew that, she had no idea. There had been no sound, no other indication.

Callie turned her head slowly.

A woman in a jewel-studded black gown stood under the tall, drooping trees. Her dark hair and eyes were so beautiful, they were almost painful to behold.

A whoosh went through Callie's stomach.

"*Mom*?" she whispered, but even as she did, she knew the woman before her was not her mother. She did not possess the same energy.

"Hello, Callie," the woman said, not refuting Callie's question, but not confirming it, either.

Callie's heart was racing and springing with hope. Maybe it *was* her mother, and there was just something wrong with her, like she was sick or something. But though Callie's heart hoped for such a thing, her gut told her otherwise. Whoever this woman was, she was *not* Callie's mom. And if she wasn't her mom, she could only be one other person--the woman from Callie's dream.

"The Raven Queen," she whispered.

Chapter Twelve

Secrets and Lies

With superb grace of movement, the woman walked across the grass toward Callie. A hint of a smile danced at the corner of her mouth. There was something coldly beautiful about her. Callie's mom had never been cold.

Callie's mind raced. She knew she was in danger, yet she couldn't leave. "How did you get here?" Callie asked.

"Is that how you greet your poor aunt, my dear?" the woman asked in a melodious voice. "I suppose you cannot be faulted. You were brought up in a strange land, and are unfamiliar with royal customs." She bent down and presented her cheek for a kiss, which she obviously expected Callie to give her. But Callie didn't make a move.

The Raven Queen straightened, took off her black gloves and flicked an eyebrow, looking slightly perturbed and amused at the same time. "So much like my sister, Ana. She was stubborn, too, you know."

Callie repeated her previous question. "How did you get here?"

"That is none of your concern. But I have risked much to be here."

"If it's so dangerous, then why have you come?" Callie asked.

The Raven Queen smiled. "To see you, of course. Can't a loving aunt wish to see her sister's only child?"

Though the Raven Queen had not threatened her in any way, Callie couldn't shake a feeling of foreboding that now swirled around her.

The Raven Queen sat down on the stone bench and patted the seat next to her. "Come and join me. I won't bite." Her smile, her face was so beautiful, it was hard to believe that this woman could be dangerous. Maybe the stories about her weren't true after all....

Yet Callie remained where she stood.

The Raven Queen gave a resigned smile, and decided not to press the issue. "Let me get to the point-- the reason for my visit. I wish to help you, Callie. You're being used as a pawn in a terrible game my mother is playing. She hasn't told you everything, has she?"

Callie paused. "Everything? Like what?"

"Like the *real* reason your mother left Albion?"

Callie tried to calm her beating heart as the Raven Queen continued, "Ana was miserable here. She was tired of being used. So was I. Ultimately, it is why we both left."

"Used?"

The Raven Queen nodded sadly. "Yes. My mother was using Ana to try to increase her own powers. The queen's powers have been fading for some time." She looked around, as if someone might overhear. "In fact, she has almost none left. That is why Ana had to leave-- Mother was trying to steal Ana's powers for herself. She would do the same with me if she could, and she will do the same with you. Since you have arrived, hasn't she been pushing you to learn how to use them?"

Callie thought about the upcoming lesson with Dr. Monsoon. Though Queen Arabella had originally assured Callie she would know how to use her powers when the time came, she *had* been pushing the issue.

"You must forgive me, but I did overhear some of your conversation with her--about your father?" The Raven Queen looked very concerned. "Personally, I think it's *horrible* that your father wants to re-marry. Has he forgotten Ana so quickly? I assure you, she would not have forgotten him so soon, nor would she want to marry another. *He* was the love of her life, and if she was the true love of his, he would not even consider taking another woman as his wife."

Her voice became filled with emotion. "Six months ago, my husband, King Gregor, died, and I can assure you, I will *never* marry another. My heart is his forever. What my mother told you is *wrong*."

Callie's stomach knotted in confusion. This was the Raven Queen--the woman who everyone said was evil--but she understood what Callie was feeling.

The Raven Queen held out a hand. "My dear, please let me take you away from this place. You remind me of my dearest Ana. Your spirit is so much like hers. I miss her terribly, just as I know you do. Perhaps the two of us could find comfort in each other's presence, if you came to live with me?"

Callie felt something twinge in her heart. The more she looked at the woman before her, holding out her arms, the more she saw the woman's resemblance to her mother. Callie imagined looking into that familiar face each day, sharing meals with her, just as she had with her mom, laughing and giggling together about silly things, seeking her guidance, the soft warmth of her arms hugging her when she was sad...

Callie felt as if she were floating in a dream. *"Mom...is it really you?"*

"Yes, Callie. It's really me," the melodious voice answered.

Callie's heart filled with warmth as she moved toward her mother's open arms.

Then a booming voice said, *"Stop right there! In the name of King Eldric, I command you to stop!"*

Callie covered her ears in pain. The voice kept shouting and echoing in her head, like a deafening gong. *"By the powers of the Ixion Stars, and the Breath of Erebus, I command you to release her, Miranda!"*

Callie heard a scream--but it wasn't coming from her, even though she felt herself hit the ground with a thud. She tried to get up, but she was so dizzy. She managed to lift her head....

A short, white-haired man with gold spectacles appeared on the lawn. He was still shouting strange words and commands as he waved his arms about in front of him, battling the Raven Queen.

A cloud of swirling green smoke surrounded them as they both hurled their magic at each other. The Raven Queen's face, which before had looked so beautiful and so much like Callie's mother's, was now dark and twisted by an evil snarl. Her eyes glowed with an unearthly, cold light.

She hissed, *"You think you can defeat me, old man? You always were so predictable. Make no mistake, you have won this battle, but I shall win the war. Tell my mother I'm coming to take the Enchanted Throne of Albion, and there is nothing she can do to stop me."* She glanced down at Callie who remained where she'd fallen. *"Not even she can save you!"*

The Raven Queen's frightening gaze pierced Callie's and her mouth curled into a malicious grin. Callie shrank back.

The Raven Queen frowned hideously. *"And by the way, your friend Wanda says hello."*

With that she disappeared.

Callie stayed where she was, panting, her heart thudding against her ribs like a sledgehammer.

The white haired man dusted off his jacket, adjusted his spectacles, picked up his brown leather satchel briefcase, and helped Callie to her feet. Then he unceremoniously introduced himself. "Dr. Pericles Monsoon, Your Highness." He consulted his timepiece. "And you're late."

With that he turned and started off toward the palace. "Come on, come on, not a moment to waste, as that dreadful episode should demonstrate. Watch your footing there, that's right, a clipping pace now, if you please. I did not come all the way from the Marpesian Mountains to have my time wasted fetching truant students. And though I am the Queen's third cousin, I am above all an educator, Your Highness, and from my students I insist upon punctuality, enthusiasm, stick-to-itiveness, and poems written in my honor." He glanced down at Callie as she tried to keep up. "I am, of course, *jesting* about the last part. However, if you are so moved to compose a verse or two about me, by all means, do so."

"Dr. Monsoon--" Callie said. "What just happened?"

"Well, that is obvious, is it not? Miranda, my former pupil and the Raven Queen herself, was attempting to work a Dark Enchantment upon you. She was making you see what she wanted you to see--that she is the mother with whom you yearn to be reunited. I daresay we were close to losing you, except for the fact that your powers were obviously too much for her."

"What powers? I haven't learned how to use them. They don't work yet," Callie explained, confused.

Pericles glanced down at her. "Nonsense! I have no use for a defeatist attitude, young lady, princess or not. Your powers have been within you since the day you were born, humming in your blood like a tune. As you can see, they protected you from Miranda's Dark Magic. It's what prevented her from just snatching you away, I suppose. She hasn't got the power. She tried to enchant you, because it would have been the only way. Once in her clutches, I have no doubt what she would do with you."

"What?" Callie wasn't sure she wanted to know.

"Though she lusts after the Enchanted Throne, and you stand in the way at the moment, there is another reason she would want to capture you. No doubt, she will want to steal your powers for her own."

Callie was stunned. "That's what she said about Queen Arabella! That my grandmother wanted to steal my powers because hers are fading."

Pericles shook his head. "Ridiculous! I have known Arabella for centuries. She would never do such a thing, least of all to her own granddaughter. It is Miranda who thirsts for power--a thirst that is seemingly unquenchable."

Callie thought back to the Raven Queen's melodious, spellbinding voice. It was shocking how easily she had made Callie believe in her lies, but that was what the Raven Queen did best, she supposed.

No wonder the people of Albion were so afraid of the Raven Queen seizing the Enchanted Throne. If she did, it wouldn't take long before the Albian people were enslaved, like the people of Tor-Enrith.

"Oh my gosh--Wanda!" Callie exclaimed.

"Who?" Pericles said, bustling them toward the hedgerow maze and looking at his timepiece again. "Drat. We have lost more than five minutes of our lesson already."

"Wanda Morris. One of my classmates. She followed me and Lewis--"

"Lewis and *me*," Pericles corrected.

"*Lewis and me*, through the tunnel from our world into Albion. We thought she'd gone back home. But the Raven Queen said--"

Pericles held up his hand to signal Callie to stop talking. You simply didn't argue with a man like Dr. Pericles Monsoon. "I wouldn't hold my breath," he said. "If your friend is with the Raven Queen--"

"We can use the Pool of Arundel," Callie said, dragging Pericles back toward it, though he tried to protest. This time it was Callie's turn to insist. "And she's not my friend. She hates me."

Pericles continued, "Whoever she is, if she is with the Raven Queen, I daresay the girl is under her spell."

They reached the Pool. "Show me Wanda Morris!"

The sliver-blue water *whooshed*, and there was the image of Wanda, trying on jewelry. The Raven Queen stood beside her, a hand on Wanda's shoulder. Then the Raven Queen turned her head and looked directly at Callie, as if she knew she was watching.

The sight gave Callie a chill. "We have to save her."

"That is quite impossible at the moment, I'm afraid," Pericles pronounced, ushering them back toward the palace. "You must put it from your mind, and concentrate on developing your powers. That may be your best hope. Don't forget, Wanda may be working together with the Raven Queen. As you say, she is not a friend."

Callie grimaced. It would be just like Wanda to join forces with an evil queen.

"Tell me," Pericles asked, changing the subject, "have you read my book, *Magic—Don't Be Afraid to Use It*?"

"It was on my reading list, but it was checked out of the library."

"Oh. Well, it is quite popular. Don't worry, I never go anywhere without a copy. That and the companion volume, *Flexing Your Magical Muscles--741 of the Most Popular Exercises*. Just came out, and it's already #1 on the *Albion Times* Bestseller List." He smiled proudly, taking the books out of his satchel and handing them to Callie. They were so heavy, she nearly dropped them.

As she struggled up the back steps of the palace behind her new teacher, Callie tried to calm her fears-- about Wanda, about the Raven Queen, and about her own future, both here and back home.

Chapter Thirteen

The Uruk Daahl

Wanda watched the capital city of Taleisin pass by as Queen Miranda's carriage rolled through the streets. She admired the old stone buildings with their arches and towers, the round puff-ball trees, the cobblestone streets, stone bridges and statuary. But the thing she liked the most was looking down her nose at the people of Taleisin and Tor-Enrith. It was something Queen Miranda encouraged. Now that Wanda was going to be the queen's daughter, it was her right to demand respect from all the less important people in the world. And that meant everyone except *them.*

Wanda raised her hand and did the "royal wave," like she'd seen the Queen of England do on TV once. She frowned. The people on the street didn't even notice. In fact, they all seemed to be staring into space like zombies. It was hard to flaunt your superiority over people when they were too stunned to notice. All the servants at the castle had been the same way, too--as if they were in a trance.

The queen had even given Wanda her very own serving girl, Dorie, and it was Dorie's job to wait on Wanda and do whatever she said. Dorie looked to be no more than twelve, the same age as Wanda. Wanda greatly enjoyed ordering Dorie around, asking her to do stupid, useless tasks just to see if she would.

"Count the stones in the wall, Dorie."

Dorie did.

"Turn the page of this book for me."

Dorie did.

"Do a somersault."

Dorie did.

Wanda never said please or thank you. She didn't have to. Queen Miranda had told her so.

Dorie always did as she was told and never complained about her treatment, which in Wanda's opinion took some of the fun out of ordering her around. Dorie acted like a zombie most of the time. She had never once spoken out loud.

To prepare for her first trip into town with Queen Miranda, Wanda had ordered Dorie to arrange her hair and help her change into a wine-colored gown with a few ruby necklaces and the ruby tiara on her head.

She looked like a princess.

She was going to be a princess. A better princess than Callie Richards...Queen Miranda had promised.

Wanda gazed at the Queen sitting beside her--the woman who was going to become her mother--and marveled at her beauty. Her real mom back home hadn't been as pretty as the queen. It was nice to have a pretty mom.

They rolled to a stop in front of a monument in the center of the city. "Behold, the Uruk-Daahl," Queen Miranda said, gesturing grandly toward the towering statue that reached toward the clouds like a hand.

It was made of shiny black stone--onyx, like the throne of Tor-Enrith--the queen explained. As Wanda and Queen Miranda looked on, thousands of slaves pulled on ropes, moving heavy stones into place. They too, seemed in a daze. They moved slowly, obediently, as if responding to silent orders that were being beamed at them. Huge scaffolding surrounded the monument. Workers chiseled strange writings and carvings into the stone. Aside from the sound of the work itself, the scene was eerily quiet.

"What is this thing?" Wanda asked, intrigued.

The queen's eyes shone with proud anticipation. "It is a device."

"What does it do?" Wanda asked, trying to control her impatience. *Sometimes Queen Miranda could be so cryptic...*

"It creates energy," she answered. "Transforms it into a power of unstoppable proportions. It is a tool of the ancient world. Legend says that the Ancient Kings of Albion first crafted it, but it was so powerful, it destroyed them. The secrets of the Uruk-Daahl itself were destroyed with them. Until now."

"How did you figure out how to build it?" Wanda asked.

"My ravens found lost ruins deep in the Forest of Theron, where ancient carvings revealed the instructions. Wars have been fought over it, you know. It would be a tragedy if such a powerful device fell into the *wrong hands*." The queen smiled. "I thank the gods it was my ravens who discovered the ruins. If Albion had gotten hold of such a thing...it does not bear thinking about, for they, themselves, are acquainted with the principles of its energy source."

Queen Miranda chuckled mirthlessly. "When I was a girl, all the royal children of the palace, were forced to study very dull subjects. Little did I know--little did *any* of us know--that two of those subjects would hold the key to the Uruk-Daahl's power: Quantum-Sorak Physics and Lyaxion Relativity." She glanced down at Wanda, looking amused. "The textbooks were enough to induce sleep, but I'm glad I kept my copies."

Wanda grinned. She liked when the queen shared little stories with her. "How long until it's completed?"

"Only a few months, I expect. When the Uruk-Daahl is ready to use, my powers shall increase a thousand-fold. No one in any of our worlds will be able to match it, and I shall rule triumphant. *We* shall rule, my dear."

Wanda smiled. She liked the sound of that. The queen had already explained Wanda's role to her--how she needed Wanda to be a bridge to the Land of Ur, in case anything happened and Callie Richards somehow made her way back there before the Raven Queen had captured her. Wanda would act as the queen's special agent, her eyes and ears in the other world. If Queen Miranda went into the Land of Ur, she would lose her magical powers--possibly forever. Her sister, Callie's mother Ana, had lost hers. She simply could not risk such a thing.

Queen Miranda continued, "But simply the building of such a device will not make it operational. According to the ancient kings, there are two missing ingredients that the Uruk-Daahl requires in order to unleash its power."

"What are those?" Wanda asked, excitedly.

Queen Miranda eyed her. "There is an ancient stone, a stone of magical powers beyond any we have known in this world. It is called The Cyn-Dorjan, the Dark Warrior. The origin is unknown. The ancient kings had found it, and one of them reportedly buried it in the hidden city of Antheon, which is where my ravens found it, in the ruins. We shall take the Cyn-Dorjan and place it atop the Uruk-Daahl. Then we need only the second item that the ancient kings describe: *the blood of your greatest enemy.*"

"Callie Richards," Wanda answered.

"Yes. Callie Richards." Queen Miranda gave a self-satisfied smile. "I was close to getting that today. If it hadn't been for that interfering fool, Dr. Pericles Monsoon, I would have. But it is a minor setback. She has many weaknesses, which we can exploit in the future."

Wanda smiled. She and Queen Miranda were two of a kind. They didn't let minor disappointments get in the way of their goals. They always had a contingency plan. Wanda had learned long ago that achieving success was really just a numbers game. It was the people who never gave up who would win, the people who kept their eye on the ball, who kept going no matter what the odds, the people who had already worked out plan A, B, C, D, E and F. Maybe even G.

People like her and Queen Miranda.

"And I have other ideas for Princess Callie."

"Like what?" Wanda asked, her heart beating faster with excitement.

The Raven Queen spoke with a dreamy expression on her face. "The ancient kings speak in their scrolls of a secret ritual involving a sacrifice to a Fire God of the Old World--Ethnor. His home is in the Cave of Eos, deep in the Forest of Dead Souls in my homeland of Albion. The sacrifice of which I speak is part of the Dark Magic.

189

It was outlawed by the ancient kings thousands of years ago, for one of their members had learned its secrets and wanted to use it to increase his own power. He was imprisoned by the others, by means of a powerful spell. Legend says that his soul is still held captive in an enchanted vessel, buried somewhere deep in the Lost City of Antheon."

She continued, "Ethnor is an ancient Fire God. There are stories of an ancient ritual in which a sacrifice to Ethnor will result in a transfer of power from the victim to the officiator. This is how I will steal Calandria's power and take it for my own. But before I do that, I'll make her bleed a little. I'll save her precious blood in a vial to use with the Uruk-Daahl. It is a perfect plan, don't you think?

Wanda's heart warmed at the prospect. That was one more thing she and the Raven Queen saw eye-to-eye on: they both wanted to see Callie Richards bleed.

oOo

Callie Richards was an ordinary girl, at least as ordinary as a girl trying to learn how to be a magical princess could be.

She batted at her hair as it fell into her face for the umpteenth time, then she took a deep breath.

"Now, *focus*, Your Highness," Pericles coached in his customary brusque voice. "Focus your energy on the target. Try to touch it with your mind." He adjusted his gold-rimmed spectacles and indicated Callie's target.

"Excuse me?" Lewis said from where he was seated across the room. "Since when did I become an *it*?"

Dr. Monsoon smiled apologetically. "My apologies, Mr. Farnsworth." He regarded Callie. "Please try again to move Mr. Farnsworth with your mind."

Lewis rolled his eyes. "Just watch the face, okay?"

Callie balled up her fists in determination. Then she stared at Lewis, and tried to lift him into the air.

He blinked back at her with an expression that said-- *Well? I'm waiting...*

She tried again.

The only result was the sound that emanated from between her grinding teeth.

Dr. Monsoon rolled up his sleeves. "Here--watch me." He took a deep breath and stared calmly at Lewis. A few seconds later, Lewis floated up gently into the air, to hang there about three feet above the chair.

"Whoa!" Lewis exclaimed. "That is *so* awesome. Cal, you gotta try it! I know you can do it."

Dr. Monsoon set Lewis back down in the chair as lightly as a feather, then asked, "Are you always this disruptive in class?"

"Pretty much," Lewis answered, smiling. "Bring it on, Cal!"

Callie took a deep breath. She focused. She tried. And tried. And tried so much she was getting a headache.

Pericles patted her shoulder. He knew his student was getting frustrated. "Like this--watch me, again." He pointed toward Lewis, lifted him into the air, and slowly turned him upside down. Lewis laughed with boyish glee. "Ha! Waaayy cool. You look funny upside down. What else can you do, Dr. Monsoon?"

Pericles waved his hand about, and Lewis turned slowly around like a wheel. Though Lewis seemed to be loving it, Dr. Monsoon said, "I don't want to make you dizzy, Mr. Farnsworth."

"No problem, dude! I'm cool."

Dr. Monsoon set him down again.

Callie rolled up her sleeves. She stuck her tongue out of the corner of her mouth (a sure sign that she was concentrating). Nothing worked. Nothing.

Callie felt her eyes begin to water as angry tears came to the surface. She didn't want to look stupid in front of her teacher, and she didn't want to look stupid in front of Lewis, either. She spent way too much time doing that back home. Knowing Lewis, *he'd* be able to learn how to move objects with his mind before she did--no matter that he wasn't magical!

"My dear," Dr. Monsoon asked, "Have you been doing your exercises? Magical muscles must be properly warmed up and toned before they can be of any use." He checked his notes. "I gave you *Chapter One--Tuning and Toning for the Novice*?"

Callie nodded. She had tried to do the exercises last night, but they were hard, and she hadn't really been able to complete them all. Lewis had tried to help her, but he was just as stumped as she was by some of the instructions, which were full of terms neither of them could understand. They had spent half the night looking up strange words in Rothman's Royal Dictionary.

According to Dr. Monsoon's exercise book, by the end of Chapter One, Callie should have been able to move objects with her mind, see through objects, and read people's thoughts.

So far, she was 'zero' for three.

Forget zapping people with lightning bolts!

"Now, try again," Pericles commanded. "This time, *concentrate*."

"I *am* concentrating," Callie said, starting to feel her temper rise.

"No, you are *not*," Pericles said, whipping off his spectacles in exasperation. "You are making excuses, and you are refusing to apply yourself! I have given you the simplest of exercises, Your Highness, but you have failed to complete them as instructed. If you are content to fail at such a serious task..."

"*I'm trying*," Callie said.

"You are *not* trying."

"Uh...hold on there, Dr. Monsoon—" Lewis interjected, standing.

"Mr. Farnsworth, forgive me, but this is a matter of National Security. The Princess *must* learn how to use her magical powers or our entire nation is doomed, do you understand that? *Trying* is not good enough, Your Highness. *Trying* is not going to save peoples' lives," Pericles said with all the warmth of a Major General.

Callie tried to calm herself, but she couldn't keep quiet. "Do you know what I've been going through the past couple of weeks? *Do you?* I've had riding lessons and dancing lessons, lessons on royal fork usage and proper princess footwear! I've had my hair curled and uncurled, braided and bunned. My head hurts from trying on tiaras! I'm up all night reading books on Ancient Albion History that weigh more than I do! I'm trying so hard, and all you have to say is that it's *not good enough?* Well I'm sorry, Dr. Monsoon, but it's going to have to be."

Pericles made a reply, but as Callie's insides churned with anger, her instructor's voice began to fade. "...would have expected more from you, a royal princess...greatly disappointed in your abilities, as well as your attitude...don't know how I will explain this to the Queen...."

Callie closed her eyes. She was so upset, she didn't know what to do.

Just then, the top of her head began to feel lighter, somehow. In fact, all of her felt lighter, like she weighed no more than a feather. Her blood began to pump faster and faster, she felt something whoosh through her, and it felt good!

She opened her eyes.

Then she blinked a couple of times.

"Dr. Monsoon," Callie asked. "What are you doing up there?"

Pericles Monsoon was floating near the ceiling with a bemused expression on his face. He was upside down. "I wanted to ask you the same thing, Your Highness, for it is *you* who put me here."

"Me?" Callie said, astonished, looking at Lewis. She hadn't done that...had she?

Lewis waved his fist in victory. "Yeah! That's what I'm talkin' 'bout!"

"I didn't put myself up here, I assure you," Dr. Monsoon said pleasantly, crossing his arms where he floated. "Well done, Your Highness! Excellent progress."

Callie's heart leapt with hope. Lewis grabbed her hand and squeezed it in congratulations. She had picked up Dr. Pericles Monsoon and dangled him upside down from the ceiling! How cool was that?

"Now, if you would get me down?" Pericles asked.

"How do I do that?"

"You'll figure it out. While you are working on it, I shall hum a tune."

He began humming something very deep and jolly, which kept Callie relaxed as she focused on getting him down without breaking his neck.

Then he started to sing in a deep warm baritone:

"Oh, there once was a pretty little princess
Who captured a dragon's heart
The dragon, he was a strange one,
He couldn't see very far

He flew into walls and he flew into trees,
And he flew into mountain sides
He fell to the ground with a heavy thud
The day he almost died

But then, the pretty little princess
Came upon the dragon's lair
She found the sightless dragon
He didn't know she was fair

She nursed him and she fed him
She won the dragon's heart
Her love restored his sight
Now they sing about it near and far

Aaaaaaaaaaannnd,

They danced and they danced, forever and a day,
The dragon and the princess fair,
They married happy ever after
And lived life without a care."

Pericles repeated the chorus a couple of times so Callie and Lewis could join in, and they sang the old legend of the "Dragon and the Princess Fair" together.

Soon Callie had gotten her teacher down from the ceiling. The only problem was that when she'd let go, Pericles had fallen headfirst into a plant.

"I do apologize for the subterfuge earlier, Your Highness--and to you, Mr. Farnsworth," Dr. Monsoon said, brushing dirt from his sleeve. "My behavior was abominable, and though I am known for my no-nonsense nature, I would never seriously insult a student like that. I was merely using a technique I thought would be helpful for the Princess. I aroused her anger in order to redirect her focus, not on trying--but on *feeling* her own power. I think it worked marvelously."

"Me, too. Thanks, Dr. Monsoon!" Callie said. She had learned how to flex a muscle she'd never known she had. Like all good teachers, Dr. Pericles Monsoon had helped to find the power within herself, and apply it.

Lewis beamed at her with pride. "Magical powers beats my first place in the Science Fair, any day!"

Suddenly, the reality of it hit her like a wall. The reality of it...her powers...they were *real*. "I need to sit down."

Pericles beckoned to the gold brocade chair which slid across the room. He plunked Callie down in it, then checked her forehead with the back of his hand. "No fever. It is just the excitement of today's lesson, I expect. Queen Arabella will most certainly be--"

The Queen appeared behind them. "*What*, Pericles? You know I cannot abide when people assume to speak for me."

"*Pleased*, Your Majesty," Pericles said proudly.

If Callie didn't know better, she could have sworn there was a flirtatious twinkle in Pericles' eye as he gazed upon Queen Arabella's majestic face.

The queen's mouth curved slightly at the corner and she turned quickly, saying importantly, "Pleased about what, Pericles?"

Pericles stepped around her, so she had to look him in the eye. "About your granddaughter's progress, Your Majesty."

This got the queen's attention. "Her progress?"

Lewis couldn't contain himself. "She dangled Dr. Monsoon upside down from the ceiling. It was *awesome!*"

Queen Arabella laughed at Lewis' exuberance. "I wish I could have seen it." Then she said to Callie, "I am so proud of you my dear! Take it from me, Pericles Monsoon is not an easy man to 'dangle.'"

Callie laughed, and the rest joined in.

"Now I believe you have another lesson coming up with Lady Nutley on Princess Posture and Propriety," the queen said. "After that Lord Sterne will be instructing you on Royal Elocution, and after that, Ignatius wants to see you about Earle."

"Is Earle okay?" Callie asked, concerned.

The queen was non-committal. "He will explain it all to you. And now--"

The door flew open loudly.

Callie, Lewis, Dr. Monsoon, and Queen Arabella all turned to see who could possibly think to disturb the queen while she was having a private meeting.

Lord Graydon strode forcefully into the room, his tall brown boots hitting the marble floor with gusto. He looked like he had just come in from riding, which, they found out, he had.

"Graydon!" the queen exclaimed. "What do you mean by barging in without announcing yourself? Have you lost all sense of decorum?"

Lord Graydon's eyes were dark and serious as he whipped off his riding gloves and pulled out a roll of parchment. "We have no time for decorum, Your Majesty." He handed her the message. "She is coming."

Chapter Fourteen

The Raven Queen's Decree

Queen Arabella's mouth compressed into a line, and Callie thought her grandmother had gone a little pale. Arabella snatched the parchment from the Captain of the Guard, flung it open, and read aloud:

"To Her Royal Majesty, Arabella, Queen of Albion, from your Royal Daughter, Miranda, Queen of Tor-Enrith:

We know that Ana's daughter, Calandria, is with you. We greatly regret the souring of relations between our two lands, but We will not put aside Our claim to the Enchanted Throne. I, Miranda, am sole Heir to the Throne of Albion, and will not relinquish my Rightful Place upon it. We will not negotiate. If Calandria Richards is not delivered to our borders by sunrise tomorrow, Darkness shall fall upon the City of Arraband.

Miranda, Queen of Tor-Enrith"

Queen Arabella quickly rolled up the parchment. It looked like steam was going to come out of her ears. "*Ungrateful child!* Unrepentant fool of a queen! To think she was once my daughter...." She shook her head in confusion. "Now, I don't know what she is."

The queen's pale blue eyes blazed with anger, then grew dark with sorrow. "I held out hope that she would come to her senses. It was a false hope. Miranda has made her choice, and now, we all must live with it." She held up the parchment, and asked Lord Graydon, "Where did you get this?"

"My regiment was on patrol outside the city gates, Your Majesty. A raven swooped down over us and dropped it. I rode straight for the palace."

"What does that mean--'Darkness will fall upon the city of Arraband?'" Callie asked.

"Her army, I suppose," Lord Graydon answered. "As we speak, our forces are mobilizing. I've sent riders out to our regiments in the North, with orders to stop anything coming through The Pass in the Adarra Mountains, which is the only route to us. I'm calling in reinforcements from the outlands, as far as Ap-Cernach. We shall be ready for her, Your Majesty. We shall guard the Enchanted Throne, and the princess, with our lives."

Lord Graydon regarded her, his bright blue eyes serious. "You must be brave, now, Princess. Everything depends upon it. No matter what happens, promise me you will not give in."

Callie stared up at him, not knowing what to say.

Pericles put a comforting hand on her shoulder. "Listen to Lord Graydon, child. You must indeed be brave, for Albion needs you now, as never before. You are our only chance at defeating the Raven Queen."

"But I'm not ready. I need more time."

"There is no more time," Queen Arabella said. She clasped Callie's hands. "For any of us."

"But I don't know how to do everything yet." Callie looked to Pericles for help. "All I can do is dangle a person upside down! How is *that* going to help?"

"You must trust your powers," Pericles said soberly.

"But what do I do?" Callie pleaded. "Won't someone tell me? How do I fight her?"

"You will know. When the time is right," Pericles said, confidently.

Callie was stunned. This was all happening too fast. "Wait a minute. The note said Darkness would fall upon the city of Arraband if you didn't deliver me to her borders by sunrise. What if I volunteer to go?"

Queen Arabella stared at Callie, speechless. "Out of the question."

"But what will happen if we don't do what the Raven Queen wants? There's going to be a war because of me? I don't want that."

The queen shot her a thunderous look. "Being a princess is not about *what you want*. It is about doing what is right, no matter what the cost."

"Even if the cost is innocent lives?"

"Yes!" the queen shot back. "That is what you will be risking if you play into the Raven Queen's hands. Every citizen of Albion--man, woman and child--will become her slaves, for eternity! They will be worse than dead. That is what you will condemn our people to, Calandria, if you give up now, if you let her take the Enchanted Throne."

Callie felt suddenly tired and helpless, and she hated the feeling. It was the same feeling that had darkened her days after her mother's death.

"Majesty," Lord Graydon said, "I cannot spare another moment. I must ready the troops."

The queen gave a nod. "Go. And Graydon...be careful."

Lord Graydon looked down at Callie, his eyes resigned. He took her hand in his, closed his eyes and kissed it. "It is an honor to fight for you."

Callie's heart pounded as she watched Lord Graydon walk away, his long, confident strides full of purpose.

"Lewis," Callie said. "I need to talk to Lewis." Queen Arabella paused. "Yes. It will be best if you and your friend are kept out of the way and safe, during the preparations. Pericles, will you escort the Princess to the library? The boy seems to live there of late. Tell Sir Reginald to watch over them, and then return to me here. I have need of you."

Pericles bowed slightly. "Yes, Your Majesty." Then he stepped closer to the queen and whispered, "Arabella... it will be all right."

The queen drew in a breath. "Thank you, Perry."

She addressed her granddaughter, "Callie, listen to me. You must do as Pericles and Sir Reginald tell you. If something happens and we are separated, you will need to rely on them." She pulled Callie into her arms. "If anything should happen to you...I would never forgive myself!"

Callie gulped back her own tears. "It's okay, Gram. Don't cry. I'll be okay. I promise. I'm going to practice my powers some more. I'll be an expert by tomorrow morning, right, Dr. Monsoon?"

"I have no doubt," he replied.

The queen stepped back, once again the picture of regal purpose. "Now, run along. And Callie—"

She turned and looked back at her grandmother, the Queen of Albion.

"Never forget that you are a princess."

oOo

When Callie told Lewis about the upcoming battle, the first thing he said was, "Cool!"

Then she reminded him that this wasn't a video game and that real people might be hurt or even die, which quickly sobered him. "Sorry, Cal. It's just, I've never seen a real battle before." Along with being a science geek and a math whiz, Lewis was also a military history buff. He had books and books on the stuff back home.

After a brief conversation, Pericles and Sir Reginald decided the best course of action was for Lewis and Callie to remain in the library and carry on as normal. Pericles was part of the Queen's War Council and was needed in the war room. Though Callie had wanted to practice her powers, Pericles actually advised against it, saying too much exercise might tire her out. What she needed right now was rest and relaxation.

Yeah, right. The Raven Queen was coming, there was going to be a huge battle, and people Callie cared about were going to be in the thick of it. Not a real restful atmosphere.

While Lewis buried his face in another book, Callie tried some deep breathing exercises. They didn't work. She tried reading a book of poetry. That didn't work, either. She couldn't concentrate on anything--she was going stir crazy.

Then she remembered her grandmother had said earlier that Ignatius had wanted to see her about something to do with Earle. Now was as good a time as any. Since she had gotten Earle, Callie had tried to spend as much time with her fledgling dragon as she could, which, with all her royal duties, wasn't as much as she would have liked. But Callie found hanging out with Earle and just petting his warm scaly head very soothing.

Sir Reginald only agreed to let her go to the Royal Dragon stables if she took four palace guards with her. A short time later, she was walking down the wide center aisle between the dragon paddocks. One beast eyed her curiously through the bars, another ignored her, another was busy chewing a dragon toy the size of a car.

She rounded the corner to see Ignatius with his visor down, doing some dentistry work on a forlorn-looking Northern Waxwing named Aegides.

Sensing someone was about, Ignatius ducked his head out of the dragon's mouth and lifted his visor. His big face brightened immediately when he saw Callie standing there. "Hello, Princess." He patted the dragon's scaly nose. "Come to see old Aegides get her cavity filled?"

Aegides blinked at Callie and gave a sad bellow.

Callie patted the dragon's nose, too. "It's okay, girl. Nobody likes going to the dentist. Trust me."

That seemed to make the dragon feel better.

Ignatius took off his gloves and helmet and ran his fingers through his graying dark hair. He led her toward Earle's stall, looking serious. "Glad you came down, Princess. There's something I need to talk to you about."

Callie's heart did a nosedive. "Is Earle okay? He's not sick, is he?"

"No. He's not sick. But there is something wrong with him, I'm afraid."

Anxiety rushed through Callie. She couldn't handle this today. Not with everything else going on...

Ignatius opened the barred door of Earle's pen, but he stopped Callie from going in. Earle sensed immediately that she was nearby. His head popped up and he jumped around excitedly, like an uncoordinated moose with wings.

"Call him," Ignatius said.

"Here, Earle!" Callie called. "Here, boy!"

Earle's head spun quickly toward her voice and he flopped around, trying to get out of the way of his own feet as he bounded toward the gate. It was amazing how quickly he picked up speed as he charged toward them. Then--SMACK--he hit the bars next to the gate head-on and fell back on his rear end.

"Earle!" Callie cried.

The young dragon seemed momentarily stunned, shaking his head quickly as if to clear it. Then, he got up again and headed for the gate. He bashed into the other side of it and fell back with a great thud. He stayed down a moment or two longer this time before getting up and standing, wobbly, in one spot.

Then it hit Callie. "Is he...*blind?*"

"Almost," Ignatius said seriously. "He can see a bit. But for a dragon, his sight is greatly impaired."

Callie tried to digest what Ignatius was saying about the creature that stood shakily in the pen, vulnerable and alone.

"That's not all, I'm afraid. Earle isn't growing at the rate he should be. He is small for his age, and by my calculations, he will never reach the full-grown size of a normal Great-Crested Ceylx."

Callie stared at the fledgling dragon before her. "But he's huge! He's the size of a moose already!"

"I have no idea what a moose is, Your Highness, but by now Earle should be almost twice the size he is." Ignatius looked down at Callie. "I know you have grown attached to him in a short time, but I'm afraid Earle is just not Royal Dragon material. Without sight, he won't be able to protect you, let alone himself, against attackers. Can you imagine him fighting one or more full grown dragons? It would be grossly unfair. He wouldn't stand a chance."

Earle looked over at Callie and bellowed, "Eehhhhhrl!"

She laughed, but there were tears in her eyes. Earle sprang up and looked in the direction of her voice. She saw now that he couldn't see her, but his big yellow eyes were bright and full of excitement. He jumped around, hit his head on the ceiling of his stall, then plopped back down and shook himself to get his bearings.

"What will happen to him?" Callie asked.

"He'll live out his days here, of course, with the other dragons. It is the kindest thing to do, Your Highness, given Earle's physical limitations."

Callie bit her lip. This was so unfair.

Ignatius continued, "I expect Aegides to be laying eggs within a few months. I'm sure you will find another one that will suit you."

Callie didn't want another one. She wanted *Earle*. "Can I have a moment alone with him?"

"Of course," Ignatius said, stepping back to give Callie some privacy with her fledgling dragon.

Callie stepped into the pen. "Hey, Earle."

Earle turned his head and sprang up, flying in a spastic zigzag pattern before hitting the wall and skidding sideways on the dirt-covered ground.

"Come here, baby," Callie said. After his initial excitement, the sound of her voice calmed him, and he managed to make his way over to her without bumping into anything. She sat on the floor, stroking the warm, lavender-hued scales on his head as he settled down next to her. Earle purred deep in his throat.

He watched Callie as she stroked him. His eyes were full of quiet devotion. It was unlike any she had ever experienced from any living creature.

Callie hummed softly, and realized it was the tune Pericles had been humming earlier. She started singing the words, about "Dragon and the Princess Fair." She sang the first few verses--then came to the fourth one:

> *"She nursed him and she fed him*
> *She won the dragon's heart*
> *Her love restored his sight*

207

Now they sing about it near and far,

And they danced and they danced, forever and a day..."

As Callie continued the chorus, a plan formed in her mind. It was a crazy plan, but then again, having a dragon for a pet was pretty crazy too, when you thought about it.

She looked into her dragon's eyes and whispered, "I'm not giving up on you, Earle. Nobody believes in you but me. And everyone believes in me *except* me. We're a strange pair, you and I. But I guess, sometimes you just have to take a leap of faith." She stood up and called Ignatius over to the pen, brushing the dirt off her jeans.

She stood at her full height (almost five feet) and emulated Queen Arabella, saying regally, "I thank you for your input regarding my dragon, Mr. Entwhistle, but I have made up my mind. Earle *will* be my Royal Dragon--physical limitations, or not."

Ignatius didn't seem too impressed. He looked like he was going to interrupt.

Callie put up a hand. "I'm not finished."

Ignatius raised his eyebrows.

Callie continued, "I believe that regardless of Earle's vision problems and his small size, there are other qualities he *does* have which cannot be ignored. I believe, Mr. Entwhistle, that he has something more important than either of those other things put together: *potential.*"

Ignatuis' expression didn't change much, though he looked slightly intrigued.

"And furthermore," Callie continued, "I believe we can overcome Earle's limitations if we work together."

"How? He can't see, Your Highness."

"He *can* see, a little bit! You said so yourself. He just needs glasses."

"Glasses?" Ignatius said, flabbergasted. "A dragon with eyeglasses? I never heard of it!"

"Well, you just did," Callie said, very pleased with herself.

He didn't look convinced. "How will they stay on his head when he's flying around?"

Callie smiled smugly. She removed the elastic from of her hair, held it out and pulled on it a couple of times to demonstrate. "Like this."

She had seen people back home with glasses which had bands on the back of them. Why not for a dragon? Though it would have to be a long band.

Ignatius took the hair elastic and tested it, a new light of possibility in his eye. "You know...." He started searching around his work area, strewn with dental tools. "I could tie them on with this!" He held up a leather-like rope, but when he pulled on it, it sprang like a bungee cord. He looked down at Callie with admiration in his crinkled eyes. "This just might work, Princess."

"I *know* it'll work," she said. "And we can do research on special food, to see if that makes him grow. A kid in my class, Wyatt Corkum, was small for his age, too, but he went to a special doctor and got some vitamins, and now he's as big as Lewis. Maybe Earle just needs vitamins." She paused. "*Big* vitamins."

She and Ignatius laughed over that, and started making plans for Earle's first pair of eyeglasses. As she watched Earle chewing on a toy in his pen, Callie hoped she'd be able to solve the other problems that faced her, and Albion, as successfully.

Chapter Fifteen

The Battle

When Callie awoke, it was still dark. Not that she had gotten much sleep, anyway. The palace had been noisy in preparation for the upcoming battle. The grounds were full of troops, some on horseback, others on foot. They practiced drills with their swords, and rode and marched in formation. Medical supplies were being brought to the palace. Part of the east wing was being set up as a hospital.

After a hasty breakfast with Lewis and Sir Reginald, they met with the queen.

Callie had never seen her grandmother look more resolute. She was dressed in a blue military jacket, decorated with medals. She wore black trousers and high brown boots like Lord Graydon's. A long, slim sword hung at her side. Callie had no doubt that the Queen knew how to use it.

"It is almost dawn," she said quietly. "Lord Graydon has sent word--his scouts have spotted the Raven Queen's army advancing just past the border. It won't be long before the battle begins."

Callie's blood chilled. Then she realized why. Besides the stress of the upcoming battle, she could *feel* the Raven Queen's army approaching, the thunder of boots pounding the ground as thousands of them marched closer and closer to the borders of Albion. Yet, something told her they were not the true threat.

Something else was coming.

Something no one could stop.

Darkness...

The queen touched Callie's chin. "What is it, my dear? You do not look yourself."

"I'm feeling a little dizzy," Callie said, putting a hand to her head.

"It is the coming battle, I expect," Queen Arabella said. "We all feel tense. It is normal."

Callie nodded, though she didn't think what she was feeling was the least bit normal. She only hoped the battle would be over soon and that everyone would be all right. Still, the possibility that she might have to face the Raven Queen today--and do battle against her--was incomprehensible.

Callie hoped it wouldn't come to that, for though everyone around her had faith in her abilities, Callie's belief in her powers was waning. She had tried to use them this morning to no avail. She couldn't even lift a rose like Pericles had done, let alone a full grown man. What would she do if the Raven Queen tried to zap her? She had no clue, but she hadn't told anyone about this morning's power blockage, not even Lewis. She didn't want them to know, not now, not when they needed to believe in her.

"What if it's a trick?" Callie said suddenly.

Everyone looked confused.

"Her army...what if it's a decoy?"

The queen exchanged a look with Sir Reginald. "A decoy...but my dear, Graydon's scouts have seen them. The army is, at this moment, marching toward us."

Callie tried to explain what her instincts were telling her. "I know, but I just can't shake this feeling...her army's going to get in here. There's going to be a battle *in here*." She looked around the palace.

"In here?" The queen said incredulously. "Graydon has regiments standing outside the city walls. Miranda's army will never advance this far. Sir Reginald?"

"I must agree with the queen, Your Highness," he said to Callie. "It is highly unlikely."

"Highly unlikely isn't impossible," Callie replied.

"Callie's right," Lewis offered. "In *Thompson's Guide to Medieval Warfare*--"

But the Queen cut him off. "Mr. Farnsworth, we have no time to debate such things. Sunrise is but an hour away. We must be in our places well before then."

Lewis said no more, but gave Callie a meaningful glance. Even in Albion, it seemed, adults often dismissed what young people said as irrelevant.

For their own safety, Callie and Lewis were relocated to Callie's room, under heavy guard. Sir Reginald brought them a strange and powerful telescope which had two viewfinders, so they could both look through it at once. The two friends were both glued to it now. In the distance, Callie could see the queen's army on the battlefield.

"They're moving into formation!" she said to Lewis. "I—I can see the Raven Queen's army. Oh my gosh...they're *huge*."

Lewis adjusted the focus. "Whoa, you're right, the Raven's Queen's guys *are* huge. They're twice the size of our guys, and our guys are big!"

Callie looked more closely at the Raven Queen's army, and felt her stomach lurch.

Towering soldiers in black armor marched swiftly, resolutely toward them. Other mounted soldiers stood at the ready, their dark steeds pawing hungrily at the ground. Spears stood straight at the warriors' sides. Dark flags adorned with the Raven Queen's standard billowed in the air.

Panic like she'd never known wedged in Callie's throat.

"They're advancing!"

Lewis and Callie watched, transfixed, as the two armies advanced at a steady, determined pace.

Lord Graydon, looking fierce on his dappled grey stallion, sword high above his head, gave the order to charge.

Callie trembled as she watched, a helpless spectator to the coming carnage....

Then, something strange happened.

A swirling, shifting shadow passed in front of the morning sun.

"The Darkness," Callie whispered.

"The *what?*" Lewis said.

Neither of them spoke, for they were unable to. They merely watched with open mouths as the sky turned black. But it wasn't darkness, Callie realized.

"Ravens," she said. "It's an army...of ravens."

She and Lewis watched helplessly as the Raven Queen's *real* army filled the air. Queen Arabella's army had been momentarily surprised, but Lord Graydon barked orders at his men, and they held their formation.

The Raven Queen's troops continued their advance, moving in perfect unison like robots...or zombies.

The ravens grew closer. Queen Arabella's army would be helpless against them. There were too many for the Royal Archers.

Then, the ravens swooped down, and darkness descended upon Albion's army. Callie screamed. The men tried to fight, but there were too many birds, attacking like screeching demons. Arrows shot through the air, striking down some, but more and more filled the air. The soldiers swung at the birds with their swords, but it was no use. The ravens kept coming and coming, like a screaming squall of destruction.

Toward Arraband. And the Royal Palace.

Seconds later, thousands of ravens smashed through the glass windows of the palace. They poured through Callie's bedroom window and filled the room, squawking and shrieking and spiraling.

"Callie!" Lewis yelled, trying to shield her with his body. She heard him cry out as the ravens pecked at him.

"Lewis!" They tore at her sleeve with their talons, and smacked chaotically into the walls. Wind from their fluttering wings blew Callie's hair about.

"The passageway!" Lewis said, dragging Callie to the far corner of the room. He hit the switch--a unicorn carving on the wall--and the door opened. Callie held on tight as Lewis hurled both of them through and whirled around to close the door on the sharp beaks of the ravens, finally shutting them out. Callie shivered at the ravens' demonic cries as they thrashed and pummeled on the other side.

"Come on," Lewis said, taking her hand. He grabbed a lantern from where it hung and shouted to the Porfirian Sweetbugs, *"If you know what's good for you, you'll give us light, now!"*

Instantly the tunnel was suffused with eerie blue light.

"Lewis...." Callie tried to catch her breath. "Did you see? The ravens...*the ravens!*"

"Yeah. I saw. Talk about crazy." He glanced at her. "Are you okay, Cal?"

She nodded, taking the lantern. "Yeah. Just bleeding a little. Thanks for protecting me, Lew. Are you okay?"

"Blasted birds pecked me a few times," he replied. "But I'll live. Come on."

Callie proceeded through the secret passageway. "Where are we?" she asked, not that she cared, as long as it was away from the ravens.

"I don't know. The library, maybe," Lewis answered. "I've sort of lost my bearings." They could hear the discordant screams like a powerful moaning wind just outside the passageway. It was unlike anything Callie or Lewis had ever experienced.

Then, all of a sudden, the sound vanished.

Callie and Lewis looked at each other in the dimly lit tunnel.

"What just happened?" she whispered.

Lewis didn't reply, but cocked his ear.

The silence was deafening.

He shook his head. "Sounds like it stopped."

They held onto each other for a few seconds and listened. Then...a moan...a human voice crying out for help.

They rushed down the passageway, searching frantically for a door.

"Help me!" a voice called from the other side of the wall.

"Is someone there?" another voice pleaded.

Other voices called out for people whose names Callie and Lewis didn't recognize.

"We're coming!" Lewis shouted.

"We'll help you!" Callie yelled, her heart racing. "There's got to be a door around here somewhere...Lewis?"

"I'm on it!" He ran his hands along the damp stone walls of the passageway.

"Help us..." a voice cried.

Callie's heart pounded with anxiety. She needed to get to her people. Now.

Lewis grunted as he struggled with something on the wall. Callie joined him, and they both pulled on a rusty lever that protruded out of the stone wall.

It finally gave way, and golden light suffused the tunnel.

Callie left the lantern where it was and reached for Lewis' hand. They walked toward the crack of light, and pushed the door open.

Callie had no idea where they were in the palace, and she doubted Lewis did, either, but all along the floor were the bodies of injured people, bleeding, struggling, begging for help.

Callie stifled a cry.

Lewis put his arm around her. "It'll be okay, Callie," he whispered. "We're going to help them."

They immediately began tending to the injured people as best they could. Others appeared who weren't as seriously injured, and they helped, too. A few dead ravens littered the floor, their glossy black feathers shiny in the morning light, their sharp beaks caked with blood. The rest of them--they'd been told by some of the injured--had simply flown away after their mission to attack the Royal City was completed.

A shiver went through Callie. "We have to find the queen."

Lewis nodded in agreement.

After being assured that the injured would be seen to, Callie and Lewis set off to find Queen Arabella. Each room they came to looked worse than the one before. Shattered glass covered the floor, doors had been broken off their hinges, tables and chairs were turned over. It looked as if a bomb had gone off.

Callie stopped in the doorway of the war room, or what *used* to be the war room. The windows were completely blown in. The draperies which had hung so grandly were in shreds. This room looked to be the hardest hit.

Fear coiled in Callie's stomach. Besides the obvious, she felt there was something terribly wrong here...

Then she saw them. Pericles kneeling on the floor, crouching over her grandmother's body.

"Gram!" Callie cried, rushing over, but Lewis and someone else, Sir Reginald perhaps, held her back. A cold, cold fear--white, icy, and dense--suffused Callie's body.

"Please...don't let her be dead," Callie whispered.

Chapter Sixteen

The Regent of Albion

Queen Arabella was in a coma.

She had been trapped under heavy debris, Dr. Monsoon explained, and had suffered several broken bones, as well as a serious head injury. They moved her to the hospital wing, which was still trying to recover from the attack, as well. The beds were full. People were lying on floors in hallways--every available space was being used. Pericles himself was on duty as a medical doctor and had his hands full.

The worst part of all was that even with her supposed powers, Callie was unable to help her beloved grandmother. As Pericles explained, Albian magic did not work that way--you could not use it to heal someone, nor could you prevent someone from dying.

Reports from the city were coming in; the damage had been extensive. Thousands of people had been injured. Some had been killed.

All because of Callie.

Lewis kept saying everything was going to be all right, but Callie was sick of hearing it. She couldn't bear to look at the people in pain on the floors of the palace, knowing that her presence alone had caused such carnage.

When they brought the wounded soldiers in from the battlefield, Callie's heart sank anew. Lord Graydon was among them. He was conscious, but in pain. His face would be permanently scarred, Pericles said--if he lived.

Callie sat beside him and wiped away a tear. She respected Lord Graydon so much. She was still trying to understand why this man had risked his life for her, a twelve-year old girl.

Lewis put a comforting hand on Callie's shoulder, then left her alone with the Captain of the Queen's Royal Guard.

"Lord Graydon?" she whispered.

At the sound of her voice, he opened his eyes. It looked like even *that* hurt. *"Princess..."* he rasped.

"I'm so sorry," Callie said.

"Didn't see them coming..." He tried to get up, seeming suddenly alarmed. *"The queen?"*

Callie stopped him. "No--you mustn't move, please! Dr. Monsoon gave strict orders." Her eyes filled up again. "The queen is hurt. She's unconscious. They don't know if she'll survive. And it's all my fault. What are we going to do?"

His eyes fluttered a bit as he whispered, *"Remember...what I told you. Remember..."* Then he slipped into unconsciousness.

Callie stared down at Lord Graydon's battle-scarred face.

Be brave...everything depends on it...don't give up...

It was hard to be brave at a time like this, harder than anything else she'd ever faced, besides her mother's death. Callie was far from home. Her grandmother and countless others--including Lord Graydon--had been injured while trying to protect her. Callie was feeling a lot of things right now: scared, shaky, and sick to her stomach. Brave wasn't on the list.

Sir Reginald approached and said gravely, "Your Highness, the Council--what remains of the Council--would like to see you in the Queen's Chambers."

Callie's stomach swirled. What did they want with her? To put her in the dungeon, perhaps? She almost hoped that they would. At least no one else would get hurt if she was locked away.

They proceeded down what had once been a grand hallway, now ravaged with the remnants of the Raven Queen's wrath. They didn't speak, but before they came to the door, Sir Reginald stopped Callie and whispered quickly, *"Don't ever forget--you are a Royal Princess of the House of Arraband. You bow to no one in that room."* He opened the door for her and gave her a meaningful look as she passed by. He followed her in and closed the door.

She stepped into the Queen's Chambers, and was greeted by serious stares from the Royal Council. Callie gulped. These were powerful, intimidating men and women, and none of them seemed to be impressed with recent events. Most of them stood, as the council table and many of the chairs had been damaged during the attack. Callie's heart brightened fleetingly when she saw a familiar face--her cousin, Roarke, the Duke of Kenryk--though the expression on his face was anything but warm.

"Thank you for joining us, Your Highness," said a white-haired man with a pointy white beard. Callie remembered being introduced to him once...Lord Radley. She hadn't liked him much then, either. His eyes were cold and he spoke in a nasal voice. "Now that the princess is here, let us proceed with our very pressing business--that of naming the Regent of Albion."

Callie felt her heart sink. There was going to be another battle in this room, and it was going to be over her....

Lord Radley read from a roll of parchment: "It is the Royal Law of Our Land that in the event of serious injury, incapacitation, or other circumstance which prevents our ruling sovereign from carrying out his or her Royal Duties, that a Regent shall be named and endorsed by the Royal Council, and shall rule in the sovereign's stead until that time whence the sovereign is declared fit and able to resume his or her Royal Duties."

He pulled off his spectacles. "Ladies and gentlemen of the Council, as you know, during this morning's attack, Her Royal Majesty, Queen Arabella, was injured, and has not regained consciousness. Doctors have reported the queen's condition as *very serious.*"

At those words, Callie felt a lump form in her throat.

"It is therefore the duty of the Royal Council to name a Regent, in accordance with our laws."

All of a sudden, Callie noticed Roarke looking very confident. The people around him were nodding to him and making congratulatory noises.

Lord Radley looked at Roarke. "As you all know, Roarke, Duke of Kenryk, is the queen's closest male heir, and has been the queen's choice as Regent for many years."

Roarke gave an appreciative nod.

"However..."

That one word changed the mood in a split second. It was as if someone had dropped a piano into the room. Callie looked at Roarke, her cousin, and saw him staring back at her, his eyes dark, giving away nothing.

Lord Radley continued, "However, late yesterday, the queen made an amendment to the document which I now hold in my hands. And I quote: '*I, Arabella of Albion, being of sound mind and body, appoint as my Regent, the Princess Calandria of the Royal House of Arraband. On this day, etc, etc...*'"

Callie was stunned. She looked around the room, at the cold, unhappy faces staring back at her. The duke's face seethed with controlled fury.

"Are you telling me," he said quietly, "that we are to be ruled by a twelve-year-old foreigner who knows nothing of our customs, let alone how to run a country?"

Callie felt herself bristle at the duke's obvious rudeness. "Hey...."

He pointed at her as he went on, "That this *child* is now to make decisions about government? She can't even use her powers yet! In fact, I doubt she even has any." He circled her, like a big, black raven. "I think she's a fraud, and as a member of the royal family and of this Council, I challenge her right to act as Regent of Albion."

There were audible gasps in the room. One of them had come from Callie herself. She had never been insulted in such a way before, especially by an adult.

Lord Radley gazed at her calmly. "Your rebuttal, Your Highness?" He folded his arms and waited, as if he didn't really expect her to make one.

225

Which really ticked Callie off.

She glanced at Sir Reginald who gave her a look that said, "You go, girl!"

Callie thought back to her school's debate team last term, how nervous she'd been, how she'd had to speak off the top of her head in response to the other team's arguments. Sometimes it was best to just start speaking and spewing out facts. So that's what Callie did.

"First of all, Duke, I *do* know a lot about your country's customs—probably more than you do."

At this, he scoffed.

Callie continued, "Have you read the entire twelve-volume set of *A Short History of Albion* by Sir Humperdinck Perkins? I have. Did you know that Prince Cadmus, the second-born son of King Eldric, was the inventor of the first Royal Albian Fork, whose design is still in use today? I did. And did you *also* know that after a fatal hairstyling mishap in the fourth century in which Queen Theophelia and her two daughters, Pythia and Sophronia, were accidentally killed, Spark-Tailed Teklins were banned from use as hair ornaments? I did. So don't tell me I don't know anything about your customs."

Her determination did not stop at that. "Second of all, last term we completed a unit on law and government, and I was first in my class. So I *do* know a bit about it."

The duke curled his lip. "It will take much more than knowing a few facts about Royal Fork Design and Hairstyling Law to convince the Council you would make a good Regent, dear girl."

"Oh yeah, I was just getting to that part. You know, the one about me not having magical powers?" Callie was just blowing smoke now, she had no idea if her powers were going to work or not, but she was on a roll and she wasn't going to stop. *"Just watch this."*

Callie concentrated.

Nothing happened.

The people started looking at each other restlessly.

Callie calmed her breathing and focused on her target.

Still nothing happened.

Finally the duke huffed. "You see? The girl has no magical powers. She is a fraud. I move that you strike the amendment from the Queen's Decree, and name *me*...."

He stopped talking just then. Probably because his feet were no longer touching the ground. He looked around fearfully as he was lifted into the air, as if by an invisible hand. Then he started to spin clockwise, like a wheel, faster and faster, until he was just a screaming blur.

"Hey, this is good practice for me, Reggie," Callie said to the man beside her. "What do you think, should I take him down now?"

The members of the Council stepped away fearfully as the Duke spun and spun, screaming the whole time.

Sir Reginald replied, "I think you've made your point, Your Highness, though I must admit, I am quite enjoying the show."

Callie stopped the spinning and plopped the duke down on the floor, not too hard, but not too gently, either. He struggled to his feet, batting away the people who tried to help him. He weaved and wobbled, unable to regain his balance, while Callie and Sir Reginald shared a laugh.

Callie decided to close by doing her best Sharon "Don't-Mess-With-Me-I'm-a-Lawyer," impression. "I'll cut to the chase, Duke. The queen named me as Regent, and you're just going to have to deal with it. If you don't like it, well, *I guess you could cry about it."*

The duke turned a strange shade of green. He put his hand up to his mouth and bolted from the room.

Callie quirked a brow. "Running away is also an option."

With the duke out of their hair, Callie, Sir Reginald, and the rest of the Council got down to business. Parchment had to be signed, seals had to be sealed, and lots of other official royal stuff had to be done. Callie was actually glad for it, because it kept her mind off the other problems at hand: the queen's and Lord Graydon's injuries foremost among them.

Callie had been made Regent of Albion, and Sir Reginald couldn't have looked more proud. He beamed down at her. "Bravo! *That* is how you take command, Your Highness--you *take* it. Excellent job."

It was kind of scary, but Callie knew she had to do this. She had no choice. The people of Albion were counting on her, and she wasn't going to let them down. She'd come here to do a job, and she was going to do it. For her grandmother, for the people of Albion, and most of all, for her mom.

They headed back to the hospital wing--Callie wanted to check on the queen and Lord Graydon. As they passed through what used to be a glassed corridor,

Callie experienced the strangest sensation. She turned and looked out the smashed window, as if someone or something had called to her.

"What is it, Your Highness?" Sir Reginald asked.

It quickly became apparent what Callie was staring at. A lone raven flew toward the empty corridor, heading straight for them. There was no time to take cover. Sir Reginald drew his sword and pushed Callie behind him. But the bird simply flew in, dropped a roll of parchment, then flew back out again.

Callie reached for it shakily, but Sir Reginald picked it up first.

"It's from her," Callie said. "The Raven Queen."

Sir Reginald eyed her and unrolled the parchment. He read it over, then regarded Callie with a grim expression. "So it is, Your Highness."

"Show me what it says."

Sir Reginald hesitated, but knowing he had no choice, handed it to his princess.

Callie read:

"To Her Royal Highness, the Princess Calandria, Acting Regent of Albion, From Your Royal Aunt, Miranda, Queen of Tor-Enrith

Be it known to you that this morning's events in the City of Arraband were but a warning only. If you wish to spare your people further suffering, you will present yourself to me at the Cave of Eos within the Forest of Dead Souls tomorrow at dawn. Otherwise, there will be more attacks upon Albion.

Miranda, Queen of Tor-Enrith"

Callie swallowed and gazed up at Sir Reginald. "How can she know I'm the Regent already? It just happened."

"I have no answer for you, Your Highness," Sir Reginald said. "But surely, you must not go."

"I think it might be the only way." She stopped and regarded Sir Reginald. "Can I count on your support, Reggie? Even if you don't like my decision?"

Sir Reginald removed his hat and held it to his chest. "I am with you, Your Highness. To the last moment, I am with you." Then he did something so touching it almost brought tears to Callie's eyes. He kissed the back of her hand.

"Thanks, Reggie. I'm going to need your help on this one. Big time."

oOo

That night, Sir Reginald helped Callie and Lewis as they prepared to leave the palace.

"It's pretty stupid that you have to sneak out of your own palace," Lewis said.

"Yeah, well, if anyone besides Reggie knew what I was up to, they wouldn't let me leave." Callie fastened another barrette in her hair.

Lewis rolled his eyes. "I don't know why you're fussing so much with your hair. We're going to meet an evil queen. What does it matter what your hair looks like?" He reached out to touch one of the sparkly barrettes and then yelled, "Ow! It bit me."

Then it snarled.

"They do that sometimes." Sir Reginald grinned. "You must be careful."

"What are they?" Lewis asked.

Callie had about four or five of the dangerous creatures in her hair. "They're Spark-Tailed Teklins," she replied. "They've been illegal for over eight-hundred years."

"Illegal? Why, what do they do?"

"Set things on fire."

"Like what?"

"People's heads."

Lewis gave her a funny look. "Is it wise to wear them in your hair, then?"

"Probably not, but they might come in handy, later. I read about them in *A Thousand and One Royal Hairstyles*, by Ephronia Trent." Callie fastened the last barrette and looked in the mirror. They *were* kind of pretty.... Then she returned to the task at hand. "Reggie, can I have the checklist?"

He handed it to her and she read aloud: "Sweetbug lantern?"

Lewis said, "Check."

"Map of the Forest of Dead Souls?"

"Check."

"Chewing Gum?"

Lewis looked up. "What do we need gum for?"

"It's very useful, trust me. Chewing Gum?"

Lewis hunted around. "Check."

"Spark-Tailed Teklins--definite check." She smiled at Sir Reginald. "Thanks for getting those for me, Reggie. I don't want to know *how* you got them, but thanks."

"Anything for the cause, Your Highness." He gave gallant bow.

She read the next item. "Talking Tiara?"

"Check!" the voices said in unison. Then they all started babbling about the "grand adventure" they were about to embark upon, and how exciting it was going to be to go on a field trip away from the palace.

"Why do we have to bring that thing?" Lewis asked. "The Raven Queen'll hear us coming a mile away."

"Because," the voices said in unison, *"we know the way to the Cave of Eos!"*

"Yes, young man," a little voice lectured, *"we were there many, many, years ago. Do you suppose it's changed much, Beryl?"*

"I don't know, Eustacia. It's been about six, seven hundred years. That's not very long."

Lewis rolled his eyes.

Callie took the tiara from him and asked it to try to keep its voices down. Then she said to Lewis, "Besides showing us the way to the Cave of Eos, it's supposed to protect the wearer from harm. Don't forget that. If something happens and you have to wear it, Lewis, don't be afraid of how silly you'll look with a tiara on your head, okay?"

"Things would have to get pretty bad before I wear a tiara," Lewis replied, placing it on Callie's head and being very careful not to disturb the Spark-Tailed Teklins.

"Famous last words," Sir Reginald said.

He walked Callie and Lewis over to the door to the secret passageway in the corner of Callie's room and regarded them both seriously. "If the queen ever finds out that I allowed the two of you to go into the Forest of Dead Souls to meet the Raven Queen, I daresay she'll hang me by my toes...and that's if she's in a good mood, which she won't be. But I must obey the Regent, as well as my Princess." He kissed Callie's hand and shook Lewis' outstretched one. "Good luck, both of you."

Callie gulped. It was really hitting her now, what she and Lewis were embarking upon. They had been so busy all night getting ready that she hadn't had time to worry about it, which she supposed had been a good thing. Now she was realizing that if things went badly, she might never see Sir Reginald, or Pericles, or the queen again. Or her dad, back home...

Yet, she had to do this.

The lives of the Albian people depended on it.

She forced herself to smile and gave a cheery wave. "Later, Reggie."

"*Later*, Princess," he replied, using the Ur slang she had taught him.

Callie and Lewis stepped into the secret passageway and closed the heavy door behind them.

"Sweetbugs, gimme light!" Lewis commanded.

The passageway stayed mired in darkness.

"I said, 'Sweetbugs, light this baby up!'"

Still nothing.

Lewis huffed. "O Wonderful, nice, intelligent and handsome Sweetbugs, would you be so kind as to illum—"

The lantern glowed blue. Even the Sweetbugs were getting tired of Lewis' over-the-top sweet talk, it seemed.

"Talk about *attitude*," he whispered to Callie, though he was sure the bugs had heard him.

They continued along the secret passageway, up, down, around; through tunnels and up stairways. They were supposed to eventually reach a door that would let them outside somewhere in the back garden.

Lewis pulled the map from his pocket and unfolded it. "I think it's this way."

"Are you sure?" a voice said from behind them.

Callie and Lewis both jumped and tried to run, but it was too late. Strong hands grabbed hold of them.

Callie's stomach twisted in fear as she looked up into cold blue eyes.

It was her cousin, the Duke of Kenryk.

Chapter Seventeen

The Forest of Dead Souls

Callie struggled against the duke's iron grip, as Lewis tried to get in a kick or two, but the duke was just too big, even for both of them put together.

She used her magic. The duke's feet lifted off the ground, but because they were all attached, the three of them flopped around in the tunnel like a beached sea creature. Callie ended up banging her head on the wall. She tried to use her powers to loosen the duke's grip, but it was hard to focus when your arm was being wrenched out of its socket. She tried to shake off the duke again, but all she managed to do was bash Lewis into the wall, and he gave out a painful grunt.

She didn't want to hurt Lewis!

"You're not going anywhere, young lady, except to the dungeon," the duke said coldly, regaining his balance. "You wanted to be Regent so badly? Then that is what you shall be. We shall lock you up for your own protection if need be. It's not like it hasn't happened before. And you shall stay here and do your duty, not go off on some fool-hardy expedition. *Come now, back you go.*"

"Let go of her!" Lewis yelled.

"Quiet, boy! I am not in the mood to thrash you, but I will."

Then it dawned on Callie. "You're the one who's been spying on us in here! It was *your* eyes I saw looking through the paintings."

The duke looked down at her smugly. "Yes, it was me. Keeping an eye on you, for your own good! Smart thing, too, or I wouldn't have gotten wind of your foolish plan to meet the Raven Queen on your own."

Callie struggled again, but it was impossible to break free. He was going to ruin everything!

"Foolish girl...without much of a brain in your head, it seems," the duke said condescendingly.

"Did he just call our princess foolish?" a tiny voice asked.

"Yes, he did, Beryl. And he insinuated that she didn't have a brain," another answered.

The duke looked around. "Who's there?"

"He is very ill-mannered," another voice added. *"I never liked him, Malcolm."*

"Nor did I, Georgina."

"Who the devil is it?" the duke thundered.

"Yoo-hoo! Up here," the voices said in unison. *"On her head."*

The Duke looked at the tiara that sat upon Callie's head.

It grinned at him, the spiked fringe growing wide like a shark's mouth. Then it opened, with fangs like knives, and roared.

The duke's face twisted into an expression of horror. "AAAAAAHHH!" He let go of Callie and Lewis and scrambled to get away from the snapping jaws that reached out to bite him.

"AAAAAAAHHHHH!!!" Callie screamed, too as the tiara snarled and snapped like an alligator on her head.

"*AAAAAAAAAAAAHHHH!*" the duke screamed anew--though this one was more high-pitched as the tiara took a bite out of his arm.

That was that. He turned and ran down the passageway, clutching at his arm and screaming in fright.

Callie and Lewis held onto each other, trying to catch their breath. They were afraid to move in case the tiara decided it was still hungry and took a bite out of them.

"*Well, good riddance to him, I say,*" a little voice said. It sounded like it was chewing something.

"*Yes. Dreadfully dry.*" This one was chewing, too. Then something spat out of the Tiara and landed on the floor. "*But what can you expect of the Kenrycks?*"

Callie didn't want to think about what the Tiara had spat out.

Another voice asked, "*Are you alright, Princess?*"

Callie and Lewis relaxed a little. It seemed the tiara had indeed only been trying to protect her. "Yes, I'm fine," she replied. "Thanks, guys."

"*Our pleasure!*" the voices said in unison.

Lewis let out a breath. "I see why you brought the tiara. Good thinking. Now let's get out of here!"

Callie agreed. Time was ticking away. They had to reach the Cave of Eos before sunrise or the Raven Queen would do something even worse to the people of Albion.

They followed the map and soon, they were climbing out of a marble statue's well-rounded posterior in the Royal Gardens. They snuck through the quiet streets of Arraband, and walked past the Grimstead Gate. The gargoyles, Terry and Kevin, were fast asleep and snoring like train engines.

"Some gargoyles they are," Lewis said. "Sleeping on the job."

"We don't have time to talk to them anyway," Callie said. "Come on, we have to walk faster!"

Their sneakers padded on the dirt road. It was the only sound in the still night, except for a few insects singing in the grass.

"Not far, now," Lewis said. He looked around. The moon was full, the air fresh and clean. "Hey, this reminds me of camping. Except for the crazy guy in the passageway, the crazy tiara, and the crazy lady we're going to meet."

"Oh, Lewis..." Callie muttered.

The closer they got to the Forest of Dead Souls, the more nervous she was getting. What if her powers didn't work when she met the Raven Queen? They hadn't worked very well in the tunnel against the duke. Was she out of juice? Or was she just blocked up because of nerves? She just hoped she got *unblocked* when the time came.

"Over here," Lewis said, pointing to the road sign that read *Forest of Dead Souls* and had an arrow pointing into a dark, silent forest. He lifted up the lantern and reached for Callie's hand. They each took a deep breath and entered.

Tall, spindly-branched trees towered over them like a latticed roof. The pale, blue light of the moon and the Sweetbug lantern cast a spooky light. They walked for awhile in silence, the only sound was the crunching of their feet on dead leaves.

"I wonder why they call it the Forest of Dead Souls?" Lewis said absently. Then he stopped. "Oh, no."

Several diaphanous beings appeared before them and grinned. *"Oh yeees!"*

Callie and Lewis screamed as a group of shrieking ghosts swirled around them and chased them down the path, further into the bowels of the woods.

"They call it the Forest of Dead Souls to make you run faster!" one of them cried maniacally.

Another one said, *"They call it the Forest of Dead Souls because that's what we are--dead!"*

Yet another breathed down Callie's neck, *"And your powers won't work on us, Princess. Neither will your tiara."* The tiara was snapping and snarling madly, but there was nothing to bite.

"We're already dead!" they sang. *"We're already dead! Dead, dead, dead--we're already dead!!!"*

The ghosts zoomed around madly, laughing and shouting things like, *"Run! Run! Run!"* and *"Here we come--we're going to get you! AAAHHHHH!!!"*

Callie and Lewis did run. They ran faster than any Olympic Gold Medalist to date.

"Hey, I know," one of the ghosts said. *"Let's play a game--Weeko!"*

"Yes! Yes! Weeko! We haven't had real Weeko balls for five hundred years!"

Callie and Lewis exchanged terrified looks and ran even faster, but it was no use. All of a sudden, they were flung high up in the air, and they were being used as balls in a game that greatly resembled tennis.

"Ow!" Callie squeaked as she was batted between two ghosts.

Lewis groaned, as a ghost sent him flying towards his Weeko partner.

"Yay! A doubles match!" the ghosts cried, batting Callie and Lewis to and fro between them and laughing like hyenas.

"Wait a minute!" Callie cried as she zoomed back and forth between two enthusiastic ghosts. "Wait a minute! *I said STOP!*"

The ghosts stopped; Lewis and Callie floated in mid-air.

"We don't have time to play Weeko!" Callie shouted. "We have to get to the Cave of Eos. I—I promised my grandmother I would do something. She's sick, and you're going to make me break my promise to her! We don't have much time. It's almost dawn. We have to go, *now!*"

"Well, why didn't you say so?" the ghosts said. Seconds later, the whole group of them--Callie and Lewis included--were whizzing through the forest at a breakneck speed.

"You didn't have to get all cranky about it," one of them said in Callie's ear.

"Yeah--we were just having a little fun," another one said.

"Excuse me, have you ever been used as a Weeko ball?" Lewis asked, dodging branches. "It's not fun."

"You want a little cheese with that whine, sonny?" one of them said to Lewis.

"Oh, brother," Lewis said, rolling his eyes. "Just get us there, okay?"

One of the ghosts put on an affected voice. *"Yes, milord. Anything else, milord...?"*

Lewis eyed the one directly behind him. A ghastly smell emanated from the ghost's mouth. "You didn't brush your teeth a whole lot when you were alive, did ya?"

The ghost screwed up its face and snarled.

"Hey, do you know anything about the Raven Queen?" Callie asked the ghost behind her as they shot through a grove of trees.

The ghost winced, then whispered in Callie's ear, *"We're afraid of her."*

"You're afraid? But you're ghosts. What can she do to you?"

"The Raven Queen is most powerful. She holds the Dark Magic, which has dominion even over the dead. We cannot help you."

The fear in the ghost's voice sent a chill through Callie's veins.

"What do I do?" Callie asked. "How do I defeat her?"

The ghost chewed her lip and shook her head.

"Please," Callie said. "Tell me."

"She has a weakness," the ghost whispered. *"You are powerful, too...She fears you...You must be what she is not. Hmmmmm...what she is not...."*

"What does that mean?" Callie asked desperately.

The ghost cried, *"We are here, we are here! The Raven Queen is near!"* The rest of the ghosts became agitated, darting around in zigzags and making low keening sounds. *"We must fly, fly, fly!"*

Like a swirling billow of smoke, the ghosts were gone.

Callie and Lewis dropped to the ground and looked up. They were completely unprepared for what they saw next: Wanda, hanging from her wrists high in a tree. The rope creaked across a branch as she kicked her legs and swung back and forth.

Callie cried out in horror, "Wanda!"

"Help me, please," she moaned. "Someone...."

Callie sprang to her feet. "We're coming!"

"We'll get you down," Lewis echoed. "Just stay calm, okay?"

Callie touched Lewis' arm. "I'm going to try to use my powers."

Focusing all of her energy on Wanda, Callie felt energy swell inside her, but nothing happened. She felt some kind of resistance. Then she noticed an eerie green glow surrounding Wanda.

"The Raven Queen must have put a spell around her or something," she whispered to Lewis. "If only I knew how to use my magic better. If only I'd had more time..."

"We'll just have to try to get her down the regular way."

Wanda moaned again, spinning slowly.

Callie and Lewis started up a narrow path that led to the outcropping where the massive tree stood. All of a sudden, the ground of the outcropping fell away beneath them. They tumbled straight down and landed with a *thunk*! onto a hard floor.

Callie rolled over as pain shot through her. "Lewis? Are you alright?"

Lewis moved next to her, groaning a little. "For the most part."

They looked around them. The Sweetbug lantern had fallen with them and now lay on its side. Lewis picked it up and shone it around. It quickly became apparent that they were in some sort of a...*cage*. It had been placed beneath the outcropping and covered over, like a bear trap. A door above slammed down, closing them in.

Lewis ran up to the bars. "Hey!" he shouted.

"Hay?" a snarky voice replied. "Hay is for horses...or didn't you know?"

Wanda Morris appeared in front of the bars, her arms folded, a smug expression on her face.

Callie blinked a couple of times. "Wanda, what are you doing here? Are you..."

"Okay?" Wanda asked. "Couldn't be better, now that you two have dropped in. *Right, Mom?*" She glanced behind her as the dark silhouette of a woman came into view. "They fell for it," she said to the woman. "Hook, line, and sinker. I told you they would. They're so gullible, it hardly makes it fun."

The woman stroked a gloved hand under Wanda's chin. "I know, my sweet. I feel a little disappointed, myself."

Callie took the lantern from Lewis' hand and approached the bars. "Queen Miranda...."

The soft blue light of the Sweetbugs did nothing to diminish the Raven Queen's beauty. Her skin was luminous, her eyes dark, liquid pools, her lips ruby red. She smiled. "Hello, Calandria."

Callie addressed her classmate. "Wanda, I don't know what she's done to you, but you have to listen to us. She's not your mom."

Wanda laughed. "Oh, yes, she is."

Lewis joined in. "No, she's not! Wanda, your mom lives back home. Her name is Marlene!"

Wanda's expression darkened. "*Marlene's* not my mother. *Miranda* is." She gazed up lovingly at the Raven Queen. "She's been a better mother to me than my real mom ever was."

"She's put a spell on you, don't you see?" Callie pleaded.

The Raven Queen stroked Wanda's hair. "Don't listen to her, dear. She's just jealous, because you're prettier than she is."

Lewis's head snapped back like someone had hit him. "Now you're talking crazy."

Wanda shot him a seething look. "I'm not under any spell, moron. I'm here of my own free will, got it? My mother is going to destroy you both, but before that, she's going to suck all the power out of Callie, and take it for her own. But first, she's going to make her bleed a little. You, too, before she finally kills you. And I'm going to watch every minute of it. So there!"

Callie took a step back.

Kill them? Then Callie remembered her powers. She was supposed to be even more powerful than the Raven Queen. She focused on her magic and got ready to use it. She sent a bolt of energy at the bars that held them captive. Too late, she saw the bolt bounce off a translucent green force-field and head straight back toward her. She dove for the ground and just missed getting hit.

When Callie looked up, the Raven Queen was laughing. So was Wanda.

"Those bars are made from the horns of unicorns. They hold a potent magic. And besides that, they're hexed," the Raven Queen explained. "Whatever you throw at them, they throw back at you." She chuckled to Wanda. "What did I tell you, my dear? She is as uncoordinated as a baby roolat! And *this* is what my mother sends to defeat me. It is an insult."

Callie raised her chin. "If it's such an insult, why do you have me behind bars? Because you're afraid?"

"Yeah," Lewis added, stepping closer to the bars. "You know, I'll bet underneath that pretty face, this queen is a real hag."

The Raven Queen frowned. "The time for jokes is over," she said.

"But I'm just getting started, Your Royal *Hagness*."

The Raven Queen pointed a finger at Lewis, and a bolt of green light sent him flying across the cell. He bounced off the bars like a rag doll and lay motionless on the cold floor.

"*Lewis!*" Callie screamed, dashing to her friend. He didn't move. Callie could feel the blood draining from her face as she stared down at him. She felt light-headed, scattered. If something happened to Lewis because of her....

Wanda and the Raven Queen were laughing. It was too much to bear. Anger and sadness swelled in her heart as Callie clutched Lewis's hand.

"I hope he wakes up," Wanda said, conspiratorially to the Raven Queen. "It won't be as much fun to throw him into the volcano if he's not awake."

Callie's blood halted in her veins.

Volcano?

The Raven Queen looked down at Lewis with mock concern. "Yes, it is true what my daughter says. The Cave of Eos would be known in your world as a volcano. At its center is a pit of liquid fire, which has brewed there from before the time of the ancient kings. Those in Albion turn away from its power--and the secrets of the Dark Magic." She smiled. "Your sacrifice will bring me much strength, Little One. Indeed, after you are given to Ethnor, the Fire God of Eos, I shall be more powerful than I ever dreamed."

Callie shot her a scathing look. "Keep dreaming."

The Raven Queen stepped back, dramatically. "Such brave words from one who is about to die." She and Wanda laughed again, as if Callie and Lewis were amusing exhibits at a zoo.

Callie tuned them out and looked down at Lewis. He was still unconscious. "Lewis, wake up! *I need you,*" she whispered.

He made no reply.

The Raven Queen called out, "Argus! Boldiszar! Daemon! Talos!" Four mammoth ravens circled around the unicorn cage and landed on each of the four corners. "Escort the Princess Calandria into the Cave of Eos!"

The ravens' thick, taloned feet gripped the sides of the cage. They flapped their glossy black wings and lifted it out from under the outcropping and into the air.

Callie gasped and tried to keep her balance as the cage picked up speed, flying rapidly towards the huge gaping mouth of the cave.

She felt so alone.

No one could help her now, not even Lewis. Her best friend lay motionless at her feet, injured, because of her. He'd followed her on this journey blindly, with all the faith and enthusiasm of a true best friend. Now, he might pay with his life. Callie had no idea if he would survive. Or if *she* would.

But it was much too late now.

They couldn't go back.

Chapter Eighteen

The Cave of Eor

Callie shielded her eyes from the fiery orange light as they traveled further and further into the cave. Wanda and the Raven Queen followed behind them, in a flying chariot propelled by more enchanted black ravens.

The cave grew hotter and hotter, and a foul smell came from somewhere up ahead.

Callie gulped as she saw their destination. Ahead lay a jagged, rocky outcropping. A menacing orange glow blazed below it. Puffs of smoke spewed into the air. An ancient stone platform was carved out of the bedrock of the cave, and it extended over the burning chasm below. The rock was an altar--for preparation of the sacrifice, most likely.

The ravens hung the cage on a hook overhead, where Callie and Lewis remained suspended, like tiny, trapped birds. Callie didn't miss the irony of that.

More ravens came above them, swooping and cawing their malevolent song.

The Raven Queen's chariot was gently set down on an overhang. She and Wanda stepped out. The queen raised her arms, and spoke in a commanding voice. "Ethnor hungers for blood. And we, his faithful servants, must sate him. But first, a tasty morsel to whet the god's appetite, and prepare his palate for the main course."

The Raven Queen's eyes glittered darkly as she smiled at Callie. Then she pointed a long gloved finger at one of the ravens who flew above them. Callie's breath caught as she watched the creature stop and struggle, as if held by an invisible hand. It flapped and flailed madly, trying in vain to escape, but Callie knew it was useless. It was trapped by the queen's magic.

Moving her hand slowly through the air, Queen Miranda dragged the helpless bird toward the fiery mouth of the volcano. The raven squawked crazily; the other birds were going mad. Then, Callie watched in horror as a whispery cloud of fire rose up out of the volcano and held the bird in its jaws. The raven's body jerked to and fro like a puppet; it screamed and flapped as the Mouth of Ethnor held it suspended in its power.

Then, with a roar, Ethnor pulled the raven down into the fiery pit of its belly.

Callie trembled with shock. *That* was what the Raven Queen had planned for her and Lewis? It seemed too horrible to comprehend.

"Now you must say goodbye to your friend," the Raven Queen said simply. She turned and proceeded up toward the platform, with Wanda throwing an I-told-you-so look at Callie behind her.

The reality was hitting her now.

If Callie didn't do something quick, both she and Lewis were going to be toast. Literally.

Callie's only hope was her power, though she had already seen how useless it was against the unicorn bars and the hex the Raven Queen had put upon them. She stood up, taking a deep breath and trying to relax....

Like *that* was possible at a time like this.

Fear coursed through her, making her almost dizzy with its force.

She looked down at Lewis. She couldn't let him die like this. She just couldn't!

Callie braced herself and focused.... She felt something happening. Then, a bolt of light shot from her hand just as it had before, bounced off the bars and headed straight back at her. Callie had to dive to the floor to avoid being hit again with her own magic. The cage swung heavily, creaking with the force of her landing. Pain shot through her wrist and up her arm.

Callie stayed down, reaching out to her friend. This was inconceivable. How could it all end like this? How could the Raven Queen win? And what was it going to feel like when they were thrown into a pit of fire?

It had all been a lie. She *didn't* have the power to defeat the Raven Queen, and because of that, she and Lewis were going to die. Because of that, the Raven Queen would be victorious.

The thought of Lewis dying...that seemed to be the worst thing of all, even worse than her own fate.

Callie looked over at the Raven Queen, where she stood making the preparations at the stone altar. A tall, black jeweled crown adorned her head, its glittering, swirled spikes like gnarled fingers reaching up to the sky. She chanted something in an ancient language while Wanda stood by, her face lit with excitement.

The preparations for the sacrifice had begun.

Callie felt so powerless...so afraid...just as she had that day in her mom's hospital room. She'd stood next to her dad in a daze, knowing she was going to lose the most important woman in her life, but unable to face it. The fear had been like a huge wall that Callie was unable to climb, so she'd just stood there, blocked by its impenetrable thickness, unable to move forward.

She touched Lewis' unruly hair. *"I'm so afraid, Lewis!"* she whispered. "What do I do?"

Callie shut her eyes, and memories swirled in her head--her mother when Callie was young, playing with her at the playground. Callie had been only two or three. She'd been afraid to climb the ladder and go down the slide by herself. Callie had kept looking back at her mom, and her mom had been smiling, saying, *"Don't be afraid, Callie. You can do it. Don't be afraid...."*

Callie gasped as something clicked into place. She remembered what the ghost had said about the Raven Queen: *She fears you--you must be what she is not....'*

That was it. That was the key.

No fear.

Then, she remembered the prophecy Queen Arabella had quoted from the scrolls of the ancient kings, about the key to the Enchanted Throne of Albion:

> *This ancient key is legend*
> *But does not yet exist*
> *It will be forged upon the day*
> *When fear fades into mist*
>
> *It will be won in battle*
> *And at tremendous cost*
> *In order to be found*
> *Something must be lost*

"Something must be lost..." she muttered. She looked down at Lewis, who still lay unconscious at her feet. She had been so afraid the prophecy meant she would lose someone close to her. And she still might. As the Scrolls said, it would come at great cost. But the key would only be forged when Callie's *fear* was lost.

That was the key to defeating the Raven Queen, it was the key to the Enchanted Throne, it was the key to everything.

Callie slowly got to her feet. Since her mother's death, fear had been with Callie for so long it had become a normal part of her life.

No more.

Callie removed the Talking Tiara from her head and placed it on Lewis as best she could. "I know you can't hear me right now," she said, "and I know it's not your style, but you may need it in a few minutes." She removed the barrettes from her hair, too--the Spark-Tailed Teklins, thinking they might be useful as well.

Then she stood. A strange, quiet calm brushed over her like a whisper. Her heart stilled, slowed, like a smooth pool of water on a windless, sunny day.

Callie closed her eyes and lifted her hands in front of her, calling to something.

And something came.

Misty billows of energy--pink, like the color of King Eldric's jeweled key and her mom's diary--swirled around her. They were memories from her past. She could see them! Her mom and dad together, laughing at Callie's first birthday party...Callie smiling up at them, holding their hands as the three of them walked through a shady park on a hot summer day...playing in the snow...falling asleep in her dad's lap...a million other memories that seemed to hum with an unparalleled power.

Lewis stirred at her feet. He looked up at her, seeing the strange energy force. "What are you doing, Cal?"

She smiled down at him. *"Letting go."*

The whirlwind of energy that encircled Callie grew stronger; it made the air shake with its force. She stepped forward.

The door of the cage blew outward and flew off its hinges, as if propelled by an explosion.

The Raven Queen's head jerked sideways, her face a mask of fury and disbelief. She rose into the air and came hurtling toward Callie, her fingers curled like talons, and though it was a frightening sight to behold, Callie stayed calm. She felt her power grow. It was unlike anything she had ever felt before.

The Raven Queen snarled and shot a bolt of green energy straight at Callie's heart.

The queen's power collided with Callie's, but Callie held her ground. She didn't give an inch--didn't give in to the fear that the Raven Queen was stronger than she.

Shock swept over the Raven Queen's face as she realized what was happening. She sent another green bolt hurtling toward Callie's face. It stopped just inches away, buzzing angrily outside the force that protected Callie--the strength of her parents' love for her, and hers for them.

With each passing moment that she failed to defeat Callie, the Raven Queen's expression became more and more hideous, more and more terrifying.

"You think to defeat me?" The Raven Queen hissed. "You--my sister's half-breed whelp? You haven't got it in you. You are so like Ana, just as weak and easy to toy with." Her face became a twisted mask of hate. "She was no match for me, and neither are you. What would you say if I told you your mother's death was *not an accident?"*

The words registered on Callie's senses. Disbelief, then rage spiked within her, but she fought to control them--

Her mother's death not an accident?

Callie's head spun; she felt her powers weaken.

No. If she let fear overtake her, she and Lewis--and all of Albion--wouldn't stand a chance.

Like a hound on the scent, the Raven Queen knew she'd just hit a nerve. "Oh yes, Callie. Just because I could not follow Ana into the Land of Ur and risk losing my powers, doesn't mean I couldn't send someone else in my stead. Someone who, perhaps, didn't know how to drive what you call an automobile very well?"

Callie felt her resolve begin to quiver. Her mother's car accident had been caused by a reckless driver. Could it be true? Had the man driving the other car been one of the Raven Queen's agents, sent into Callie's world to assassinate her mom?

It was too awful to comprehend.

"That's not all," the Raven Queen continued, looking very smug, and completely evil. "What if I told you that I did it for one reason, and one reason only: to hurt *you.*"

Callie felt sick.

"That's right, my dear. The ancient kings had predicted your arrival; the Priestesses of Arundel, too. They told of a girl from a strange land who would challenge me, whose powers would be great." The Raven Queen gave a look of mock innocence. "I had to do *something* to diminish your chances. Call it a pre-emptive strike. 'All's fair in love and war.' Isn't that what they say in your world? And I must agree, it worked well. You mother's death has weakened your strength considerably, just as I knew it would."

If what the Raven Queen said was true, Callie's mother had died because of her, and for no other reason. It was too much to take in all at once.

The swirling force that encircled Callie started to fade, short-out almost. She couldn't concentrate. Her emotions were all a jumble as she tried to process what the Raven Queen had said. The ravens screeched louder, as if they were laughing.

The Raven Queen smiled. A bolt of green light flew like a javelin toward Callie. She ducked, her head spinning as it sailed past her, mere inches from her face. She tried to catch her breath, but the Raven Queen's assault was relentless. She sent bolt after bolt of her magic toward Callie, and Callie felt like she was playing a deadly game of dodge ball.

"Don't let her get to you, Callie!" Lewis said, scrambling to his feet.

"*Lewis!*" Callie cried. Fear was circling again, like a cloud of dark ravens.

The Raven Queen called to Wanda, "I leave him to you, my dear. Show him what happens when he angers a princess of Tor-Enrith!"

Wanda's face screwed into a dark sneer that matched the Raven Queen's. She raised a scepter covered in rubies and pointed it at Lewis. A bolt of red energy shot out of it and zoomed toward him. But the Talking Tiara clung to Lewis' head and opened its jaws wide...and ate the bolt of magic like an appetizer at a banquet. Then it smacked its jaws together, waiting for another bite.

Wanda's nasty sneer grew nastier. She leveled the scepter at Lewis with a vengeance, and shot bolt after bolt of magic at him. The tiara ate up each one--literally. Lewis shouted and tried to keep his balance as the tiara jerked him to and fro in its quest to protect him.

"She's just playing you, Cal!" Lewis called, doing a strange dance indeed. "She's afraid of you, 'cause you're stronger than she is. Don't let her win!" He picked up Callie's barrettes and pitched one at Wanda. It landed in her hair, and appeared miffed at being hurled so rudely across such a distance. What happened next made it easy to see why Spark-Tailed Teklins had been banned from public use. The hair accessory hissed and spat, then sparks shot from the tip of its tail.

Wanda screamed and leapt around, batting at the sparking creature in her hair. Lewis seized the opportunity to throw a few more at her, which kept her occupied.

Callie sucked in a breath. She couldn't worry about Lewis right now, though he seemed to be managing okay. She had her own battle to wage against a queen who played dirty.

Callie cleared her mind, and heard her mother's voice. *"Don't be afraid, Callie...don't be afraid..."*

That was it. The Raven Queen knew Callie's weakness: fear. That was why she had been trying so hard to bait her by using her mother's death as a weapon. For a few horrible moments, it had worked. But Callie realized that even if what the Raven Queen had said was true, it didn't change anything. Her mom's love for her still lived within Callie's heart, as it had since the day she'd been born, as it *always* would.

Callie felt her power returning, saw the misty-pink force swirling protectively around her again.

No fear.

No matter what.

She regarded the Raven Queen calmly. "I never knew you were this afraid of me."

The queen's mouth compressed into a tight line. She glared back at Callie. "I'm not afraid of you, *whelp*."

"Yes, you are, and you're jealous, too--just like you were of Mom, and of her and Dad, their love for each other, and our love as a family."

The Raven Queen seethed.

But Callie continued, "You've brainwashed Wanda, you want to enslave the people of Albion, and you want to throw Lewis and I into a volcano because you're full of hate. But I'm not going to let you do it." Callie stood tall, resolute, but calm, as she faced her enemy. "I don't want to hurt you, Aunt Miranda--but if I have to, I will."

The Raven Queen laughed. "Is that so, *Little One*?"

Callie kept her focus. "Little One" was her mom's pet name for her; she had no doubt that the Raven Queen knew that. But Callie stood firm.

"Yes. That's so."

The Raven Queen's mouth curled into a snarl. "Well, then. Let the real battle begin!"

In moments Callie and the Raven Queen were in the air, locked in a deadly contest as bolts of magic zoomed all over the cave, hitting the bedrock and sending shards of stone and dust into the air. The Raven Queen wrapped her hands around Callie's neck. Callie struggled, fighting with all her might.

All at once, Callie heard her mom's voice in her ear: *"Turn, now! Duck. That's it, you've got her...You can do it, Callie,"* and *"Mommy and Daddy love you, no matter what."*

That was the crux of it, right there. No matter what happened to any of them, nothing could change the love Callie and her parents felt for each other—not death, not moving on with life, not even an evil queen who was trying to kill Callie.

That was all Callie needed to know.

Her power surged, then; she felt almost dizzy with it. Callie saw the Raven Queen's eyes fill with fear as she looked on helplessly while Callie's power grew ten times, then fifty, *then a hundred times* stronger than what it had been before.

The ravens circling above went crazy, shrieking and flying in zigzags, sensing Callie's unbelievable power.

The Raven Queen growled while she struggled to regain her position. But it was too late, now. She and Callie were zooming precariously toward the edge of the volcano--the Mouth of Ethnor--wrestling for their lives.

They hit the bedrock wall and bounced off it like billiard balls. The Raven Queen lost her grip on Callie.

Her frightened eyes looked up into Callie's as she began to fall toward the red-hot Mouth of Ethnor.

Callie's first instinct was to try to save her aunt, but then the whispery cloud of flame rose up out of the volcano like the jaws of a beast. It encircled the Raven Queen and held her suspended above the blazing mire. She began to writhe in pain, screaming, reaching out to Callie. *"Help me! Help me, Calandria!"* she shrieked. The cry sent a chill through Callie's blood as she, herself, struggled to maintain her footing on the edge of the rocky outcropping.

The Raven Queen was being jolted about like a puppet--just like the poor raven she had used as a demonstration--her limbs like a rag doll's as the Mouth of Ethnor held her in its grip and tortured her with invisible teeth.

Callie looked behind her. Wanda and Lewis had stopped their battle too, transfixed by the ghastly scene.

The Raven Queen's body bowed like an unnatural thing, writhing in torment.

It was almost too horrible to watch, and yet Callie knew she must. Just as she knew she was helpless to do anything to save her mother's twin.

The Raven Queen's eyes were white with terror, her piercing scream like a knife in Callie's heart. Then the force that held her took her slowly down, writhing and screaming all the way...down into the Mouth of Ethnor, to feed the Fire God's hunger.

Callie stood on the edge of the volcano and looked into the orange depths of liquid fire. She couldn't see the Raven Queen anymore. The woman with her mother's face was gone.

Callie turned around, and ran toward her friend. "Lewis!"

Lewis stood there panting, a mist of sweat on his brow and the Talking Tiara perched jauntily upon his head. He opened his arms and pulled Callie in for a tight hug.

"Are you okay, Cal?" he said. *"I thought I'd lost you."*

She stepped back, tears in her eyes. "I thought I'd lost you, too. I'm so glad I didn't!" She threw her arms around him again and hugged him with all the strength she had left.

"Mom?" Wanda said fearfully, walking slowly toward the edge of the Mouth of Ethnor and looking down into its fiery depths. She stood at the edge, her hair singed from the Spark-Tailed Teklins. *"Mom, come back!"* she cried.

Callie went to Wanda and touched her shoulder. "It's okay, Wanda. It's over. You're going to be fine."

Wanda turned. The despair in her eyes almost broke Callie's heart, no matter that Wanda had just tried to *kill* Lewis. Even if she had been brainwashed, Wanda had just suffered a tremendous loss.

And Callie knew exactly how that felt.

She put her arm around Wanda and pulled her close. "It'll be okay," she said. "I promise. We're going to take you home, now."

Wanda seemed to be in a daze as Callie and Lewis led her toward the cave's entrance. The ravens were going crazy--screeching and flying madly, arcing in wide circles at tremendous speeds. It was as if they knew their Queen was gone, and they were disoriented.

Callie, Lewis, and Wanda emerged into the misty dawn to find the ghosts flying around, keening their strange song. The ghost that had helped Callie before swirled around her as the others picked up Lewis and Wanda and zoomed all of them back toward the road to Arraband.

"You have defeated the Raven Queen," the ghost said. *"You are most powerful, indeed! But beware, Princess...*

Callie jerked her head to look at her diaphanous friend. "Why should I beware? The Raven Queen is gone."

"She is gone...but where? But where?" the ghost sang.

"What? What does that mean?" Callie asked, a feeling of foreboding creeping through her veins like ice-water.

"I cannot say what happened to the Raven Queen," the ghost answered. *"But know this: the Mouth of Ethnor is not as deep as it seems! Not as deep as it seems!"*

Then all of a sudden they were back at the road to Arraband. The ghosts dumped them off and disappeared in a swirl of smoke.

Callie turned to Lewis. "Did you hear what she said?"

Lewis nodded and started leading them down the tree-lined road. "Yeah, I heard it. What--are you going to believe a bunch of crazy ghosts who used us as Weeko balls? She fell into a pit of lava. She's gone. Toast. Crispified. End of story."

Callie gulped. Lewis had a point, but the ghost who had told her this latest information was also the one who had given her the key to defeating the Raven Queen. And she'd been "spot on" about that....

"Yeah, you're probably right," Callie said weakly, glancing at Wanda who was still in a daze from the Raven Queen's spell. "I'm sure she won't be able to hurt anyone, again."

Why did those words sound so hollow, even to Callie's own ears?

Chapter Nineteen

The Coronation

Callie and Lewis returned to a hero's welcome.

Queen Arabella had regained consciousness and was on the mend. The city was re-building. Palace life was getting back to normal. The Raven Queen was dead. Everyone rejoiced at the news--except for Wanda, and Callie, herself.

Callie had immediately given Wanda into Pericles' expert care.

"I think she needs to see a counselor," Callie had said. "She's been through a lot." Pericles assured Callie that Wanda would receive the best care the Albion medical community could offer until she returned home to her family doctor in the Land of Ur.

Wanda was led away. Even though Wanda had personally caused Callie and Lewis a lot of grief, both here and back home at school, neither one of them could find any victory in their classmate's pain. It wasn't Wanda's fault that she'd been kidnapped and brainwashed by an evil queen.

The headline in the *Albion Times* read:

Princess Callie Defeats Raven Queen at Cave of Eos; Albion Saved!

Bureau Chief Tertius Lombardi reporting:

The ancient kings predicted it, and now it has come true! Princess Calandria has outdone herself, utterly vanquishing the Raven Queen in a legendary battle deep in the Forest of Dead Souls at the Cave of Eos.

Eyewitness accounts report a dazzling display of magic from the young princess, the likes of which Albion has never seen. Apparently it was too much for the Raven Queen, who could not match our princess' power. The former Princess Miranda met her unhappy fate in the fiery Mouth of Ethnor, deep in the Cave of Eos.

One Albian citizen, upon hearing of the Raven Queen's demise was quoted as saying, "Well, good riddance." Another said, "I knew our princess could do it!" Princess Calandria, or 'Callie' as she is known to her friends, will officially be named as Heir to the Albian Throne tonight, in a spectacular coronation ceremony at the palace.

Even though the mood in Arraband and the royal palace practically sparkled with joy, Callie felt conflicted. It was time for her to go home. She'd done her job and defeated the Raven Queen. At least, that's what the newspapers said....

All that remained was Callie's official coronation ceremony, which Queen Arabella, in her customary I-Am-The-Queen-Don't-Argue-With-Me way, insisted upon, with all the pomp and circumstance that Albian tradition called for. Which was a lot.

The short list for the celebration read as follows:

Three-hundred Royal Jugglers

Six-hundred Royal Trumpeters

Five-hundred Royal Drummers

Three-hundred-fifty Royal Cymbal-Clangers

Nine-hundred Royal Choristers

Two-hundred Royal Firework Technicians
Four-hundred Royal Chefs
Three-thousand Royal Guests

It was enough to make anyone dizzy!

Callie was tired of the endless dress-fittings, and shoe-fittings, and tiara fittings, and hair-style experiments. She just wanted it to be *over* so she could go home and be a normal twelve-year-old kid again.

Three days after the Raven Queen's defeat, the day of Callie's coronation arrived. Everyone who was *anyone* was there, including Dr. Pericles Monsoon, the Royal Dragon-Master, Ignatius P. Entwhistle, and a young Great-Crested Ceylx named Earle.

Callie had burst out laughing with joy when she'd seen her baby dragon, who wasn't so much of a baby any more, and who now sported a thick pair of glasses which Ignatius had fashioned for him. They made his eyes look twice their normal size. Still, Earle looked very proud to be taking part in the ceremony, which started with an official procession around the royal palace and through the streets of Arraband.

Callie and Lewis stood together on the Royal Float, drawn by six white Royal Albian Unicorns. Lord Graydon, not fully recovered from his wounds, but insisting on a return to active duty, led the mounted procession. He looked marvelously handsome in a pale blue jacket with silver buttons, ruffled white shirt, black trousers, boots and a black ribbon tying back his queue.

Queen Arabella sat upon a throne, doing the "royal wave," and urging Callie to do the same.

Wanda had a place on the float, too. She was dressed in a pale green gown. Queen Arabella had loaned her several pieces of jewelry from her own personal collection, but Wanda barely acknowledged it. She was still recovering from her trauma, the Albian counselor had advised. She would need more time in order to fully heal.

Callie's Coronation gown was beautiful--a confection of pure silver-white, encrusted with diamonds. She wore the Talking Tiara proudly upon her head. It gave a running commentary as they traveled along the procession route.

They passed by the gargoyles, Terry and Kevin, who waved madly with big grins on their scary faces. "*We know her!*" Terry said to someone down on the street below. "*Personal friend of ours, the princess. We gave 'er directions once!*"

Wanda seemed oblivious to theirs or anyone else's comments. She merely clutched the ruby scepter to her chest--it was no longer enchanted by the Raven Queen and therefore harmless--and stared off into space miserably.

For Callie, all the royal hub-bub was bittersweet. The people of Albion loved her--she could see it in their smiling faces as they cheered and waved--and she loved them. She loved her grandmother, and Earle, and Pericles, and Sir Reginald, too. But nothing lasted forever. She knew that, now.

It was time to go home.

But first, there was this little matter of her coronation to get through. Callie was about to be officially crowned Princess Royal and Heir to the Enchanted Throne of Albion, and that was pretty cool.

The procession soon passed through the palace gates and Callie felt her stomach whoosh with nerves. Soon they were standing in their places in the Throne Room. Queen Arabella--looking every inch a queen in a sparkling gold, jeweled gown--read from the Ancient Scrolls, held with panache by a proud-looking Sir Reginald, while Lord Graydon looked up at Callie with serious eyes.

Callie was going to miss all of them. A lot.

She looked around the Throne Room and saw more old friends, the Hamburgers beaming up at her, Ignatius looking on stoically, quickly wiping a tear from his eye, and the many people in the palace she had come to know during her stay here.

"I hereby proclaim the Princess Calandria my One True Heir and Protector of the Enchanted Throne of Albion," Queen Arabella pronounced grandly.

She motioned for Callie to ascend the steps and join her next to the dazzling jewel-covered throne. As Callie moved into position, she caught sight of someone else in the crowd--her cousin, the Duke of Kenryk. Callie noticed his arm was in a sling. Obviously he was still recovering from the Talking Tiara's attack. Still, when his dark blue eyes met hers, Callie got the distinct impression that the duke was by no means down for the count. But she couldn't worry about that right now.

She had to take her vows and become an official princess.

Callie stood in front of the throne as Queen Arabella handed her the Royal Scepter of the Ancient Kings, then the gold Orb of Atria. She took a deep breath, as the enormity of the occasion hit her. These people were investing their trust in her. She wasn't going to let them down.

Callie took a deep breath and sat upon the Enchanted Throne. As soon as she did, she felt an energy begin to swirl around her. The pink, misty swirls danced around her, humming with a high, bright sound that echoed the feeling in Callie's heart. Then, she understood. The pink swirling stuff, the sound, the power...it was coming from Callie's own heart.

That's where her power came from!

As Queen Arabella raised the spectacular crown of diamonds, pearls, and other colorful gems, Callie smiled proudly. The queen placed King Eldric's Coronation Crown upon Callie's head as the room erupted into cheers from the Albian people.

Callie looked at Lewis, who beamed back proudly and gave her a "thumbs up."

Then she saw another face smiling back at her in the swirling pink mist--her *mom*. She was a diaphanous image on the edge of the Royal Dias, just out of Callie's reach. But Callie knew she couldn't reach out and touch her, even if she tried. Her mom lived within Callie's own heart, just as she always had, and always would.

Her mom said nothing--she didn't have to. *"Thanks for everything, Mom,"* Callie whispered. *"I love you, too."*

Callie's power swirled even stronger. She heard gasps from the crowd as they watched in awe. The Enchanted Throne was *doing something*. It was beginning to hum, to sing a full, rich, ethereal chord, like an other-wordly choir. Light spilled out of the jewels that adorned it, shooting colorful laser beams across the Throne Room.

A few people near the Royal Dias stepped back, but Callie wasn't afraid. This was what she had been meant to do--to overcome her fears, realize her full potential, and share her gift with her people. And it felt pretty good.

Queen Arabella proclaimed proudly, "The Prophecy of the ancient kings has come to pass. Princess Calandria is the One for whom the Enchanted Throne was crafted."

Chapter Twenty

Into the Land of Ur

"What was all that stuff about the Enchanted Throne being crafted for me, Gram?" Callie asked, packing away some souvenirs to take back home with her.

The queen, wearing a simple gown of sky blue, finished packing some jewelry into a drawstring velvet bag for Callie's trip. Last night had been so busy that they hadn't had much time to talk privately after the coronation.

"Exactly that. The Scrolls of the Ancient Kings tell of the Throne being crafted for the One Protector of Albion. Many kings and queens have sat upon it, I assure you, and there is no record of that "singing" business of last night ever happening before. You have unleashed a powerful magic, which will serve to protect our land until your return."

Queen Arabella smiled proudly and reached her arms out for a hug. Callie rushed into them as the reality of their separation loomed before her. She didn't want to leave all her friends here, or her grandmother.

But she and Lewis had to go home. Wanda wasn't doing very well. She still hadn't really spoken since the horrible scene with the Raven Queen in the Cave of Eos. She was getting paler and thinner by the day, and she had started out pale and thin to begin with. Callie was worried about Wanda's health. She had to get her back to the Land of Ur so she could be treated by her own family doctor.

Callie, herself, had to face certain difficulties in her own life back home. She had made great strides at conquering her fear here in Albion, but would it last when she got home and had to face her dad's marriage to Sharon? Callie hoped so. But she knew one thing--she couldn't hide here in Albion forever, no matter how tempting it was.

She was a princess, now, and princesses faced their problems head-on.

There was another reason Callie was anxious to get home: her mom's diary. The key was back home in her mom's china jewelry dish. Callie wanted to learn more about her mom's life here as a princess of Albion, and since the Raven Queen's revelation that her mom's death might not have been an accident, Callie wanted to see if the diary revealed any clues about the twins' early relationship. Had Miranda always been so evil? If not, what had made her so? Callie hoped to find out more about her mother's mysterious twin sister.

Since Callie's return from the Cave of Eos, Queen Arabella hadn't really spoken about the Raven Queen's defeat. It was understandable; Miranda had been her daughter, after all. Now, both of the queen's children were gone.

Or were they?

Callie couldn't stop thinking about what the ghost had said to her. *The Mouth of Ethnor is not as deep as it seems!* Was it possible that the Raven Queen could have survived?

Callie was the only one who seemed to consider it a possibility. Lord Graydon reported that his scouts had heard nothing about the Raven Queen surfacing anywhere, that the people of Tor-Enrith had been released from the spell that had enslaved them. It certainly seemed like she was gone for good.

Callie hoped so.

Queen Arabella regarded her with a brave face, but Callie could see her grandmother fighting to control her emotions. "It's okay, Gram. I'm going to miss you, too."

The queen sniffled softly and put her arm around her granddaughter's shoulder. They gathered up Callie's things and took their last walk alone together through the glittering halls of the palace.

"I'll be back before you know it," Callie continued.

"For you, perhaps, but here, it may be years before I see you again. I hope it shall pass quickly."

"You can send me messages in my cereal," Callie pointed out, "like you did before. Only this time it won't freak me out, because I'll know it's you!"

The queen smiled. "I will. I'll tell you all about what's going on at Court, who I'm throwing in the dungeon on any given week, how Earle's coming along. And how much we miss you." She kissed Callie's hair.

Soon they were at the palace door where Lewis, Wanda, Sir Reginald, and Dr. Monsoon stood waiting for them. Callie's heart sank. She hated goodbyes....

Callie flew into Sir Reginald's arms. "Reggie, I'm going to miss you. Thanks for everything."

Sir Reginald cleared his throat a couple of times and managed to say, "It has been my great honor to serve you, Your Highness, which I will continue to do until my dying day." Then he stepped back, took out a hankie, and sobbed into it loudly.

Callie patted his arm and regarded the next person in line.

Dr. Monsoon stepped forward, looking serious, but jolly just the same. His eyes twinkled down at her.

"Thanks for being such a patient teacher," she said. "You taught me so much."

Pericles cleared his throat as his eyes filled up a little, too. "As you taught me, Your Highness. In this life, we are all each other's teachers." He handed her a signed copy of each of his books. "In case you need to refer to them in the Land of Ur."

Callie thanked him, though she didn't know how often she would have to refer to Dr. Monsoon's books on magic, since her powers wouldn't work in her own world.

"Lord Graydon," The queen commanded, "please see the princess and her party safely to the tunnel."

Outside in the courtyard, Lord Graydon sat astride his gray charger, next to the queen's waiting carriage.

"This is it, then." Callie gulped looking up at the queen.

"Not yet. I have something to show you." Queen Arabella pulled out something from a pocket of her gown.

"Sunglasses!" Callie exclaimed.

The queen laughed and put them on. "I believe the correct term is *shades*."

Callie and Lewis both chuckled at the sight of Queen Arabella of Albion, smiling and looking cool in a pair of shades.

"And there's someone else who wants to say goodbye." The queen pointed toward the sky. Something was flying at them at an alarming speed.

"*Earle!*" Callie exclaimed, her heart leaping with happiness at the sight of her dragon swooping down to greet her--but not before he did a few difficult loop-the-loops in the air. Ignatius rode on Earle's back, looking very proud of his prodigy. "It worked, Princess! His glasses are staying on!"

It was true. Earle flew around in zigzags and figure eights, but his thick eyeglasses stayed on, fastened around his head by Ignatius' special bungee cord. They landed very smoothly nearby, and Callie thought it was great not to see Earle crashing into things! He bounded over to her like an enthusiastic puppy, his eyes bright with affection for his princess.

Callie ran to greet him. She threw her arms around his neck--what she could of it, as he was bigger than an elephant now--and hugged her dragon. Earle purred and cuddled beside her. "I love you, Earle," Callie whispered. "I have to go away for awhile..."

Earle looked as if he understood what she was saying. He bellowed sadly and rubbed his big, scaly head gently against her.

"I'll be back soon," she said. "I promise." She stroked his nose and tried to keep her own tears at bay, but it was hard. "So, I need you to be a brave boy while I'm away, okay? And listen to Ignatius, because he's going to teach you how to do all kinds of neat things. You can practice them and show me when I get back."

This seemed to peak Earle's interest as his huge eyes blinked from behind his thick lenses.

Callie rejoined the group. Then came the hardest goodbye of all: to her grandmother.

The queen had pushed her shades up onto her head so she could look unhindered into her granddaughter's eyes. Callie thought she saw Queen Arabella's lip tremble but she held it together. She was, after all, the Queen of Albion, and they were in public.

Callie didn't care if anyone saw her lip tremble, which it did. Queen Arabella pulled her close for a tight hug, and whispered into Callie's ear, *"I love you, Callie. Never, ever forget my dear, that you are a princess."*

Callie nodded, wiping her eyes. "I love you, too, Gram. I won't forget."

The Queen stepped back as Sir Reginald opened the door to the carriage and helped Callie and her friends in.

Lewis poked his head out the window. "Thanks for everything, Your Majesty. And thanks for the books, Sir Reginald. I'm going to do a *wicked* science project on Quantum-Sorak Physics and Lyaxion Relativity!"

"I have no doubt, Mr. Farnsworth," Sir Reginald replied. "Take care of yourself, young sir. And our princess."

"I will," Lewis said gravely, and waved goodbye.

Wanda said nothing to anyone. She merely sat on the carriage seat, looking out the other window as if she just wanted the whole thing to be over.

The queen commanded, "Lord Graydon, please escort the princess to her destination."

The young captain turned his mount and signaled for the regiment to depart.

The carriage lurched as it pulled away. Though Callie knew it was anything but princess-like behavior, she leaned out the window and waved. "Goodbye, everyone! I'll miss you. I'll be back soon, I promise."

Sir Reginald, Pericles, Queen Arabella, and Ignatius waved goodbye; even Earle flapped a wing.

The carriage turned onto a busy Arraband street and her friends were gone from sight. Callie sat back, trying to compose herself. It was painful to say goodbye to people you cared about. But she would see them again. She knew it.

Lewis seemed perfectly fine, as usual. He was busily working out some equations on a sheet of paper. "By my calculations, we've been gone from our world for about fifteen minutes. No one should even have missed us."

Wanda glared at Lewis, as if accusing him of being a know-it-all. Maybe she was feeling better after all...

If what Lewis said was true, that meant their own world was still virtually the same as when they'd left it. But they had changed. Even though Callie had faced and conquered many of her fears in Albion, she still wasn't quite sure how well she was going to do with the whole "Sharon" thing. It was going to be an adjustment, for all of them. She'd just have to face it like a princess.

Soon they were at the Grimstead Gate. The carriage stopped, and the door opened. Lord Graydon helped Callie out. He helped Wanda out next—she didn't bother to thank him. Lewis came out on his own, of course. They all stood solemnly in the golden morning light. Callie's stomach sank like lead. She looked up into the clear blue eyes of Lord Graydon.

He looked down at her. "Your Highness--"

"*Callie*," she corrected.

"Callie...." He looked so serious. "It has been my great honor to serve you. Your bravery knows no bounds. You have defeated the Raven Queen and saved our nation from a horrible fate." He took her hand in his and raised it to his lips. "I am your humble servant, now, and always." Then he pressed his lips to the back of Callie's hand. She thought she might faint.

Lewis muttered, *"Oh, brother..."*

Callie ignored her friend, and looked up at Lord Graydon. "Thanks, Hugh. That means a lot to me."

Lord Graydon stepped away from her, and gave a short bow. "I shall count the days until your return to us, Princess." He looked at Lewis, then, and said gravely, "Take care of her."

Lewis crossed his arms across and puffed up his chest. "You can count on it."

Lord Graydon mounted his charger and gave the order for his regiment to pull out. As he rode toward the city gate, he looked back and met Callie's gaze. Then he was gone.

Lewis let out a big breath. "Well, I'm glad *that's* over. I don't know who that guy thinks he is."

"Oh, Lewis!" Callie said in exasperation.

Wanda followed along sullenly as they passed under the gate and came out onto the dirt road that led back to the tunnel, which was only a few feet away.

"Bye, Princess!" a familiar voice called from above.

Callie grinned as she looked behind her. The gargoyles, Terry and Kevin, peered down at them and waved cheerily.

"Take care, now," Kevin echoed. *"And don't forget us, Princess!"*

Callie laughed and replied, "I could never forget you two. Trust me."

The gargoyles seemed pleased with that, and then went on to argue with each other about which one of them was the princess' favorite. They were still going on when Callie, Lewis and Wanda reached the entrance to the tunnel.

Lewis lifted up his flashlight and flicked it on. The flashlight had been in safe-keeping at the palace since the night they'd arrived. Callie and Lewis had requested it, as they were unsure whether Sweetbugs would survive in the Land of Ur. "Come on," Lewis said, leading the way.

Callie directed Wanda into the tunnel ahead of her. As soon as they stepped over the threshold, the torches on the walls came to life. Wanda stepped beside them, still clutching the ruby scepter in her hand. As they walked, Callie thought she heard Wanda...talking to it.

"Mom, I hope wherever you are, you're okay," she whispered fearfully.

Callie's heart sank. It was no use telling Wanda that the Raven Queen couldn't hear her. At least, that was what everyone seemed to think. Callie could only hope that the ghost in the Forest of Dead Souls had been wrong--that the Raven Queen had died in the Mouth of Ethnor and would never be able to hurt anyone again.

They proceeded into the tunnel. Dampness seemed to penetrate their very bones as they walked deeper and deeper into the ancient passage. Callie reached for Lewis' hand.

They passed the smooth stone walls, then they reached the carvings. Lewis shone the flashlight at the wall. Callie gasped.

"These carvings are new!" Callie said. "When we passed through before, this part of the wall was smooth. I remember!"

Lewis agreed, "I remember, too."

Wanda stepped forward and studied the chiseled stone wall, too.

The wall showed a new scene--one that showed the Raven Queen and Callie locked in a deadly battle in the Cave of Eos. It depicted them wrestling with each other in the air, shooting magic at each other, and then the Raven Queen falling into the Mouth of Ethnor. That was all.

Wanda cried, *"No!"* and flung herself at the stone wall. She clawed at the pictures like someone possessed.

Callie and Lewis stepped back, not knowing what to do.

Then Wanda turned on them, her eyes glowing unnaturally. She glared at Callie. All of her old acid personality seemed to have been restored in a heartbeat, only worse. Wanda pointed her finger at Callie accusingly. *"You killed my mom!"*

"Wanda, I--" Callie stammered.

Wanda got right in her face, though Lewis tried to push her away.

Even pale and thin, Wanda was a lot stronger than she looked. She snarled at Callie, "You killed my mom, and I'm going to make you pay. If it's the last thing I do, I'll make you pay!" Then she pushed past them and ran down the tunnel and out of sight.

"Glad to see Wanda's back to her old self," he said dryly. "Are you okay, Cal?"

"Yeah. I guess so." Callie took a shaky breath. "Do you think she was serious, about making me pay?"

Lewis replied, "You never know with her. But don't worry. I promised Lord Graydon I'd take care of you, and that's what I'm gonna do."

Callie's heart filled with emotion. Lewis was the best friend anyone could ever hope for.

Still, Wanda's threats echoed in Callie's mind. Was her troubled classmate serious? If so, what steps would she take against Callie? That was all she needed now that she was returning home. Her dad's upcoming marriage still hung heavily in her heart, and now she had a vengeful classmate to deal with, too.

Soon, they came to the end of the tunnel and the Land of Ur. Callie saw the spiral, wrought-iron staircase up ahead and paused for a moment. As soon as she emerged from the Door in the Floor she would be...*normal* again. She had kind of gotten used to being a magical princess. It was going to be hard to give that up.

But it was only for awhile, she told herself. One day, she would return to Albion, to her friends there, and become the magical Princess Calandria once again. Knowing that was enough. For now.

Soon, she and Lewis were back in the garden.

Wanda was nowhere in sight.

The cool night air was a contrast to the sunny Albian morning she and Lewis had just left. Callie looked up and saw the familiar sight of her house, the golden light spilling out of the back kitchen window.

Her dad was in there. Her old life...and her new life. Callie stood tall and took a deep breath. Like the princess she was, she forced herself to make that first step, no matter that it was hard.

Lewis walked with her. They didn't say too much as they approached the back door to the kitchen. He just followed her in like he had done so many times before.

Callie could hear the TV in the family room. She walked silently through the house, motioning over her shoulder for Lewis to be quiet. She stopped at the threshold to the family room. She stood still for a moment, watching her dad with the woman he was going to marry. They sat next to each other on the couch comfortably, engrossed in the movie they were watching.

She thought of her mom then, of the times *she* had sat next to Callie's dad on the couch, just like Sharon was doing now. Callie knew her mom would approve.

"Hi," Callie said tentatively.

Her dad immediately turned his head, then rose to greet her. "Is something wrong, honey?"

Quite unexpectedly, Callie flung herself into his arms. "Oh, Dad! It's so good to see you!"

Lewis stood back quietly while Callie hugged her dad. Sharon, too, got up, looking concerned.

Callie's dad laughed and stroked her hair. "Sweetie, you've only been outside for fifteen minutes or so."

"I know, but I just gotta tell you--*you look great, Dad*. I'm sorry if I 'weirded out' a little, before. I guess the whole twelfth birthday thing hit me a little hard. Right, Lew?"

Lewis stood by, ready to lend his support. "Right, Cal. Don't worry, Mr. Richards, I straightened her out."

Callie shot Lewis a pseudo-scathing look.

He shot a playful one right back.

She didn't care, she was just glad to be home. Callie stepped out of her father's embrace and went to Sharon. Though it felt a little strange, she gave her dad's new fiancee a hug, too. "I just wanted to say, congratulations on your engagement. I hope you and my dad will be very happy together."

Sharon looked a little surprised by Callie's statement, but she smiled. When she smiled, she looked truly beautiful. "Thank you, Callie."

"I think I'll go up to my room, now, if you don't mind," Callie said. "It's been quite a day."

That was an understatement. Her dad didn't know that his only daughter had recently learned how to use her magical powers, had defeated an evil queen, and been crowned Heir to the Enchanted Throne of Albion.

Her dad nodded, but pointed to the satchel she carried, which contained her souvenirs from her adventure in Albion. "What's that?"

Lewis stepped closer and put his arm around her. "Oh, that's my birthday present to her. Just some books and stuff."

That seemed to be a sufficient answer for Callie's dad, who shrugged and took his seat back on the couch next to Sharon. "Well, happy birthday, honey."

285

"Thanks," Callie replied, and hustled Lewis out of the room to give her dad and his fiancee a little privacy.

She saw Lewis to the front door. The two friends exchanged a look--it was one they had exchanged many times before. But this time it was special. "Thanks, Lew. I couldn't have done it without you."

He smiled broadly. "You're right. You probably couldn't have."

Callie punched him lightly in the arm. "See you tomorrow at school."

"Yep. Back to the old grind." He made his way down the front steps. He only lived around the block. He'd be home in about thirty seconds.

Callie shut the door and headed upstairs to her room. The satchel she carried grew heavy. It was full of treasures from Albion. Bo, her dog, trotted in to greet her, his tail wagging as he sniffed all the interesting smells that remained on her from the other land. She patted his head. "I'll bet you smell Earle, don't you?"

He answered with a soft bark, his brown eyes bright and happy. Then, he walked around in a circle and lay down on the rug beside Callie's bed, letting out a big, doggy sigh of contentment.

Callie plopped onto her bed and dug through the satchel. There were Dr. Monsoon's books on magic. There was her beautiful coronation gown. Inside a velvet bag was a collection of royal jewelry that Queen Arabella had packed for her. She opened it just to remind herself that it hadn't been a dream. She had really been to Albion. The jewels Queen Arabella had given her proved it.

Callie smiled as she lifted out the next item. She unfolded the velvet cloth and looked down at the Talking Tiara. Callie peered closely at the sparkling diamonds, expecting to see the familiar faces there.

Out of habit, she called to them, "Beryl? Stan?"

There was no answer.

Callie placed the tiara on her head and looked at herself in the mirror. Magic or not, it still looked pretty impressive on her.

Then she took out the last item in the satchel: her mother's secret diary. The swirling gold 'A' on the front glistened in the soft lamplight of Callie's room, and the pink cover sparkled brightly.

Callie went to her bureau, to the china dish that held her mother's everyday jewelry. It had to be here, somewhere...Yes! She found it, a small gold pendant in the shape of a key, with the letter 'A' on it. There were still so many questions about her mother's past.... She would find some of the answers within the pages of this diary.

Callie's past and her future were now forever changed. After hers and Lewis's adventures in Albion, her life would never be the same. But maybe that was how it was meant to be.

No matter what challenges she faced, here at home, or in the magical kingdom of Albion, Callie vowed to meet them head-on.

She looked at her reflection in the mirror, at the sparkling tiara on her head, and took a deep breath.

She was Princess Callie.

And she would never, ever forget that.